KILLER INSTINCT

ALSO BY BRADLEY WRIGHT

Tom Walker

Killer Instinct

Holy Water

Alexander King

THE SECRET WEAPON

COLD WAR

MOST WANTED

POWER MOVE

ENEMY LINES

SMOKE SCREEN

SPY RING

Alexander King Prequels

WHISKEY & ROSES

VANQUISH

KING'S RANSOM

KING'S REIGN

SCOURGE

Lawson Raines

WHEN THE MAN COMES AROUND

SHOOTING STAR

Saint Nick

SAINT NICK

SAINT NICK 2

KILLER INSTINCT

For Danica and Kade. Three 2.

"The very essence of instinct is that it's followed independently of reason.

— CHARLES DARWIN

"If the single man plant himself indomitably on his instincts and there abide, the huge world will come round to him."

— RALPH EMERSON

KILLER INSTINCT

1

A s soon as Tom Walker shut the car door, he knew that the three men who'd picked him up were going to have to die. Otherwise, it was going to be him.

It wasn't the driver sitting in front of Walker who gave it away; he'd known about Jim Randall for a while. He was the big man with the lisp. Intimidating in appearance, but not much more than a driver with a good right hand. It wasn't Dan Reed in the passenger seat either. With his horseshoe bald spot and his grating Boston accent. Word was he had become more of the guy who handed out the next assignment rather than the cleanup man he used to be.

Walker, however, didn't know the man in the backseat beside him. All he knew was that it didn't take three men to deliver an assignment.

Walker was the assignment.

Inside the black Lincoln Continental it was dark. Just as it was outside. Dan had been smoking before they picked Walker up. The stench was still clinging to the interior. He wouldn't stop fidgeting in his seat because he couldn't wait to have another. The air conditioning was cold. Jim was the kind of man who'd sweat in a refrigerator. He would be greasy whether it was eighty-five or forty-five. The back of his neck was glistening. It was embarrassing really.

The man beside Walker? He was the professional. His large hands rested flat on his knees as he stared at the back of Dan's head. He fit the same mold as Walker. Big and strong, but not so much that it took away his agility. It was easy for Walker to spot because for the last twenty years they'd been giving him top dollar to kill the killers. Walker couldn't help but think that somehow these people had forgotten that that's what they paid him to do.

Jim had introduced the man in the seat beside Walker as "Trevor Sthimpsthon." He must be one of their up-and-comers. He was young, but old enough to have more than a few jobs under his belt. He kept his light brown hair trim, same for his midsection. But his broad shoulders were where his intimidation factor came in. The problem this young man had in his current situation was that he didn't know what he didn't know. Walker had been the same way when he started. Up to now this young man's talent had always been enough to survive his dumb decisions, but he had never been in a car with Walker.

The only smart thing they'd done, other than keep the third man a secret until Walker was already in the car, was to make sure they picked him up just outside the airport. It would ensure that Walker had no weapons. Not that he needed any. They should have known that too. But Walker always had his pen with him. It wasn't some James Bond gadget where a blade slipped out the other end with the push of a button. He used it to write, which he very much liked doing. And the pointed end would be plenty sharp enough to penetrate a man's flesh. Walker fished it from the band of his watch, down into his left hand without Trevor noticing.

By the body language from the two in the front seats—fidgety and restless—killing him was supposed to happen in the car. Walker was going to have to make his move before they made it to the spot where they were planning to bury him. Every so often the car tires would whoosh as they ran through a puddle. The conversation on the way to pick up Walker had probably been a happy one due to the rain; Dan probably told Jim it would be much easier to dig a hole for Tom Walker when the ground was soft.

They'd been driving for about twenty-five minutes and hadn't been on a main road for ten. They had crossed the state line into Kentucky just before they turned left. The trees had grown thicker as the road became narrower. Walker needed to pick the right spot to get out of the car. He needed a place to stay for the night and didn't want to have to walk too far in case he was injured in the car wreck.

"You guys always so talkative?" Walker said.

Both men in front of Walker jumped at the sound of his voice. They were on edge. It was about to happen.

Dan cleared his throat. "Just giving you the courtesy of letting you rest after a long travel day."

How sweet.

The reason they had given Walker for having him fly into the small regional airport in Huntington, West Virginia, then driving him somewhere out in the sticks in Kentucky was, of course, secrecy. Also because the job they were giving him was supposedly local. That's supposedly why they'd chosen Walker—he'd grown up in the area. But after what happened last week, Walker knew this day was coming. He couldn't just stand there and let the organization's veteran assassin murder a pregnant woman in cold blood. Their favorite assassin was operating outside the only code that mattered to Walker in his violent business: only the bad people die. So their assassin had to die too.

Walker had agreed to traveling to Kentucky because they told him that Karen Maxwell, the head of their little secret organization, would be waiting at the place they were driving him. That she wanted to discuss a raise now that Mitchell was dead. It's not that he believed that; it was just that he wanted a face-to-face so he could decide how he wanted to handle the situation. Now, that wasn't important. Since they were going to kill him, it meant they'd chosen to side with a bad man. Walker was no saint, but he'd never willingly accepted a job where he knew good people were the target. He wouldn't be a part of something like that, even if it was the only job he'd ever known. Besides, it was clear to him that he wasn't headed to visit the boss at this point, so his choices were limited.

Walker watched the rearview mirror for Jim's eyes. When he looked over at Trevor beside him, it was time. The pen was ready. Walker hoped his next move wouldn't break the pen. It writes better than any other he'd found. Ideal situation would have been Trevor on Walker's left side so Walker wouldn't have to reach across his body. But Walker had to play the hand he was dealt. If Trevor was quick, he could get to the pistol in his shoulder holster before Walker got all the way to Trevor's neck. Walker supposed he was about to find out why they chose Trevor to kill him. He had to assume the young man was good.

The road began to veer to the left. In the right corner of

the windshield Walker caught a glimpse of a wooden fence in the headlights. The kind of fence that keeps horses in. That meant there would be a barn. Perfect for a night's rest without disturbing anyone's sleep. The road straightened back out so Walker jabbed right with his pen. Instead of blocking his attack, Trevor went for his gun. He thought Walker was only throwing a punch. A fatal mistake on Trevor's part.

His talent wasn't good enough to overcome his error. He didn't kill Walker, but he was quick enough to pull the trigger as Walker sank his pen into his carotid artery. His gun fired just as soon as it cleared his leather coat. The first round shot where Walker's seatbelt connected, unstrapping it. When the seatbelt came loose, it pulled Walker's arm as he grabbed Trevor's gun hand, and when Trevor squeezed the trigger again, the second round darted through Walker's left thigh. Though he was already bleeding out, Trevor pulled the trigger again, but only after Walker was able to redirect the nose of his gun toward the back of Jim's seat. Trevor was too busy trying to keep the blood inside his body to get off a fourth shot. He wasn't going to be successful; Walker had hit the artery flush.

Walker's next move was to brace for impact. Trevor's third round had gone right through the top of Jim's neck, who slumped in his seat as his foot went heavy on the accelerator. The engine wound up. The road followed the creek below them on the right and was about to bend back to the left again. But the car wasn't going to follow. From the passenger seat, Dan was desperately trying to slow the speeding, but it was out of control.

Walker tucked his pen inside the lapel pocket of his coat as he curled up into a ball. Next to him, Trevor was still leaking blood from his neck. As the car sped through the turn, it went airborne. It felt like the wheels of a jetliner lifting from the runway at takeoff. Walker's body was suspended in midair—rising completely off the seat. Then, with the force of a runaway train, the car slammed into the embankment on the other side of the creek.

2

When Walker's eyes opened, he stared at what looked like old dusty beams in a barn. It was hard to tell because his vision was blurry and the pain in his head was unlike any he'd ever felt. Like his brain was in a vise and the squeeze would pop it at any moment. The light was faint. That didn't help. It had a blue hue that seemed a pre-sunrise glow.

He attempted to sit up but fell back immediately. Blinking didn't much help his sight, but he could see enough to tell that what he was holding was a handful of hay. His senses were overloaded from the ache in his head, but the smell of horses slowly crept in. He couldn't understand why the hell he was in a barn. And he couldn't comprehend why the hell he was in so much pain.

A second attempt at sitting up was successful. Then came the pain in his leg, and it was sharp. He wiped at his eyes, but the blurred vision was still coming and going. Walker's jeans were blood-soaked above the knee. There was a hole straight through his bloody pant leg. When he tested it with a squeeze, it was clear there was a hole in the top of his thigh as well. That wasn't the strangest part. What really spooked him was that he didn't even recognize his own hand. What the hell is going on?

Walker rolled his neck to try to work through the pain, but that only brought more.

Where the hell was he?

What the hell happened to him?

Movement helped a bit. He could see clearly around him now. He was lying in an oversize stall, surrounded by square bales of hay. There was a light brown leather messenger bag beside him, sitting alongside a lightweight jacket, neither of which looked familiar. Off in the distance Walker thought he could hear a buzzing sound. Maybe a small engine? Then the horses in the surrounding stalls began to rustle. A whinny and a grunt followed. Someone the horses knew was coming, and here Walker was in a strange barn, bloodied, concussed, and God only knew what else.

The buzzing grew closer, so he did all he could to get to his feet. As soon as he made it upright, the barn spun, and Walker couldn't keep the vomit from exploding from his mouth. The horses didn't appreciate his hello, and they all began talking to each other. There was no door in the middle of the stall where he was at the back of the barn. Easier for loading and unloading hay, he supposed. The barn stretched out in front of him. All stalls down the left side. Stalls down the right as well, but they ended in what was probably a tack room closest to him. Beyond the stalls the double doors of the barn were open. Framed like a picture were rolling hills of green grass. A dirt path the size of two tire treads disappeared off to the left.

Before he could move from where he was feebly standing, a utility four-wheeler pulled up and shut off just outside. Walker limped to his left as quickly as he could and hid himself behind the adjacent stall. A golden light popped on in the barn, and the horses whinnied their approval. Through a slit in the stall's yellow pine, Walker could see a woman saying hello to the first horse on her right.

"Y'all hungry?" she said.

A couple grunts and squeals came in response.

"Yeah. I thought so. Sorry I'm late. Got caught up watchin' the news. I'll get you fed and out for some exercise in no time."

The woman walked from the stalls straight into what Walker supposed was the tack room. She was medium height, probably close to five foot seven. In good shape. Tight blue jeans, untucked plaid button-down with the sleeves rolled up, and a brown ponytail bobbing behind her. Walker had no idea who she was. She made a few noises rustling around in the room, but then there was silence.

That's when Walker heard the unmistakable *click-clack* of a pistol being readied to shoot.

"All right, where are you?" she said.

She moved back into the barn. She was scanning for an intruder. Walker felt like a kid hiding from his teacher after he'd thrown a penny at the chalkboard. There was nowhere for him to go. She was going to find him. He thought it better to surrender on his own than surprise her. Bad things tend to happen when guns and surprises are involved. Walker had no idea why he knew that, he just did.

"Come on now," she said. "I don't really feel like killing anyone today. But I will."

Walker believed her. She didn't seem the slightest bit shaken. Just ready.

"I'm back here, ma'am. And I'm unarmed," Walker said.

She turned his way and extended the gun. She looked him up and down.

"Trespassing's an easy way to get shot on a farm."

"I know it is."

She studied him for a moment. "If you know that, then why the hell are you here?"

"I-I really don't know, ma'am."

"What the hell kind of answer is that?"

"Not a good one," Walker said. "But it's the only one I've got."

"Okay, well, let me start you out with an easier question then. Who the hell are you?"

"Name's Tom, ma'am. Tom Walker. I'm going to walk on out, hands up. I don't want any trouble."

Walker took a couple steps into the open and faced her.

"If you didn't want trouble, you should have stayed off someone else's property." Then she pointed at Walker's bloodstained jeans. "Besides, looks like trouble already found you."

She looked younger than Walker had initially imagined. A lot of natural beauty.

"Okay, Mr. Walker, I'll ask you one more time. Slower, so maybe you can understand this time. What the hell are you doing in my barn?"

Walker lowered his hands but didn't move forward. "It's not that I don't understand the question. I just don't know the answer."

Her face scrunched in confusion. "What am I supposed to do with that answer? That you don't know how you got here. Did you bump your head or something?"

Walker stared at her. Then gave a sheepish grin.

"You don't know that either, do you?"

"I do not."

"I suppose you don't know how you got the bloody jeans either?"

"I do not."

A siren sounded in the distance. She turned and looked outside, then back to Walker. "That for you?"

Walker shrugged. He had no idea.

She let out a short laugh. "All right. Well, other than your name—Tom Walker—just what in the hell do you know?"

Walker had to think about it for a minute. It was the first time he had the chance to ponder the fact that not only did he not know how he got a hole in his leg and ended up in this woman's barn; Walker didn't really know who he was other than his name. It was hard to process. He clearly was a full-grown man at the moment, but the last memory he had was of when he was a boy.

"That bad, huh?" she said. Still holding the gun on him. For that, Walker couldn't blame her. "Okay, let's try this." She let her gun hand down and held it by her side. "Take a deep breath. In through the nose, out through the mouth."

Walker followed her instructions. But all he felt was the pounding in his head and the burning in his leg.

"Anything?" she said.

"Nothing."

"Last one," she said. "What's the last thing you remember happening to you?"

Walker reached inside his mind. He was trying to pull something—anything recent. Anything that would tell him how he had become a man with zero recent past, shot in the leg, concussed, and alone in a stranger's barn. But the only memory he could compute was one that felt both like it was yesterday and also many years ago, and regardless, it didn't explain why he was standing where he was right now. And it was making his head swim, because in that memory he was only fifteen years old and he had just choked the life out of his foster father who had just finished nearly beating Walker's foster mother to death.

The barn began to spin again. This time, Walker wasn't going to vomit. Instead, the floor of the barn came toward him fast and knocked him unconscious.

3

"What the hell do you mean, he's gone?"

Karen Maxwell peered down at John Sparks as she stood behind her desk, leaning forward, both palms flat on the mahogany top. Her white open-collared shirt was covered at the top by her black and silver hair. Karen was anything but intimidating physically, but she'd always been one of those people who was imposing since the day she just up and decided to be. Size mattered not. Right now she was trying to impose herself on a man who'd been the intimidator ever since he'd hit puberty.

"No sign of him," John's deep and raspy voice rumbled. His military-green T-shirt hugged his muscles that were still hanging around well into his fifties. He was a G.I. Joe clone if ever there was one. "Three dead bodies, a completely mangled Lincoln Continental, and not so much as a foot-print leading away from the muddy scene. That kind of gone."

Karen stared at John. He could tell the five-foot-nothing ticking time bomb was about to explode. It was written in the throbbing vein on the side of her neck that was dancing beneath her salt-and-pepper hair.

"That's it? That's all you have to say, John? You trained him. You—"

"Yeah, I trained him. And I told you when you took over for your father that Tom Walker wasn't just a hornet but an entire hornet's nest. And that shit you pulled last week, when I told you not to, was you taking a stick to that nest. You play stupid games, you win stupid prizes."

Karen pounded her desk. "You will not talk to me like this in my office!"

John stood from his chair. Though his fifties had come along and stolen a little of his vigor, he was still built like an old oak tree—six feet, four inches of solid muscle. And somehow the white that had come for his dark hair only made him look meaner. But Karen didn't wilt. Nor had John expected her to. He just wasn't going to be shouted at. He'd had enough of that in his long military and post-military career.

"I'm just shooting you straight, Karen. I told you when it was time for Walker to move on, just let him go. You didn't listen. Now here we are."

"And where exactly is that, John? Where are we now?"

John pointed back and forth between himself and Karen. "*We* aren't anywhere. *You* just put a target on your back. A target that's been etched by the best killer I've ever trained."

Karen walked around her desk. Her square jaw jutted defiantly, her chest peacocking. "That supposed to scare me?"

"That's the intent. In more than twenty years of serving your secret organization, and therefore our government's contracted whims, Walker only refused one job. One. A job he didn't want because he didn't want his last one to help overthrow Congress. And more than that? He wouldn't kill an innocent woman and her unborn child. But what did you do? You tried to kill him for it."

"He knew the consequences of seeing a classified document, then refusing it. He knew what that meant because he's killed other men for doing the very same thing."

"He ain't other men, Karen."

"Then find him, John. Or it'll be you getting a visit from one of your other students."

John couldn't believe his ears. "You've lost your mind, Karen. The *only* reason I've stayed long enough for you to take your father's noble work and turn it into yet another political arm, used for corruption to the highest bidder, was because he took me in when I was a young man with no direction. He wanted to train men and women to be used as a weapon for good. Not for profit. So you can take your demands of me and shove them up your tight ass!"

John turned to leave, and he could tell that Karen had motioned for the two men guarding the door to not let him go. John stopped and put his hands on his hips.

"Mike!" Karen shouted.

A man in his mid-thirties, with dark slicked-back hair and an even slicker leather jacket, walked into the room.

"Mr. Sparks," Karen announced, "your services will no longer be needed here at Maxwell Solutions."

The man called Mike brought his arm up, and before it could register to John that something like this could be happening, there was a hole in his forehead.

"Find Tom Walker," Karen told Mike. "And while you're at it, find anything he loves. We'll use whatever we need. I don't care who he's been to this company, I'm not letting one man take everything my family has worked for away from me."

"Transportation?" Mike said.

"Take the plane. And take Alison Brookins with you."

"I work alone, Ms. Maxwell."

"Not with Walker. You'll need Brookins."

Mike was hesitant. "Yes, ma'am."

"And keep your shit tight. You've been warned."

Mike nodded, then left the room. The phone on Karen's desk began ringing. She walked over and picked it up.

Janice, Karen's secretary said, "Senator Davidson is on line one for you, again."

It was the third time he'd called in the last hour. He was starting to panic. Karen had been dodging the call, hoping to get an update from the local police department in Ashland, Kentucky. But the hillbillies had proved as worthless as she thought they would be.

"Tell him I have a team en route," Karen said.

"Ms. Maxwell, I told him that last time he called. He sounds pretty worried. He literally *demanded* to speak with you."

"Demanded?" Karen said with a laugh. "The only reason he became a senator at all was because my father put him there. And my money has kept him there . . ."

"I can tell him you have a call scheduled to get an update in an hour," Janice said. "Maybe that can buy you a little time?"

"Do that. And tell him I just sent our best man to Kentucky, so stop worrying."

"You got it."

Karen ended the call.

"Get this cleaned up," Karen said to the two men

guarding her door. She was pointing to John's body lying in a pool of blood on the floor.

Her father would not be happy about that. John had been one of the reasons Maxwell Solutions had flourished as one of the world leaders in security and many other off-the-books jobs. Much less the extracurricular program that became its hallmark in the covert world. He had been such a big part of why the CIA and other agencies around the world trusted Maxwell to do jobs no one else could. His training of assets such as Tom Walker had been everything. But just like everything else, things have a shelf life. And John Sparks had far outlived his expiration date.

Karen knew she needed to focus forward. Maxwell had three major jobs that week, but she needed to pull all her resources to the podunk town in Kentucky where they'd found Tom Walker to begin with. The man had information that could bring down empires, so there was no stone she could leave unturned to find him.

The least of it was that her company was on the line. The worst of it was that her life hung in the balance. As did the legacy of her father, Gordon Maxwell. For that, she would fight with all she had. No matter what it took. And no matter what Tom Walker had ever meant to her company in the past.

4

Something cold and wet woke Walker up. He was still in the barn, but this time the woman who'd just been pointing a gun at him was kneeling over him, reaching toward his forehead.

"There you are," she said as she dabbed his forehead with a damp cloth. "You went down like a strapless dress on prom night."

His head was pounding.

"Whatever happened to you that you don't remember must have been pretty nasty. You definitely have a concussion, if not worse. One of your pupils is larger than the other. I'll call an ambulance when we get up to the house."

"You act like you know what you're doing," Walker told her.

"That's because I've seen my fair share of injuries. I was an ER doctor until about a month ago. Whoever you pissed off must have thought you were dead. 'Cause that's a bullet wound in your leg there."

Just hearing her say it seemed surreal. How the hell did

he end up getting shot? Why would someone want to kill him?

She left the cloth on his head, stood, and took a step back. "I was going to move you back over to the hay, but you're a pretty big boy, so you had to lie where you dropped."

"Thank you for trying to help me."

He didn't really know what to say to her. She was no longer holding her pistol, so watching Walker drop to the ground must have taken away any real threat she may have been feeling.

"I did notice you have a phone in your pocket. Maybe that can help you figure out how you got here."

Walker reached for his left pocket. It was the first time he'd noticed his jeans were a little wet. When he slid what she was talking about out of his pocket, he had a very odd moment. Almost like déjà vu. Walker knew he was holding a phone, even though it didn't look like any kind of phone he'd ever seen. It was just a screen without buttons. But he knew how to use it, even though he hadn't ever seen one before. Somehow he also knew it wasn't good that there was water dripping from the hole in the bottom of it.

"That's not good," she said, pointing at the water.

Walker stared up at her blankly.

"No . . ." she said, acting as if shocked. She pointed to the screen in his hand. "You're looking at me like you don't know what that is. But you do know what that is, right?"

"I know what it is, just don't know *why* I know."

She moved forward and put one arm under the back of his neck and one around his chest. "Here, you need to sit up."

Walker scooted with her until he was sitting up against the wall of the tack room.

"What the hell's wrong with me?" he asked.

"I think I know, but you're not going to like it."

"Yeah? I don't like any of this, so it's going to be hard to surprise me."

"You were getting ready to tell me the last thing you remembered, and then you passed out. Know what that is yet?"

Walker stared off into space. In his mind's eye, he could see the blood running down his foster mother's battered face. He could hear his three younger foster sisters screaming and crying.

"Earth to Tom," she said.

Walker snapped out of his trance. "It'll sound like I'm crazy."

"Hmm . . . well, at least it will match how you look," she said, smiling. "Might as well give it a go."

"The last thing I remember is being fifteen."

Walker paused. She didn't need to know the details.

Her eyes studied his face. She looked at his hair, then all around from his forehead to his chin.

"Well, you aren't old. But you certainly aren't fifteen. I'd say you're somewhere around my age of thirty-two."

"So what does that mean?"

Her face changed to sad, but the shift was very dramatic. "I'm sorry, Tom, but you're dying."

It caught Walker off guard, and he couldn't help but laugh. She laughed too. It would have made for a nice moment if Walker had known who the hell he was . . . and didn't have such a pounding headache. She stood and backed away.

"You've got a very serious concussion. You need to go to the hospital to make sure there's no swelling in your brain. Short-term memory loss is pretty common with a head injury, but it makes me a little nervous that your last memory goes back so far. Let me guess—that memory isn't a good one?"

How could she know that? "What do you mean?" Walker stalled.

"I mean, usually when this happens, a patient will revert back to a very traumatic memory. That what's happening to you?"

Traumatic was an understatement.

"You could say that."

"Yeah. I don't like that, but I think you'll be fine. You need some water. Then we'll get you to the hospital."

"I don't think I have a car, or any idea where a hospital is."

"Oh, you can't drive, even if you had a car, sweetheart. I'll take you. Even if you are a bad guy, you can't remember that, so I'm safe, right?"

Walker couldn't tell if she was joking or not.

She jumped back in. "I mean, clearly someone didn't like you. But you seem nice enough to me."

"I don't want to be a bother."

"Too late for that. But I don't get much excitement out here, so I don't mind a little distraction."

She walked over with an outstretched hand. Walker took it, and slowly she helped him back to his feet. She kept his hand and moved it like she was shaking it.

"Leila."

"Nice to meet you, ma'am."

"Enough with the ma'am. That was my mother."

Walker nodded.

"Feeling okay?"

He was.

"Better," he said.

"Come on then, Tom."

Leila walked over to where Walker was lying when he first woke up, and picked up the brown leather messenger bag and the coat still on the ground. "These yours, I assume?"

Walker had to laugh. He was getting pretty tired of saying he didn't know.

"Right," she said. "Well, they ain't mine, so my brilliant deduction powers say they're yours. Maybe something in here will help jog your memory."

She walked by Walker and toward the exit. She spoke to the horses as she went. "I'll be back to feed you guys shortly. I'll bring an extra treat since you had to wait."

The horses didn't respond.

Walker limped after her. When he made it outside the barn, a gold-and-pink filter had settled over a pale blue sky. Cicadas were spinning up in the surrounding trees. The heat of the day was already on the rise. It was a summer morning that felt very familiar to the fifteen-year-old memory Walker was holding. But it told the current, much older Walker—who was limping toward a total stranger sitting on a four-wheeler—absolutely nothing. And it was the loneliest feeling in the world.

5

fter a couple-minute ride on the four-wheeler, through a dark brown wood-plank fence and over a couple of deep green pastures, Leila and Walker were winding around the corner to her ranch-style home. It was wide but not very deep. Dark red brick with white trim. It seemed old but in great shape. It was surrounded on both sides by large oak trees. The back porch looked out over the property toward the barn, and as they came around the front, there was a large half-circle driveway with a separate entrance/exit at each end. A cherry-red Jeep Wrangler sat right in front of the door.

Leila steered the four-wheeler up to the concrete walkway leading to the front door and shut it down. Walker wasn't sure why this woman was going to let him—a total stranger—into her house.

"Bet you're wondering why I'm going to let you in my house. Especially with a bullet wound in your leg there."

"You're bored." Walker wasn't sure why he said it.

She looked at him as if he'd offended her; then she shrugged and laughed. "I was going to say because you really do seem lost, and because if you wanted me dead, you would have already done it. But I suppose there might be some truth in your response. Life isn't quite as exciting out here as it was in the ER." She stood and walked around the front of the four-wheeler. "Wrong as it may be, this is at least a little something different than shoveling horse shit. I used to love helping people. Suppose I miss it."

Walker eased off the four-wheeler and followed her up the path. "Happy to spice up the day. But I have to warn you, it could be all downhill from here."

"Yeah, I'm kinda counting on that, seeing as how I'm about to walk you into my house."

"Yes, ma'am."

She looked at Walker, annoyed.

"Yes, *Leila*," he said, correcting himself. Walker had no idea why, but "ma'am" seemed ingrained in him. She nodded and opened the door.

Leila had her pistol tucked inside her jeans at the small of her back. Walker followed her inside. The interior wasn't as feminine as he'd expected. Cherry hardwood floors, same for the trim of the windows and doors. Seemed as though this may have been her parents' place. Everything seemed dated. Even to his fifteen-year-old memories of home décor.

"Let me get a sheet for the couch, some towels, and a needle and thread to sew you up with."

"We're not going to the hospital?"

She shouted back from another room down the hallway. "I got to thinking it might not be the best idea. Someone shot you, and or hit you *real* hard on your head. If you go to the hospital without knowing who you are, and with those injuries, trust me, there's going to be a whole lot of questions you can't answer, and they'll be asked by the sheriff himself."

Walker was standing in the living room. The popcorn ceilings were vaulted in the wide room. He could see a kitchen off to his right, and she'd gone down a hallway to the left. There was an old wooden TV sitting on more cherrywood furnishings on the far wall. The floral couch was green and white with maroon and yellow accents. The yellow about the same color as the paint on the walls. He just couldn't see a way a thirty-year-old woman would pick out any of that. Not that Walker had an eye for decoration, but he was her age and hadn't seen that mix of colors since he lived with his foster family. At least he didn't think he had.

Leila'd had bacon for breakfast. It was still strong in the house. Walker's stomach growled to let him know it had been a while since he'd been fed. On the coffee table in front of him were a few periodicals spread about. *Women's Health* and what looked like maybe the *Wall Street Journal*. Probably the only two things that were hers in the entire place. Those and maybe the daisies on the side table next to the lime-green lamp.

"All right, I think I've got everything." Leila came back into the room with her hands full.

She had let her hair down. It fell down below her shoulder blades. She looked nice. She dropped everything onto the coffee table, then began spreading the sheet out over the couch.

"Don't really know why I'm covering this old couch. My daddy wasn't exactly an interior designer. But I don't feel like replacing it if you happen to bleed all over it."

"We can do this outside if you'd be more comfortable—"

"Nonsense. It's starting to get hot out there." She flattened out the sheet, then raised up and pointed at his jeans. "Okay, off with those. You are wearing underwear, aren't you?"

"I am." Walker answered before he was sure. But a quick check down inside his belt line revealed an elastic waistband.

"Okay, then let's go. I don't have all day. Those horses get cranky when they haven't been fed. You can just set your coat and bag on the *gorgeous* chair my mother bought a quarter of a century ago or longer."

Walker did as told and set them down. Then he removed his boots, followed by his jeans.

"Oh, wait," she said as she rushed over to Walker. "Give me your phone. I'll get it in a bag of rice, see if we can salvage it."

He reached back into his jeans and handed it to her.

"Probably too late, but worth a shot. Get comfortable. I'll be right back."

Fresh blood leaked over the dried patch above his knee. She motioned Walker forward. He walked over and gingerly laid himself down on the sheet. He couldn't tell what hurt worse, his leg or his head. Either way, the pain wasn't nearly as unsettling as the confusion. Not knowing who he was or what the hell he had done to get shot and end up in a stranger's home pained him more than any physical wound. Worse than that was there was no stitching or bandaging that could put an end to the mental anguish. Walker could only hope that the next time he fell asleep, he would wake up with a lot more answers than questions.

Only time would tell. But if someone was trying to kill him, he wasn't sure how much time he had to figure it out.

6

Mike Hudson pulled the rented Nissan Altima to a stop just outside the home address he'd been given by Ms. Maxwell when he landed. She'd given him access to the company plane, so they'd flown into the Ashland Regional Airport. Mike didn't have much experience with small towns, so he was confused when you couldn't even rent a car there. Maxwell had to have a car there waiting for him. He was even more confused as to how the Ashland Regional Airport could be located in Worthington, Kentucky. And in five miles, he'd passed through three other "cities" just to get to the address in Flatwoods, Kentucky, where they were currently sitting.

"Where the hell are we?" Alison said from the passenger seat. "This looks like it could be in the movie *Deliverance*."

Mike had thought the same thing as he tapped his finger to the Motley Crue song playing on the radio. They were a mile or so off the main drag, some country road, and the broken-down, dirty white-planked house they were looking at sat at the foot of a farm that looked like it hadn't been touched in a decade. But what would Mike know about that? He grew up in the Bronx. People didn't have wood-planked houses, and they certainly didn't have enough land for a farm. In fact, no one had land at all. And that's the way he liked it. If he got too far away from concrete, like he was right then, he started feeling like he was about to break out in hives.

"Who's supposed to live here again?" Alison kept talking nonstop. He'd been listening to her the entire flight to Kentucky, and she hadn't let up in the car either.

"Walker's step-mom, or foster mom," he said. "I don't know. From the looks of it, they are probably all related anyway."

"What's that sound?"

Alison was referring to something that was making the most irritating, incessant buzzing sound. It was rising and falling, but not getting any quieter. Whoever the bug, or whatever it was, was trying to talk to, Mike and Alison seemed to be the only ones listening. And not by choice.

"Some kind of bug maybe?" Mike said. "You're asking the wrong guy. Rats are the only thing we really dealt with where I'm from."

"Well, it's pretty damn annoying," Alison said.

Mike turned and looked her dead in the face. "Yeah? Gee, I wouldn't have any idea what the hell that's like."

"You trying to say I'm like the bug? You think I want to be here with you? With your hair gel greasing up the seat, your Old Spice stench, and your Mr. Too Cool attitude? Even though you aren't cool at all? You think this is an assignment I wanted?"

"I don't give a rat's shit what you wanted," Mike said as he press-checked his Beretta, ensuring a round was chambered. Then he tucked it in the concealed shoulder holster he was wearing beneath his black leather jacket. "What I want is to get this job done so I can get back to my own thing. And it would be nice if, while we have to be here together, you'd keep your damn mouth shut. At least gimme a break for a minute or two. Is that too much to ask?"

"I should just shoot you and handle this myself, you prick," Alison said.

Mike turned and grabbed her by the throat. Her blue-green-rimmed hazel eyes bulged as he squeezed. "Don't forget who you're talking to here, Alison. You got me? I'm not some punk you can intimidate. I've been doing this about as long as you've been alive." He shook her head by her neck. "You hear me? Show me some respect, or I'll earn it the hard way."

Mike let go, and Alison sat back in her seat, rubbing her throat.

"That's your one pass," Alison said. "Next time I'll cut you wide open."

Mike leaned over the center console. "Oh, it's my one pass, is it?"

Alison slapped him on the shoulder, then pointed to the house. "Would you just relax and pay attention. We have movement."

Mike turned his attention to the house. An old, beat-up sky-blue pickup truck pulled into the gravel driveway. The two of them watched an older woman, rail thin, long gray hair, step out of the driver's side. She limped to the truck's back door, opened it, then pulled out what looked like a couple of plastic grocery bags.

"This is what we came to Kentucky for?" Alison said.

"Apparently. What, you don't like old ladies?"

"My biggest fear actually," she said.

Mike looked over. "You're serious? Don't you kill people for a living?"

"No, I'm research. You're the killer. And yes, old people are reminders of the slow and painful decline that lies ahead of us. It's the one thing we can't control. And it scares me."

Mike laughed. "Shit, my old man is seventy-five, and he can still whip my ass."

"Like that's saying much," she said. "Besides, aren't *you* seventy-five?"

"You're a real comedian, aren't you?" Mike said with a laugh. Then he let out a sigh. "Sorry about a minute ago. My temper has always been a bit . . . out of control. Got that from the old man."

"You're in the right line of work then," she said. "And it's fine. I know I run my mouth. I'm hyperactive, so all this sitting around has to come out somehow. You took the brunt of it. I'm like a puppy. You don't get me any exercise and I bug the piss out of you all day. Just keep your hands off me, okay?"

"Deal."

"Speaking of deal," Alison said. "Let's go deal with this lady. If Walker's in town, he's probably visited. But let's make sure he's not watching us first. Guy like him probably sees all the angles. Let's not make it easy for him."

"Maxwell said you were smart," Mike said. "Keep it up, and I just might enjoy having you around."

"Well, lucky for you, I like it rough, or I would have already turned this into a solo mission."

"Feisty too. Maybe research isn't your thing. You might be better at my part of the job."

"Great, so you're saying we're both born to be killers?" Alison said.

"I know *I* am. So I'm going to do what I was born to do."

"Just let me do the talking. Don't shoot her. Let me get

the information we need. Try using a little patience for once in your life."

Mike smiled as he put his hand on the door handle. "Patience is for passive people. I see a move, I take it. No hesitation."

"You sound like you've seen a few too many mob movies."

They both got out of the car and began walking the perimeter.

"You mean Scarface isn't your hero?" Mike said.

"Nah," Alison said. "I'm more of a *Live and Let Die*, James Bond kind of girl."

7

L eila first poured the bottle of water over Walker's wound. Dabbed it dry with a towel, then went at it with some sort of spray. By the burn, it was clearly some form of antiseptic.

"Looks pretty good," she said as she began dabbing again with a towel. "You were lucky. The bullet went through the meat and doesn't seem to have hit anything vital on the way out."

"You're saying I'm going to make it?"

"Ah"—she smiled—"you have a sense of humor at least. And yes, I believe you just might make it," she said as she concentrated on threading the needle. Her sharp jawline made her look strong. "I'm using silk for the stitches. It'll hold up pretty good if you don't get too rowdy."

She finished threading, then looked at Walker with a serious face. "I know you're a big, strong guy, but this is gonna hurt. I don't have anything to numb you. Except for whiskey. You want any of that?"

Walker didn't even know if he drank whiskey.

"I'm okay," he said. "I wouldn't want you to take advantage of me in my weakened state."

She smirked. "That's the second time you've tried a joke. Whoever you are, at least you aren't a total stick-in-the-mud. That should give you some hope for when you get back to being you in your head."

Walker just gave her a smile. He had no idea where his joking was coming from. It just felt natural.

"Just bore me to sleep with tales of how a doctor comes to live out here on a farm. That'll be numbing enough."

She raised an eyebrow. "Three jokes. All misses. I promise I won't let that affect how gentle I am on the wound."

"Appreciate your mercy."

"As for the tale about a doctor-turned-farmer," she said as she sank the needle into his skin—Tom jerked. She wasn't wrong; it hurt like hell—"it's not a long one. It's just life. This farm was my daddy's life, and when he died, I just couldn't see it go to hell. Truth be told, after over a decade of school, then straight into work full-time, it's been a nice change of pace."

"Sorry about your father."

The pain wasn't getting any less as she continued to stitch.

"Yeah, it was rough. My brother is taking it even harder than I am. It's one thing to lose someone to cancer, or even some sort of accident. But to pills? It just feels different somehow. You ever lose anyone you love to an overdose?"

"Not sure I've ever had someone to love," Walker said. Then he winced as she weaved back through the wound. "Much less someone I've loved and lost."

"Sorry," she said. "I don't have much practice conversing

33

with someone who can't remember anything. I'll try to stop asking you about yourself."

"That's okay. I don't have a lot of practice being someone without a memory. At least I don't think I do."

She stopped what she was doing and stared at him for a moment. Her chocolate-brown eyes wandered as she was cooking something up. "So, you don't know anything about yourself—well, your recent self—but you know how to walk, *attempt* jokes, and so far you've been very mannerly. And you knew that iPhone was a phone, but you don't know why you know it . . ."

When she trailed off, she started stitching up his exit wound, the entry wound was finished. "You know who the president is?"

"George W."

"Mmm mm. No. That was twenty years ago or so." She leaned back and pulled the pistol from the small of her back. Walker sat up, unsure what was coming next.

"Relax," she said. "I'm not going to shoot you. I just have an idea."

"Can't your idea involve something a little less violent? Like a sandwich?"

"Just follow me here." She stood and grabbed a throw pillow from the chair beside her. She helped him sit up a bit more, then propped the pillow at his back.

"Now what?" Walker asked.

He watched as she ejected the magazine from the pistol, then the chambered round. She put both of them in the front pocket of her tight blue jeans. To his surprise, she then extended the gun toward him. Walker didn't take it.

"What do you want me to do with that?"

"It's empty. Just take it."

Begrudgingly, he took it from her and held it in his right hand.

"Anything?" she said.

"It's a gun. Not sure what else you want from me."

"I'm not sure what I want either. Just following a hunch."

"Okay, so . . . now what?"

She took a seat on the couch beside him. Walker scooted over to give her some room.

"All right," she said. Her tone had changed to a soothing voice. Like she was about to hypnotize him. "Hold the gun with both hands."

Walker did as she asked. His right hand on the handle, the barrel cradled in his left. It was a Smith and Wesson SD9 VE. So it said on the barrel.

"Now close your eyes."

Instead of closing his eyes, Walker gave her the side-eye.

"Just do this, then I'll leave you alone."

He closed his eyes and waited for his instructions.

"Have you ever used a gun before?"

Walker thought about it for a minute. The pistol didn't feel unfamiliar in his hand, but he couldn't remember ever using one.

"No," he said. "Not that I remember."

"All right. Now I'm going to ask you to do something, and I don't want you to think. Just react. Got it?"

"No thinking," Walker said. "Got it."

"Okay, now take a deep breath. In through the nose, out through the mouth."

Walker did as told. In . . . then out.

"Remember, no thinking. Just react. One more deep breath for me."

Walker took another deep breath and exhaled slowly.

He didn't know what she was driving at, but he obliged. He relaxed and completely cleared his mind.

"Take the pistol apart."

She said it fast. Almost as if barking an order. And without thinking, Walker's hands began moving, independent of his mind. His fingers moved to the center of the bottom of the barrel, just above the trigger guard. With his left hand, he pinched both sides and pressed down as his right hand pulled back on the slide then pushed it forward, releasing it from the stock. He let the stock fall into his lap as he removed the spring and the barrel from the slide. He knew there were no other pieces without the memory of knowing why.

"Wow," she said. "That was impressive. You can open your eyes now."

Walker opened them and looked down. The pistol was lying on his lap in four pieces. Leila held an amazed look on her face.

"What just happened?" Walker said.

"You don't know why you knew how to do that, do you?"

"I don't. How did you know that would happen?"

"I had no idea that would happen. But I do know about short-term and long-term amnesia and how certain functions work, even without consciously knowing about them yourself."

"Okay. But why the gun?"

"A lot of things, really. One, you're built like a soldier. Tall and muscular, but not bulky so you won't be slow. I mean, look at your legs." She pointed down at Walker's muscular thighs. "My cousin was a Marine and you're built a lot like him. The 'yes, ma'am' thing you do is also very soldierly, but that could also just have been someone from your past teaching you some actual manners."

36

Walker thought of his foster father. The irony that he used to beat Walker for not saying ma'am and sir to him and his foster mother before he would go beat the hell out of her was never lost on him. But it was why he used those words. He had beat it into Walker. Walker didn't know why, but he didn't feel like sharing that memory with Leila.

"Lastly," Leila said, "you have a gunshot wound in your leg, so there's that. So I thought you might know guns. Turns out, you do. Very well."

"Diagnosis?" Walker said, confused about the direction she was taking.

She moved down and tied off the stitch. "Telltale signs of amnesia. No real memories, but you have the automaticity of things ingrained in you. That can be something as simple as walking and talking, or as complex as field-stripping a pistol in under five seconds. My dad was a gunman, too, so I know the lingo."

"Automaticity?" Walker said, smiling. "You're going to have to talk slow and use smaller words for a man in my condition."

Leila playfully smacked him on the arm. "Okay. Layman's terms. You may have forgotten some things, but you're still in there. Don't worry."

But Walker was worried. Waking up with a bullet hole in your leg and no memory of the last decade or more will do that.

"You can put the pistol back together for me now."

Walker stared at her blankly.

"Go on," she said as she stood. "You *can* do it."

Walker reached down to his lap, replaced the barrel and the spring to the slide like he'd done it a thousand times. Moved the slide across the stock until it clicked back into place. Then presented it to her as she'd asked.

"Impressive. All of who you are and what you know is still inside that handsome head of yours. Now, whether you actually want to know those things again is a different story."

She was smiling because she was joking. But what she said rang true. Walker clearly was in some sort of trouble when whatever happened to his brain erased years of his life. Maybe he really didn't want to know what he'd forgotten.

As she began wrapping his stitched wound, she recognized the uneasiness Walker was feeling. "It's a joke of course, but sometimes, don't you think it would be great to have a clean slate?"

Walker cocked his head. "Guess that's hard to say when you don't know just how good or bad you've had it."

"True. A real conundrum for you then."

She applied some tape to hold the bandage.

"I need to get back down to the horses. It will take me a while to get them sorted. Why don't you try to get a little rest. Who knows, maybe something will come back to you when you wake up."

"You've been awfully nice to a stranger who's in a bad way. Not sure what I would have done today if not for you. Thank you."

"Well, like you said, maybe I'm bored. I don't even handle the crops on the farm. Tyler is the one who looks after all that for me. So it's pretty much just me and the horses. Haven't worked on a human in a while. It was a good change of pace. So thank you."

"I'll be out of your hair before nightfall."

"I'll fix you something to eat before you go. Now, get some rest. I'll be back shortly."

Leila flipped off the light, and Walker lay there for a

minute just staring at the popcorn ceiling. He was almost asleep when he remembered that he had yet to look in the bag that was apparently his. Maybe there would be some answers in there and hopefully not just more questions about who the hell he really was.

8

B efore Leila walked out the front door to go feed the horses, she fixed Walker up with four ibuprofen, a tall glass of cold water, then a separate empty glass and a bottle of Maker's Mark bourbon "just in case the desire should strike." Since Walker was born in Kentucky— at least that's what he remembered from his birth certificate he'd been made to carry from foster home to foster home— he figured he *should* love bourbon, even though he didn't know exactly who he was. He remembered a few of his different foster dads saying something along those lines several times during his childhood.

Walker felt it was possible that he might need the bourbon more after he checked the messenger bag, so he held off. After swallowing the pain medicine and downing the water, he took the bag and found a bedroom down the hallway for a little privacy. The light coming in from the open curtain showed him the room was as dated as the front of the house, if not more so. He flipped on the light switch. Floral wallpaper, dark ornate wood with a large mirror attached to the dresser with gold handles. He depressed the bed, and sure enough, it was filled with water. An '80s special.

Walker had looked around the room long enough. It was time to do what he'd been dreading and look in the bag. Call it a gut feeling, or maybe his subconscious already knowing what was inside, but he just knew he wasn't going to like what he found. Of course, knowing someone was trying to kill him and considering his handiwork with the pistol on the couch, his thoughts weren't exactly going out on a limb.

Walker took the distressed tan leather messenger bag from his shoulder and set it and the jacket next to him. Both he and the bag wobbled on a waterbed wave. He unlatched both of the belt-like fasteners on the bag and folded back the top. There were two slots inside with a center divider. He pulled apart the front pouch. It was thinner than the back. Less room. There was only a sealed bag of trail mix and a bottle of water. So far, so normal.

He closed off that slot by moving the divider toward the front. When the back pouch opened, he could see at the bottom four rows of miniature notebooks stacked in groups of five or so. That was all that was in the opening, but there were pockets stitched into the inside lining of the back. The first pocket on the left held a row of pens—one missing. The third pocket on the right had a tin of breath mints poking out the top. But it was the pocket in the middle that drew his attention. The unmistakable navy blue cover with the word PASSPORT stamped in gold foil at the top was staring right at him.

Walker pulled the passport from the pocket, and behind it was a fairly large lump. He fingered it from the pocket, and just like that, he was holding a wad of cash. All one-hundred-dollar bills. At least five grand worth. Okay . . .

He placed the cash back in the pocket, then opened up the passport. Walker thumbed past the first few pages until he found the one with the picture. He stared at it for a moment. It was like looking at a stranger. He looked to his left and studied the mirror. It was the same man. Himself. He was wearing a similar tan. Same square jaw, covered in brown stubble. Brown hair was mostly the same. It was a little longer in the mirror than in the picture, but still a similar messy look with all the hair tousled to the left side. He couldn't see the color of his eyes that far away, but they were light, just like in the picture. So he assumed they were still blue. There was no question it was him. What he didn't understand was why the last name beside his face wasn't his own. Instead of reading Walker, it said Marshall. And the first name below it said Evan.

What?

Walker moved the passport closer to his eyes as if it would somehow magically morph into the name he knew was his own. It didn't. He did notice, however, that the birth date, two lines down, matched what he knew: April 10, 1989. But the line below it read FLORIDA, USA. While Walker never actually had a real home, having bounced around from family to family his entire childhood, he knew his birthplace was Kentucky. The one document that had given him any idea who he was—his birth certificate—plainly read ASHLAND, KENTUCKY. He'd read it a million times. Along with the signatures of his parents at the bottom. The parents he'd never met.

As far as Walker's memories were concerned, he'd never even been to Florida. Traveling that far had only ever been a pipe dream for an orphan. The closest he ever got was a pond near one of his many foster homes. With the right imagination, the muddy bank that surrounded it resembled a beach. He and Kelly Clark would sit there on summer days when Rick, their foster father, was on one of his road trips. He was a trucker. It was the only time he wasn't beating them up.

Kelly's blonde curls used to mesmerize Walker as they bounced around during their search for honeysuckles. They would build mud castles and pretend the tide was coming in. Walker didn't even know what a tide was, but what he did or did not know never mattered when it was just him and her. When the cardinal landed by their make-believe shore, they fed it as if it were a seagull. It got so hot in August they would strip to their underwear and wade in the pond for hours. That's where she gave Walker his first kiss.

Maybe those memories were the reason Walker chose Florida on his fake passport. Or maybe he was living there at the time this one was made. Whatever the reason for having a different name and identity in general, he had no idea, but somewhere inside Walker it didn't surprise him. The one thing he always wanted to be when he was growing up was somebody else. Anybody else. Looks like for some reason Walker was able to make that dream come true. The bullet hole in his leg told him, however, that it might not have been under the best of circumstances.

Walker searched the rest of the bag but found nothing else. He had to have a wallet, with a driver's license and some credit cards somewhere, right? But his jean pockets had only held the watered-down phone. The navy jacket he'd been carrying along with him stood out against the white bedspread. He pulled it over and fished both outside pockets. No wallet, but he did find a piece of heavy stock paper on one side. He pulled it out and looked it over. It was an airline ticket. Washington, DC, to Huntington, West Virginia, dated last night, for the one and only Evan Marshall.

Opening the bag had done the opposite of what he'd hoped. Instead of offering clarity, it served a heaping portion of confusion. Walker went to set the jacket back down, but when he grabbed it, he felt something hard near the chest area. When he opened up the jacket, the white-and-blue plaid lining had a dark red stain over the interior pocket.

He eased his hand down into the pocket to avoid cutting himself on the blade of the knife. But instead of finding a handle, his fingers felt the top of a metal ink pen. Confused, he pulled the pen from the pocket and found the source of the stain. At first he thought it could be red ink, but the way it had dried at the tip of the pen, he knew it wasn't. It was blood.

Walker placed the pen back in the pocket and set the jacket down. His eyes found themselves in the mirror. The man staring back at him was a stranger. But what else? A wad of cash, a fake name on his passport, a bullet hole in his leg, and a bloody ink pen in his jacket. Not to mention the muscle memory of taking apart and putting together a pistol. Sounded more like a spy novel than what could be his actual life. How the hell was he going to figure any of it out without a memory?

The notebooks.

The twenty or so notebooks in the bag. Maybe one of them could help him get a grip on something tangible to start working through.

He picked up his bag and pulled the first one from the pile. And just as he did, he heard the front door open.

"Leila?" a man's voice called. "You in here?"

Walker jumped to his feet. There was a lot he didn't know about himself in that moment, but there was one thing that was clear. Trouble didn't just have a way of finding him; he was a full-powered magnet for it.

9

"Leila?"

the man called again from the front door.

Walker slipped out into the hallway for a peek. His troubles compounded when he saw a man in a police uniform standing there. He also noticed that his jeans were still lying on the chair that was only a couple of feet in front of the officer.

His bloody jeans.

Shit.

Walker watched the officer find them, then pull his gun from his hip holster. "Leila!"

Walker moved back into the bedroom. There was a door on the wall to his left. He gently pushed it open. A bathroom. The man in the other room was probably either a lover or the brother she'd mentioned. Either way, he wasn't going to be happy to see a strange man in his girlfriend's or sister's house. Walker turned on the shower, slipped off his shirt, found a towel under the sink, and wet his hair with the water that was just turning warm.

The only move Walker had was to play Leila's guest. A

cop was going to investigate. That's what they do. It would look a lot worse if he found Walker hiding. He wrapped the towel around his waist and stepped into the hallway.

"Hello?" Walker said. "Leila, that you?" He did his best to sound convincing.

"Come out here with your hands up!" the officer said. "No sudden moves!"

Walker tucked the towel at his hip and did as the man commanded. When he walked out of the hallway, he moved his gun right over Walker's chest.

"Who the hell are you?" he barked.

"Can you please put the gun down?" Walker'd had enough guns for one day. He was going to do his best never to pick one up again.

"Tell me who you are."

That's complicated, officer, Walker thought. *I'm either Evan Marshall or Tom Walker*. Walker wanted to make sure to say the name that would be the path of least resistance, but he had no idea what that would be. Remembering that the only form of ID he had on him said he was Evan, he had no choice but to go with that. Along with investigating, cops also make a habit of asking for identification. He knew the situation could get tricky if Leila walked back in. Might be worse if she didn't.

"Well? Who the hell are you, and what are you doing in my sister's home with a pair of bloody jeans?"

"Take it easy. I'm a friend. I cut myself trying to help with the horses. I came back up to the house to clean up."

"A friend? Leila doesn't have friends. Not guys anyway."

"I'm an exception to the rule."

Leila's brother stared at Walker blankly. He was a large man. Maybe a linebacker in high school. Broad shoulders and a thick neck that held an even thicker head with a high and tight buzz cut on top. He was trying to decide what to do. So far, he hadn't asked again for Walker's name.

"How do you know her?" he finally said.

Walker had to use the only information he knew about Leila and hope it was enough.

"The hospital," he said.

Lying seemed to come easily. Par for the course for what he'd recently been discovering about himself.

The man was waiting for more, but Walker wasn't going to elaborate until the officer made him.

"And?"

Shit.

"And . . ." Walker stalled. "I was there for her when her father died. We've been close ever—"

"You took advantage of my sister when our dad died? You sick son of a bitch."

Her brother. The words Leila said about her brother taking their father's death harder than she had echoed in Walker's head as the officer holstered his gun and charged him.

"Look, it's not like that," Walker pleaded, holding his hands up. "I don't want any trouble."

"Too late!"

Instead of retreating, Walker stepped out into the room and made sure he didn't have the wall behind him. He had no idea why, but it felt natural, so he went with it. As Walker stepped left, Leila's brother cocked back his right hand. As if working independently of his brain, Walker's feet immediately changed course and started walking him back to the right. And somehow he sensed the benefit of moving away from the officer's power right hand.

Then suddenly Leila's brother threw a punch. Walker's body jerked left, causing her brother to miss wildly. The punch never had a chance of landing. Leila's brother stumbled forward, off balance, and stopped himself against the wall. Walker circled around, again keeping enough room between himself and the wall for plenty of movement. Walker could have hit him when he went stumbling by, but he didn't, for more than one reason. First, he's a cop. Hitting a cop has never in the history of mankind been a good idea. Second, Walker didn't want to hurt him, then have him get mad and reach back for that gun. Lastly, Leila had been good to Walker, and it sounded like she and her brother had been through a lot lately, so out of respect he had no intentions of piling on with a beating.

The question floating in Walker's head was, how did he know without a doubt that he would actually win the fight? But Walker knew it as sure as he felt the pain in his head and leg.

Leila's brother turned toward him. His face told Walker he was a little less sure now about his advantage in the fight.

"A fighter, are you?" he said.

"I don't want to fight."

"You should have thought about that before taking advantage of my sister."

The bull charged again. He was already huffing and puffing from fatigue. He was a long way from the game shape of his playing days. This time he didn't punch, but instead fell back on his abilities as a football player and went for the tackle. But again, Walker's body somehow knew exactly what to do. When Leila's brother's shoulder hit Walker's waist, Walker's legs kicked back and spread out wide. Walker's weight fell onto her brother's shoulders as he attempted to wrap Walker up with his arms. He couldn't. With heavy hips, Walker rode him to the ground, then spun around to his back. Leila's brother felt Walker's arm reach beneath his chin like Walker was going to choke him. Walker had to physically stop himself, pull his arm back, and push off him to get back to his feet.

"Please stop," Walker begged. "I'll leave. Just let me get my things."

Leila's brother was already on his feet and stalking back toward Walker. Now his ego was bruised, and he wanted redemption. He could have it, for all Walker cared. Walker just needed to remove himself from the situation. Instinctively, Walker once again started circling away from Leila's brother's power hand. He was coming slower this time— another round of punches was coming. Walker put his hands up, but for defensive purposes only. Her brother threw his jab, but when Walker weaved left, he saw Leila open the door behind him.

"Larry, what the hell are you doing?"

Larry stayed focused. He threw his right hand over the top, and Walker parried it as he bobbed back to the left.

"Stay out of this, Leila!" Larry shouted.

Then he threw two more punches. A left, then a right. When Walker weaved away from the right, his body took over once again, and Walker's hips twisted hard to the right, carrying with it a left hook that slammed into Larry's right side. Walker's conscious mind may not have known, but his subconscious instinct absolutely meant to hit Larry in the liver. Walker knew it without knowing that it would end the fight.

Larry moaned as he dropped to his knees and grabbed at his side.

"I'm sorry!" Walker shouted down to him. Then he looked at Leila. "I'm sorry. I told him I didn't want to fight."

Leila rushed forward and moved Walker back away from Larry.

"Enough!" she shouted.

Larry was still moaning.

Walker stood back, holding his hands up, palms forward. She gave Walker a scolding look. Then she bent over and helped Larry back to his feet. Still hurting, he tried to charge through her to get to Walker again. Walker continued to step away.

"Larry, stop it!" she said, pushing him back. He came forward, and she pushed him back again. She was a lot stronger than she looked. "I said stop it!"

"I'll just get my things," Walker said.

"You will do no such thing," Leila said. "Stay right there where you are."

Walker did as she told him.

"Larry, what the hell are you doing? Did you knock on the door or just walk right in?"

Larry finally stepped back. He was still trying to find his breath. "I—"

"You can't just walk in here like you did when Dad was living here, Larry. And you can't try to fight my guests."

Larry seemed as though he was finally recovering. He glared over at Walker and said with labored breath, "Who the hell is he, Leila?"

"Like I said, he's my guest."

"I heard you, but how do you know him? Do you even have any idea what just happened in the creek behind your house last night? Please tell me you've known this man longer than a night."

Walker's feeling of *needing* to leave that house was as strong as a stranded man in the desert needing water. But he also wanted to know what happened behind Leila's house. It sounded like some sort of major event, and there wasn't a fiber of his being that doubted he had something to do with it. Leila knew it too. She turned and looked at Walker for a moment. Then back to her brother.

"Of course I've known him longer than that. But that's none of your business. Now, what are you talking about happened behind my house last night?"

Larry nodded toward Walker. "Not in front of him. It's police business. Only reason I'm telling you is because you're my sister. And because it happened just off the farm's property."

Walker picked up his boots from the floor and his jeans from the chair.

"I just need a few minutes," Leila said.

Walker gave her a smile. "I have some things in my bag I need to read. I'll find a quiet spot outside. You all take your time."

She nodded.

Walker moved over to the bedroom as the house filled with awkward silence. He dressed, zipped up his bag, and walked back out.

"We won't be long," Leila said.

Larry eyed Walker all the way to the door. Walker opened it and walked out, as much as he wanted to stick around and find out what happened behind the farm. The thing Walker was sure he was part of.

But he couldn't. It was time for him to move on before someone found out something about him that wouldn't allow him ever to leave as a free man again.

10

M ike knocked on the storm door three times, then wiped the sweat from his brow.

"Why didn't you leave your jacket in the car?" Alison said. "It's like ninety degrees out here."

"Just worry about getting Walker's location from this old bag, and stop worrying about me."

"Just saying, it's hot. You're going to start sweating; then I'm going to have to smell you for the rest of the day."

Mike ignored her and knocked again.

"I'm comin'." The lady's muffled voice came from inside the house. "Hold your horses!"

The two of them waited another few seconds; then the knob on the door turned, and the door swung open. The gray-haired woman didn't look as old up close as she stood sheepishly behind the half-opened door.

She squinted at them. "I thought they quit sellin' encyclopedias since the internets came along."

"We're not selling anything," Mike said. "We need to talk to you—"

"What my friend, Mike, here means to say," Alison said

as she gave Mike a look, then shuffled over in front of him. "Is that we are trying to locate someone who used to be in your foster care. Would you mind helping us out?"

"Well, honey, that was a whole other lifetime ago. Who are you anyway?"

"I'm sorry," Alison said. "We're with the FBI. We—"

"Oh," the woman interrupted. "You must be here to ask about Tommy then. He okay? He's not dead, is he?" There was genuine worry on her face.

Alison glanced at Mike, then back to the woman. "Well, ma'am, that's why we're here. We can't find him, and we think he might be in danger. We want to help him."

The door opened wide. The woman stepped forward. Her face was emotional. Her green eyes were beginning to water. "Oh, I always worried this day would come." She opened the storm door. "Come on in out of that heat. I'll do anything I can to help that sweet boy."

Alison and Mike followed the woman inside.

"Sorry 'bout the mess. I don't get much company."

When they walked in, Alison noticed there wasn't really a mess at all. But she understood the woman because she'd grown up in Wichita, Kansas. It was just the midwestern way to apologize for everything. The tan carpet was a little worn, but overall not bad. The white walls were bare. The woman walked them past the kitchen into a living room with a floral print couch, and an old telephone still sat beside the nightstand.

"The place looks great, ma'am," Alison said.

"Bless your heart," the woman said as she showed them to the couch. "Aren't you sweet. I just love your dark hair." The woman twirled her own hair. "Mine used to be the same way, but time has a way of washing the color from things. But man oh man, I wished I had your long legs." The woman looked at Mike. "You sure is lucky to be with such a tall and pretty woman."

Mike rolled his eyes.

"Well, your hair is beautiful just the way it is, Ms. Kidwell," Alison said as she and Mike took a seat on the couch.

"Oh, call me Kim. Can I get you two something cold to drink? Tea? Lemonade?"

"Got any beer?" Mike said.

Kim laughed. "You got you a tough one here, don'tcha?"

"You have no idea," Alison said. "I think we're okay. We don't have a lot of time."

"Oh, right. My sweet Tommy," Kim said as she took a seat in the brown paisley chair on the other side of the mahogany coffee table. "All that boy went through before he made it to my crazy house and he was still just the sweetest, funniest kid. Always wanting to help. Even if it hurt him. Please tell me he's all right?"

"That's where we were hoping you could help us, Kim," Alison said. "Last night Mr. Walker got into an accident not too far from here after flying into the Tri-State Airport. "You haven't—"

"My Tommy is here? In the Ashland area?"

"Yes, ma'am. And I guess that answers my question. You haven't heard from him?"

"Oh no. Tommy doesn't call. The sweetheart still sends me money every month, but I haven't spoken to him since that man came and got him out of jail and took him to work for the CIA, or the FBI, I don't know what it was. Lots of people 'round here speculated, but no one really ever knew. I'm sure you know, but he killed my husband. Choked the damn life out of him for hitting me. That's why he was in jail, poor thing."

Kim stopped talking for a moment. She was getting emotional.

"It's okay, Kim," Alison said.

"No, no it isn't. I let that man beat on Tommy and the rest of those poor kids. I didn't know what to do. Then Tommy still stopped him from beatin' on me. I've never forgiven myself for being such a coward."

"Look"—Mike stood up—"All due respect, but we don't have time for history lessons."

Kim recoiled a bit as she sat back in her chair.

Mike continued. "So just tell us where the hell he is, and no one gets hurt."

Alison stood up. "What are you doing?" she said to Mike, then looked at Kim. "I'm sorry, ma'am. He's an asshole. What he means is that it's urgent that we find Mr. Walker. Someone might be trying to hurt him, and we want to find him before they can, so we can keep him safe." She elbowed Mike in the ribs. "Right, Mike?"

"Whatever, Alison. Kim, just tell us where the hell he is."

Kim stood, but took a step away from them both. "Well, like I said, I haven't heard from him. But one thing I know about Tommy is that he can take care of himself. That said, I sure hope you find who's after him and stop them. He's a good boy. The world needs good boys like him."

Alison stepped forward and handed Kim a generic business card. "This is my number. If you hear from him, please call us immediately. He may not know who to trust, so we need to find him and bring him in safely."

"Oh, please do help him. He saved my life a long time ago and gave up his own in the process. He deserves to be happy."

"Yes, ma'am," Alison said as she began walking toward

the door. "We'll do all we can, but you sure could be a big help."

"You'll be my first call."

Mike and Alison stepped back out into the sunshine.

"Thank you for trying to help him," Kim said from the door as they walked away.

Alison turned and waved as Kim disappeared back into the house.

"Well, that was bullshit," Mike said.

They crossed the street for their car.

"What do you mean? She clearly hasn't heard from him."

"Like I said, bullshit," Mike said as he got in the car. He immediately turned the AC on full blast. "She was way overselling. 'Such a good boy'? Are you kidding me? The man's killed more people by himself than half the militaries on Earth."

"Yeah, because it's the only thing he's ever been trained to do. Besides, you really think she knows the real scope of a secret assassin's life? Hell, you think she even knows he's an assassin?"

"I think I know that she knows where the hell he is. And if we go talk to the cops and they still don't know where he is, we're coming right back here and doing whatever it takes to get that bitch to tell us where he is. Period. And if you don't like it, go back to Maxwell and get another assignment. Or quit entirely, for all I give a damn."

"You're a pompous asshole, you know that?" Alison struck back. "How your know-it-all-mentality hasn't killed you before now is beyond me."

Mike reached for his pistol. "You want me to show you why it hasn't killed me?"

"You think because you put your hands on me earlier,

and put your hand on your gun now, that I'm afraid of you? Get over yourself."

Alison pulled out her phone and pressed call on Karen Maxwell's contact. She picked up on the second ring. The phone was on speaker so they both could hear.

"Any luck?" Maxwell said.

"The foster mom knows nothing."

"Bullshit she doesn't!" Mike said.

"Your neanderthal and I disagree, I suppose," Alison said. "But either way, we have nothing. Is there someone in particular you want us to speak with at the Ashland Police Department?"

"Yes. But the two of you better pull it together. Mike, let her do the talking. You know what your worth is, so leave what you do best for when you find Walker."

"Whatever," Mike said.

"The police contact?" Alison prompted.

"Yes, speak with a Detective Rick Pelfrey. He's already been advised that two agents would be there to see him. Use your FBI credentials if necessary, but the call to the detective that you were coming to see him was made from Senator Davidson's office. So it should all go smoothly."

"On our way there now," Alison said.

"The longer it takes to find him," Maxwell said, "the harder it will be to kill him. Every second for a man like him, he's building a plan. Let's just hope he was hurt in the accident. Maybe that will slow him down. If he does manage to make it here to Maxwell Solutions, I'm sure I don't have to tell you what that means for the two of you."

"Yeah, yeah," Mike said. "We copy. This will all be over tonight."

"Make certain that it is."

11

E avesdropping on Leila and her brother's conversation really hadn't been Walker's intention. However, when he was walking around the back porch, he couldn't help but hear Larry say the words *car crash*. Walker looked up and noticed that the kitchen window overlooking the back of the property was open to the screen. And Larry's adrenaline was running, so he was speaking louder than normal. Walker walked up the stairs of the white-painted wooden deck and stood between the window and the back door where no one could see him.

Walker figured he might as well know as much as he can about what happened before he goes walking off to nowhere.

"Why does it matter that there was a car wreck behind the farm, Larry? There's been plenty of accidents around that creek. That road is dangerous as hell."

"Leila, three people died."

They both were quiet for a moment. Walker could hear the robins whistling their tune from the canopy of the oak trees.

"Damn," Leila said. "That's terrible. But what is so secret about that? Why are you acting all weird about it?"

"Because, sis, only one of the three men in that car was actually killed by the car accident itself."

Here it was. Walker could feel a wave of knowing wash over him. Though he had no memory of how he came to be shot and concussed in Leila's barn earlier, there was zero doubt he was about to find out.

"What the hell does that mean?" Leila said. "Did they have heart attacks or something?"

"Or something," Larry said. "I need some water."

The next thing Walker heard were footfalls across the kitchen tile. Then the clink of a glass followed by the running water from the sink that couldn't have been more than two feet behind him. He tried to make himself as small as possible. But Walker isn't small. He heard Larry let out a satisfied sigh after a cool drink of water.

"Or something what?" Leila said.

"Who is this guy in your house, Leila? For real. He told me he knew you from the hospital. That true?"

"Yeah, it's true. Why? What does it matter?"

"What's his name?" Larry pressed.

"Tom."

"Tom what?"

"Tom Walker. Now, enough about my friend. Tell me what the hell happened that has you so damn paranoid, Larry. This isn't like you."

"Leila, two of the men in that car last night were murdered. One of them was shot in the back of the head, and the other was killed with some sort of pointed object."

Walker's mind began spinning, and the first place it jumped was to the bloody pen in his jacket pocket. Who the hell was he? And what was he doing in that car?

"Now, the way these men were situated in the car, whoever used the pointed object to kill a man had to have been in the backseat with the one who was stabbed. And the other two men in the car were not in the backseat."

"So you're telling me someone is missing?" Leila said.

"No, I'm telling you there is a murderer on the loose. And I show up here to make sure you're all right, and you have a strange man with a bloody pair of jeans in your house. He told me how he hurt himself, and it seems like bullshit to me. So how did his jeans get bloody, Leila?"

"What are you, my brother? Or the local detective trying to solve a crime? I told you I know Tom from the hospital, Tom told you he knows me from the hospital. Whatever the hell else happens here is none of your damn business. I'm fine. Good luck finding the man on the run, and have a nice day."

"Leila, it don't have to be like this. I'm just trying to make sure—"

"I'm fine, Larry. Now go on and get back to work where someone actually needs you."

"Fine, but I'm just trying to help. And so if this Tom fella is who you say he is, what the hell do you think Andy would think about you having another man over?"

Leila didn't immediately answer.

"What?" Larry broke the silence.

"Get the hell out of this house right now, Larry. Now!"

"What did I say?"

"You know good and well I don't give a flying shit what Andy thinks about anything. You come in here barking all this crap about wanting to protect me, but are you going to make me say it?"

"Say what, Leila? What are you so riled up about?"

"It's odd you're here trying to be so protective now.

61

Where were you last month when Andy beat the hell out of me? Huh?"

"What? I—"

"You what, Larry? Didn't know? Didn't notice the bruises? Didn't notice the way me and Andy were no longer together immediately after the bruises? You aren't trying to protect me. I'm protecting you! The only reason I didn't go to the police was because I was afraid you'd lose your job. That and we've all had enough to deal with, with Dad killing himself and all."

"Dad did not kill himself!" Larry shouted.

That was Walker's cue to exit. If he stayed any longer, he was afraid he would have to go back in. Hearing that someone had hit Leila was tough. But hearing her own brother did nothing about it triggered Walker. He had to move. He stayed low, crossed the deck as softly as he could walk, then started out away from the house. As soon as his feet hit the grass, he jogged as fast as his gimpy leg would let him. Across the grass-covered field on his right, he noticed the horses Leila must have turned out. Walker envied their station in life at that moment. A lazy graze in the rising sun. Not a care in the world. Must be nice.

The hill he was on rolled down and put him out of sight from the house. More of the farm came into view. It was beautiful, and it was big. In the distance where the land leveled out, he saw endless rows of corn. The crop fields Leila mentioned she had someone tending for her. And like a dot at the other end of the corn was some sort of structure. Probably where they kept the farming equipment. Walker hoped that maybe no one would be there and he could take a minute to form a plan. A few minutes out of the sun wouldn't hurt either.

A few hundred yards and a hopped fence later, Walker entered the corn maze. It was like being transported to a Kentucky jungle. The stalks provided shade from the sun and passed along a rich and fresh aroma. The scent of greens that were the stalks was mixed with honey and floral overtones. As a kid he'd spent many a day hiding from his last foster dad among blooms just like the ears of corn surrounding him.

Walker's foster mom had made a trip to the drugstore for some first aid supplies after taking a beating, and surprised him when she got home with a set of Jacks. It was the first gift Walker had ever received, so it had been a big deal to him. He would never forget the way she hugged him and thanked him for trying to keep Jim from hitting her. Then she told Walker if he ever tried to stop Jim again, she'd kill him if he didn't get himself killed first. Same went for if Jim found the Jacks. She didn't want Walker to get hurt trying to help her. So Walker kept the Jacks hidden. He used to find the hardest dirt in the cornfield and bounce the little red ball as he picked up the Jacks for hours. He forgot to hide them under his mattress that last night. It was inadvertently the reason Jim had gotten himself killed.

According to Larry's account of Walker's actions in that car wreck, Walker must have never stopped killing people after that.

The more he was getting to know about himself, the darker things turned. Walker didn't *feel* like a killer. But he also didn't feel like Mr. Bloody Pen—Evan Marshall—from Florida either. He had to get someplace where he could start to figure some things out. While he wasn't looking forward to getting to know more about himself, it was the only way he was going to keep himself alive, or at least out of jail. If that ship hadn't already sailed. And though Walker didn't know of anyone he could turn to, he did have a bag full of notebooks. Hopefully there would be a different story of him written in there. One with a little happier beginning.

12

W alker wiped the sweat from his forehead as he finally stepped out from the rows of corn. His shirt clung to his chest as if he'd hopped into a swimming pool. On his left stood the structure he'd seen from the other end of the cornfield. It was much bigger up close. The wood was similar to that of the barn where he'd awoken. About the same size planks as well. He took another step forward and saw the back end of a pickup truck. He stopped. It was quiet. All he could hear was the breeze rustling the cornstalks behind him. The truck's door opened and shut. He took a step back.

There was a gravel service road leading to the entrance on the other side of the shed. Walker couldn't see it crawl up the hill, but he could hear tires rolling over it. Someone was coming his way. He stepped back into the corn but moved to his left, closer to the shed. When the rolling tires stopped, someone stepped out and shut their door.

"What the hell is going on out here?" a man's voice shouted.

Walker was forty feet away with a shed between him

and them, so he barely heard well enough to make out the words.

"Señor?"

"Did your boss have something to do with what happened in that car accident last night? 'Cause it seems awfully cartel-like to me."

Whoever the man was, he wasn't happy. Walker moved farther left to the other side of the building. He could see the back end of a police car, but going any farther would risk being seen. And what the hell did "*cartel-like*" mean?

"Señor, we don't know what you are talking about."

"No? Y'all didn't kill some men in a car last night? I told you when all of this started that there wouldn't be any of that bullshit here. Where's Pedro? I want to talk to him right now."

"Pedro is back in Oaxaca. He left me to watch over things."

"So he killed these men, why?"

"Señor, I don't know what you are—"

"Have him call me immediately. I don't have a choice but to let officers search the area for the missing killer. I'll do my best to steer them away from here, but it happened right behind the farm. This is just sloppy is what it is. Clear out of here for the rest of the day."

"We really need to stay and finish, señor. Plus, we are already behind on orders as it is."

"I don't give a flying shit what you're behind on or not. You'll be making toilet chardonnay in prison if the search comes here and we aren't buttoned up. Now, finish what you're running, then close up and get the hell out of here by nightfall. Comprendes?"

"Yes, we understand."

"And Pedro's going to call me?"

66

"Sí, señor."

"Good. Now, get moving."

The door shut, and the police car shot rocks from its tires as it spun and sped back up the hill. Walker knew he might be having memory problems, and overall lacking the ability to understand who he was, but it didn't keep him from being beaten over the head with the fact that something very illegal was going on in that shed. And he would bet all the money in his bag that Leila didn't know the first thing about it.

But what did Walker care?

The dirt below his feet was still a bit damp from last night's rain. Walker crouched down and picked up a handful, then let it fall between his fingers. He had enough to worry about. Whatever was going on there, whether Leila was privy to it or not, wasn't his concern. He was fresh off a triple homicide and didn't even recognize the name on his passport. Besides, since the police, or someone from the police, was clearly aware of whatever was going on in that shed, there was nothing he could do for Leila anyway, right? Walker wondered if he had always talked to himself like this. They say you're not crazy unless you answer, but he was the only person around to have a conversation with. Walker thought he might would go crazy if he *didn't* answer.

There was movement and some noise coming from inside the shed. The Mexican men whom the officer had accused of being responsible for the car accident seemed to be closing up shop like he'd demanded. A fly buzzed Walker's ear, and he nearly jumped out of his skin. Walker just needed to be patient, wait for them to finish, then get the hell out of there. That farm and whatever was going on around it was none of his business. And it wasn't his fight.

Walker's head was throbbing. Other than the fact that

he had obviously hit it extremely hard in that car, he felt dehydrated. At least his leg felt pretty good, considering. Gravel on tires sounded off once again up the hill. He leaned forward to peek around the cornstalks. A cherry-red Jeep Wrangler was coming down the path. Same one that was sitting in the driveway at the house.

Leila.

Whether Walker cared or not, whether he wanted to or not, he was about to find out if Leila was involved with whatever was happening on her property. He didn't know why, but he couldn't help but hope she wasn't. Maybe he wasn't a total monster after all.

The Jeep pulled to a stop, once again where Walker couldn't see what was going on. He couldn't have picked a worse hiding spot, but it was really the only choice he had. He heard the door open and a Mexican man's voice speak up.

"Excuse me, you can't be here."

"Excuse me, but I can." Leila sounded defiant, caught off guard by a stranger telling her where she couldn't be. "This is my property you're standing on. Who are you? Where's Tyler?"

"Sorry, Señora Ward. I am Juan. Tyler hired me and my cousin to help with the farm."

"Okay, well, is he around?" she said.

"No, señora. He should be back soon. Can I give him a message?"

"N-no. Listen, have you seen a man walking down here? About six foot three, two hundred and twenty pounds or so. Muscular . . . maybe limping a bit?"

Leila was looking for Walker. Why? Why did she care so much?

"No, señora. We haven't seen anyone."

"All right, well, it's nice to meet you. Tyler didn't tell me he had to hire more people."

"Sorry, señora. You have a nice farm. We'll take good care of it."

"Thank you. Please have Tyler come see me when he gets back. I'll be at the house."

"Yes, ma'am."

Her Jeep door shut, then crunched the gravel as she drove back up the hill.

Now Walker had a decision to make.

Leaving a moment ago was easy. He had no ties there. And he had a whole lot to figure out about himself. But now . . . now that he knew something bad was going on under Leila's unsuspecting nose—the woman who not only took him in as a stranger, cleaned him up, but even lied to her cop brother about him, even after the word *murder* was involved—to walk away from that made Walker the man he feared was on the fake passport. Just a cold-blooded killer in a car accident. But he didn't feel cold-blooded. Walker felt like Leila had stood up for him in a way that no one ever really had before. He couldn't just leave her now, could he?

But who the hell was he to do something to help her? Just because Walker thought he may have been responsible for killing people in a car doesn't mean he's actually equipped to help Leila with her problem, did it?

The men on the other side of the barn began speaking in Spanish. Somehow Walker could understand them. In the small amount of schooling he had, bouncing from family to family, he never took any foreign language classes. They were discussing how upset their boss would be if they didn't finish "bottling up" the rest of the shipment he wanted, and how they were going to stay despite what the "gringo" told them about leaving. Because they had nothing to do with any car accident that happened behind the farm. Then they went inside. Walker heard the shed's door close.

So, Walker could speak Spanish. He had a fake passport. A roll of cash. Skills enough to kill more than one man in a moving vehicle, and judging by the scuffle with Larry inside the house, he also knew how to fight. Whoever he was, Walker thought he just might have the skills to help Leila. Or he might not. But he just didn't feel right about leaving her without at least warning her. He turned into the rows of corn, back toward the house. Walker's troubles weren't going anywhere. Maybe he could at least help relieve Leila of some of hers.

13

Mike parked the car just outside the Ashland Police Department. The heat was still sweltering, and it was especially concentrated around all the blacktop. The police department was nestled into Ashland's downtown area. To Mike, calling it a downtown was a stretch. There was really only one building, maybe a couple, that even reached over ten stories high. It wasn't Mayberry small, but it was small by Mike's standards. There were really only two main drags that ran the length of the downtown area, and they were lined with small-town car dealerships, chain restaurants, and all the banks and churches one could handle.

"This is a cute little town," Alison said.

"Emphasis on little," Mike groaned.

"You are a real bundle of joy, aren't you?"

"What's to be joyful about? We're stuck here in podunk Kentucky. Looking for someone who's meaner than me and you put together, and we have no leads on just where the hell he might be."

"I just said the town was cute. Next time just don't respond."

"Can we just go in now?"

Alison sighed. She looked across the street. Down the alley past a barber shop was a flood wall. She remembered on the flight in that they had landed by a river. It must run through town. She didn't see any real growth around the river. Seemed like a wasted opportunity for a smaller town. Would be a really great place to gather with family to shop, eat on the water, or see concerts and such. Where she grew up in Wichita, they had done a marvelous job of using the river to live and play around.

Alison looked back to Mike. He was sweating and they hadn't even gotten out of the car. "I'm assuming the goal is to see if they know where Walker is? Or if they've seen him?"

"No, Alison, the goal is to find out if Bethany from down in the holler . . . if her black lab had puppies yet or not."

Alison just shook her head and got out of the car. She waited for a couple of officers to walk by before she rounded the front of the car. Mike got out and caught up with her. She decided that ignoring his outbursts would probably be the best way forward.

"You heard Maxwell. She said let me do the talking. So for once, Mike, keep your mouth shut."

Mike put his arm around Alison and dug his fingertips into her shoulder. She wanted to wince in pain, but she couldn't because two more officers were walking out of the building. Both she and Mike smiled and gave the men a nod. As soon as they passed, she threw his arm off her shoulder.

"You'd be doing good just to keep your mouth shut,"

Mike said. "You always have something to say. It's getting real annoying."

They approached the glass double doors with the APD logo printed on the front. Alison stopped.

"I'm the annoying one? Me?"

Mike rolled his eyes, and they both went inside. Alison strode up to the front desk and gave the female officer a smile.

"Agent Brookins and Agent Hudson here to see Detective Pelfrey?"

"Hello," the officer said. "Let me see if he's in his office."

"He's there," Mike blurted. "And he's expecting us. We're kind of in a hurry."

Alison kicked his foot as she smiled at the officer. "Sorry about him, Officer Clark. He's not good at having to leave his desk and do any *real* work."

"It's fine," she said. "We get all types in here. Just one second." The officer picked up the phone. "Detective Pelfrey? Yes, there are a couple of agents here to see you?" A beat. "Okay, I'll send them on back." She hung up the phone and pointed at the door on Alison's right. "Right through there, then three doors down on the right."

"Thank you," Alison said.

Alison reached over and opened the door. She didn't have to count doors to get down to the detective's office. He entered the hallway and stood waiting for them. He was thin in his navy polo shirt. His face was pale beneath his thinning light brown hair. But he had a kind smile. He extended his hand.

"Agent . . ."

Alison gave him a firm shake. "Brookins. This is my partner, Agent Hudson," she said as she thumbed back to Mike. "Thanks for giving us a few minutes of your time."

The detective ushered them inside his office. It was pretty bare. White walls, one small bookshelf, and what looked like a faux cherrywood IKEA desk. Alison took a seat at one of the chairs facing the desk. Mike didn't sit.

"Well, I'm sorry to say it's going to be a quick minute, because we really don't have anything for you. Other than to confirm that the name the senator's office gave us does in fact match what the DNA pulled up."

"Evan Marshall?" Alison said.

"That's right. We found blood in the backseat of the car —on the inside of the door actually—that didn't match the three dead men. Got a hit in the system for an Evan Marshall. No real priors on him, though. How did you know to be looking for him again?"

"None of your business," Mike said.

Alison cleared her throat. "What Agent Hudson *means*, Detective, is that we can't tell you that."

Detective Pelfrey nodded. "Yeah, kinda figured that. Can you at least tell me if he's dangerous?"

Alison looked back at Mike, then to the detective. "Didn't he kill three men in that car?"

"Well, possibly two. The front passenger died from a head injury in the crash."

"How'd he do the other two?" Mike said.

Alison gave him a scolding look.

"I don't follow," Detective Pelfrey said.

"Sorry I have to keep translating," Alison said. "He never lost the Bronx from his dialect. What he means is how did Evan Marshall kill the other two?"

"Will you stop acting like my translator?" Mike said. Then he turned to the detective. "How did he kill them? Gun? Knife? Bare hands? Come on, man. I didn't expect much out of this small-time outfit you've got here but give us something. You're tracking him? You have a lead on his location? What?"

Detective Pelfrey stood. "I assure you that though this might not be a big city, we are very good at what we do."

"I don't give a rat's ass. Just tell us—"

"That's enough, Hudson!" Alison stood. "You're out of line. The detective is just trying to help us. Now, get the hell out of here. There is a coffee shop on the corner. I'll meet you there."

"Coffee? On a ninety-degree, hundred percent humidity day? Are you nuts?"

Alison walked over and shoved Mike until he was out in the hallway. "Get the hell out of here. We need this guy. Now, go!"

"I don't need shit but the location of the car wreck. Then I can go—"

Alison shut the door in his face. The face that was now turning red. She pointed toward the exit of the police station and mouthed the word "Go!" Mike put his hands on his hips, gave his best scowl, then turned and walked away.

"You guys under a lot of pressure on this or what?" the detective said.

Alison turned toward him with a sigh of relief. "Sorry about that. Yes, we are under a lot of pressure, but Agent Hudson is just an asshole."

"Glad you said it."

"Now, where were we? How Evan killed the other two?"

"Right, well, we aren't sure he killed them both. The driver was killed with a gunshot wound to the back of the head, but Marshall's fingerprints aren't on the gun. So we really aren't sure if he's a killer or a victim who was just trying to defend himself against the man with the gun who was sitting beside him. However it went down, Evan Marshall sure was crafty."

"Crafty?" Alison said.

"Yeah, killed the man who had the gun with what seemed like an ink pen to the jugular. We, uh, haven't found the pen, but there were traces of ink at the site of the wound."

"An ink pen?" Alison said.

"Yeah, you believe that?"

"Actually, yeah. I kind of do."

"I know you're not supposed to say, but is this Evan guy some sort of killer for the government or something? Just need to know who might be running around my city, ya know?"

"Like I said, I can't tell you that, Detective. But he is dangerous. That said, he's probably gone into hiding at this point if he's been injured like you think he has been. He won't want to draw any more attention to himself."

"I don't know how bad he's hurt, but his blood was definitely in the car and on the bullet we found."

Alison was quiet for a moment. She had heard many stories about Tom Walker. She hadn't really believed them all, but maybe she would reconsider that now. He hadn't seemed like that sort of man the few times she had been with him, but you never really know. He was pretty quiet. As were most men in their line of work. Assholes like Mike notwithstanding.

"All right. Well, can you give me the location of the crash? We'll stay out of your officers' way, I promise."

"Sure, but I'm actually headed out there now. I can give you a ride."

"Thank you, Detective, but that's okay. We have a car. Besides, I'll spare you a ride with Mr. Personality out there."

"Well, I do appreciate that," the detective said as he wrote on the back of a business card, then handed it to her. "Here's the road it happened on. Just go a couple of miles out. You won't be able to miss it."

"Thank you. We are really more interested in the surrounding area. Any leads on where we can look?"

"There's a farm just beyond the creek where they crashed. Our sheriff has already been out to talk to the owner, so no need to waste your time there. Other farms and houses scattered about, but we've canvased them all."

"Well, if you don't mind," Alison said, "might I have the name of the person at the farm closest to the crash? Just so we can tell our bosses we checked it out ourselves?"

"Sure," the detective said. "Leila Ward. Real nice woman."

"All right, thank you for your time. And your help, Detective Pelfrey."

"No problem. My number is on the other side of that card. Do me a favor?"

"Anything I can," she said.

"If you find him, or find something, please check in with me?"

"I will." Alison reached out and shook his hand. "Thanks again."

She turned and walked out into the hallway. When she made it outside, Mike was sitting in the car. She walked up and pulled on the door handle, but it was locked. She tapped on the window. Instead of unlocking it, he rolled down the window.

"You pull that shit again, you'll be getting a different car of your own. You understand?"

"Go to hell," she said.

Mike glanced down at the pistol resting under his hand on the console.

"Are you serious right now?" Alison said. "You're threatening me?"

"I'm not threatening you. This is me telling you not to step on my toes again like you did with that detective. So, do you understand?"

Alison looked up at the blue afternoon sky. There looked to be some dark clouds way off in the distance. She understood all right. She looked back down and nodded. The door unlocked and she got in. She showed Mike the card with the road on it but didn't say another word.

14

Leila's Jeep wasn't in the driveway. Since she'd been looking for Walker down at the shed by the cornfield, he assumed she'd driven on down the road to continue the search. Or she just went to the store. He was going to have to stop assuming things. Either way, after the third time he knocked, it was confirmed she wasn't home.

Walker had notebooks full of paper in his bag. And of course he knew he had a pen. The blood-crusted writing tool he'd found in his pocket wouldn't soon leave his memory. He could leave a note, but what exactly would he say? *Leila, it's Tom—the murderer—Walker. Just wanted to let you know some bad shit is going down on your property. You might want to look into it. Trust me?* Though his idea of the note was ridiculous, he knew no matter what he wrote, it would read that way to her. The real problem was more about who might find the note before she did. It was clear the men down by the shed knew they were working without Leila's knowledge, so a note from Walker explaining what was going on in the shed would then show the people working criminally on property that she knows things she shouldn't—only putting her in more danger.

Before a decision could be made about the note, Walker heard a vehicle coming up the hill toward the house. There was nowhere for him to hide, so he turned and began walking down the driveway. He'd hoped to see Leila's Jeep crest the hill, but instead, a patrol car came into view. A pit formed in Walker's stomach. He didn't stop walking, but he knew he was about to be forced to.

The officer whipped the car around through the half-circle driveway and sped up before stopping right behind Walker. The officer blipped the siren once before stepping out of the car. As if it wasn't already obvious enough that he or she was a cop.

"Hold it right there," a man's voice said.

Walker did as he asked but didn't turn around.

"Who the hell are you?"

Walker didn't answer.

The patrol car door shut, and the man raised his voice. "I said, who the hell are you? Put your hands above your head where I can see them!"

Walker reached skyward as the man asked. The officer came walking around in front of him, his gun extended. The man was tall. Thick dark hair combed back, but not wet. His face was red behind his golden aviator sunglasses, and he was relatively thin save for the beer gut he was sporting out front. His badge read Sheriff Taylor. Walker was going to make a joke about Mayberry or ask how Opie was doing, but even if the cop got the *Andy Griffith Show* references, it wouldn't improve the situation any.

"Are you deaf? I said, who the hell are you?" The gun waggled in front of him.

"Name's Tom, Leila's friend from the hospital," he said.

The story had worked on Larry, so he decided to stick with it. "There a crime against knocking on a friend's door?"

The officer looked him over. Paused for a second when he noticed the his bloody jeans. "What happened to your leg there?" Then he looked around the driveway. "And where's your vehicle? You teleport here?"

This cop was a little more astute than Leila's brother, Larry. Larry hadn't even noticed Walker was without transportation.

"I rode here with Leila. You mind pointing your weapon somewhere else, Officer?"

"What happened to your leg?"

"Cut it opening a bag of feed when I was helping Leila with the horses. You always just roll up and pull a gun on someone without probable cause?"

"I sure do, when I see a strange man outside my girl-friend's house. Especially when I got a murderer on the loose."

Girlfriend? Not this guy. He didn't seem at all like Leila's type. Not that Walker knew her type, but he just didn't seem like he was in her league.

"Murderer?" Walker said. "Sounds terrifying. Makes more sense now. But seeing as how I'm not a murderer, can I put my hands down?"

The officer stabbed the pistol forward. "Hell no, you'll keep them up, right where I can see 'em."

Walker nodded. He knew he shouldn't antagonize this man any more. There was a good chance his next step was taking him to the police department.

"Now, Tom, show me some ID. And go slow."

Walker didn't have an ID. *Evan* did. And that was a problem.

"I can't do that, Officer."

"Why the hell not?"

"Well, I didn't drive here, as I said before. So I didn't grab my wallet before I left the house. I knew I was staying here with Leila."

"You stayed the night here?" The officer puffed out his chest.

Walker wasn't doing a great job of defusing the situation. Maybe he should let his alter ego, Evan, do the talking. Couldn't be worse than he was doing now.

"Turn around, slowly, and walk over to the car. Put your hands on the hood and don't make a move."

Walker stayed put. "That really necessary? Leila will be back any minute. She'll tell you who I am."

"Yeah? I have a feeling that's not true. In fact, I don't think you know her at all. That's why you're *leaving* right now without her giving you a ride. Now, put your hands on the hood of the car, right now, or I'll make you."

Walker turned and walked over to the car. He leaned palms down on the hood. The fiberglass was hot from the morning sun. The officer holstered his gun and began frisking Tom.

"Anything sharp in your pockets I need to watch out for?"

"No, sir."

He started at Tom's back and frisked down his right leg.

"You wouldn't happen to know anything about the accident on the road behind this farm, now would you?"

"Only what Larry told Leila this morning."

The officer stood. He was surprised. "You know Larry?"

Walker shook his head. "No, but I met him inside earlier. Jumpy fella."

"He just left here after seeing you all bloodied?"

"It's a cut on my leg," Walker said. "I wouldn't exactly

call me *bloodied*. And, yes, he left after Leila told him to leave her friend alone."

"And that's you?" the sheriff said as he finished his frisk. "You're her friend, whom I've never heard of, in the year we've been dating?"

"Well, I'm friend enough to know you're not dating now."

Sheriff Taylor grabbed a handful of Tom's shirt as he spun him around. "That right, smart-ass? You think you know our situation?"

Walker held up his hands. "I don't want any trouble. I didn't sleep with Leila. She just needed a friend. Now, unless you're going to charge me with being in the wrong place at the wrong time, do you mind letting me go?"

The sheriff loosened his grip, but not the anger in his face. Walker wasn't sure what the sheriff was going to do, but when Leila's Jeep came into view out on the road, he was hoping it would provide a better outcome. Leila honked the horn and sped into the driveway.

"Don't you say a word when she gets out of that Jeep," the sheriff said. "You understand me?"

Walker nodded.

Leila was out of her car almost before it came to a stop. "What the hell do you think you're doing, Andy?"

No, Walker thought. He couldn't believe the sheriff's name was actually Andy Taylor. He'd already heard all the Andy Griffith jokes throughout his entire life by then.

"You stay right there, Leila," Andy said. "Who is this guy?"

"You don't tell me what to do on my property. Now, get your hands off him, and get the hell out of here."

Leila kept her distance. Walker could tell that whatever

she and the sheriff had as a relationship, it was over. In *her* mind at least.

"Calm down, Leila. A strange man was walking outside your house—"

"Don't do that. Don't tell me to calm down!"

"There is a murderer on the loose. I'm sure Larry told you that. I'm within my right to ask who the hell this is."

Leila softened a bit. "As I'm sure he has already mentioned, he is my friend. So go find your murderer somewhere else. He ain't here."

"What's his name?" Andy said, defiant.

"Tom Walker."

"The cut on his leg?"

"Helping me with the horses. Now, enough questions, Sheriff. You aren't welcome here anymore, in case you forgot."

Andy took a step away from Walker, toward Leila. Leila took two steps back.

"Don't you come near me."

Andy stopped. Then looked at Walker. "This isn't over, Walker. You work at the hospital, you said. Who's your boss?"

"I didn't say I worked at the hospital. I said I knew Leila from the hospital."

The sheriff smiled, then looked at Leila. Still smiling, he pointed at Walker. "No ID. Shady story. No car here, leaving before you got back. I don't know what the hell is going on, but I'm gonna find out." Andy looked back at Tom. "Give me your address and where you work. And if—"

The radio attached to the sheriff's upper chest squawked, forcing him to stop talking. A woman's voice came through.

"Sheriff, Detective Billings needs you down by the crash

site. Says he found something that might help, but says you should hurry. The creek water might affect it."

Andy depressed the button on the radio. "On my way." He began walking toward his cruiser but turned back to look at Tom. "Don't leave here. I'll be back within the hour. We have more to talk about."

"That's up to Leila," Tom said.

Andy looked to her.

"Don't look at me. He's welcome here. You aren't."

The sheriff shook his head, then turned his shades toward Walker. "Don't leave here." Then he got in his car, shut the door, and sped away. Not more than an inch from running over the tips of Walker's boots. That left Walker and Leila in the driveway alone.

"Nice guy. I see what you saw in him," Walker said, trying to break the tension.

Leila held up her finger. "Don't." She studied him for a moment. "I may have just traded the devil I know for the devil I don't."

Walker didn't know whether she was right or wrong about that himself. So he kept his mouth shut.

15

"We getting close yet or not?" Mike said. "It feels like we've been in the middle of nowhere forever."

"I'm just going on the address the detective gave us," Alison said. "I'm sure it won't be much longer."

The two of them had driven by the car accident that killed three of their colleagues and lost them Tom Walker. There were still a couple of police cars where it happened, and a few officers making sure no one was going to mess with the crime scene. Realizing they weren't going to get anything from the scene of the crime, Alison called Detective Pelfrey back, and he was nice enough to give the actual address of Leila Ward's farm so they wouldn't have to chase their tails on those back roads trying to find it. Mike was becoming more irritated than his already normally irritated self the longer they went without a real lead.

"I don't even understand why the hell we are out here," Mike said. "I don't know about you, but I'm not a detective. Never have been. My job is to act on the intel that our intelligence officers give us. Not gather intel myself. I'm the guy that ends the threat, not pokes his nose around looking for it."

"That's probably why Maxwell paired us. I'm usually the intel gatherer."

"You mean you've never killed anyone?"

"I didn't say that, did I?"

"Well, have you?" Mike said.

"I had the misfortune of killing someone before I ever got involved with Maxwell Solutions. I was US Army in my previous life."

Mike looked over at her like she had two heads. "Pretty girl like you? I bet those fellas couldn't keep their hands off you."

"Unlike you, Mike, some men actually respect women. Pretty or not."

"What the hell is there to respect about an ugly woman?"

Alison didn't respond, because a response wasn't merited.

Mike continued, "And what do you mean you had the '*misfortune*' of killing someone? There's nothing misfortunate about ending someone who's an asshole. It's not like we're tasked with killing Gandhi or Mother Theresa, for God's sake."

"Yeah?" Alison said, then shook her head. "And what about Tom Walker, Mike? What's your excuse for plotting to kill him? He's the same as you. Should I kill you?"

Mike laughed. "You could try."

They shared an unloving glare.

Mike looked back at the road. "And there's plenty of difference between me and Tom Walker. I didn't kill four of our own, now did I?"

"It was three men, and they were going to kill him in that car, Mike. You know that."

"I don't know that for sure. And if you listen to the chatter, it was *four* of our men in total. The three in the car, yes, but the reason they may have been in that car to kill Walker, if that was the case, was because—from what I hear —he disobeyed a direct order and stopped Mitchell from taking out his mark about a week ago. He shot Mitchell instead."

"Maybe so, but he saved an innocent woman's life. And from what I hear, Walker only wounded Mitchell so he couldn't carry out the bullshit mission. He died later because someone didn't want him talking."

"Shit, whatever, Alison. Why are you here then if you are so up this Walker's ass? Huh?"

"I'm not up Walker's ass. I don't even know him. I'm just objective. Not biased for the company, like you. You think everything Maxwell does is aboveboard?"

"Again," Mike said, "then why are you here doing work for them?"

"You think I have a choice now? With what I know about our little secret, government-funded organization?"

"What I think is you should keep your damn mouth shut. We make a lot of money doing what we are told to do. What *we* signed up for."

Alison sighed and sat back in her seat. "And you think everything we do is right? On the up-and-up?"

"I think that you'd better comprehend what I learned a long time ago, sweetheart. We are who we are. Killers. Killers who get paid to manage and change situations in the world that no one else on the planet can. That's why they pay us so well. To do what we do best. What we were trained to do. Not ask questions about why the government does what they do or wants what they want. That's for the politicians to worry about."

"And that's how you keep your conscience clear?"

"Yes it is. Would work for you too. We are simply tools of the machine. The machine that keeps the greatest country in the world, the greatest country in the world. Champagne and rainbows don't do it. Dirty work in the shadows does."

Alison pointed out the front windshield toward the road. "Might want to slow down. Looks like they want you to stop."

A police car was veering over into the middle of the two-lane road they were on. Its lights began flashing.

"Great," Mike said. "Local bumfuck police. Always a treat to work with."

"You are the saltiest son of a bitch I've ever met."

Mike pulled the car to the right side of the road and came to a stop.

"Thank you," he said.

A man in uniform stepped out of the police cruiser and began walking to the driver-side door.

Alison clarified, "It wasn't a compliment, Mike."

Mike rolled down the window. "How can we help you, Officer . . ." Mike waited for the sun's gleam to move from the man's metal name tag. "Taylor?"

"Would y'all mind stepping out of the vehicle for me? We have a manhunt in the area. I'd rather not take any chances."

"Actually, Officer," Mike said.

"It's Sheriff actually."

"All right . . . actually, *Sheriff*, it's hot as hell out there. You mind if we stay in here? If you just let me reach for my wallet, I think you'll oblige."

"Why? You cops?"

"FBI actually."

"I was afraid you might show up. Reach slow for your credentials, if you don't mind."

"Not at all," Mike said as he slipped his hand down into his back pocket. He pulled it out, opened it, and showed the fake FBI ID that Maxwell had made for them.

"All right," Sheriff Taylor said. "What is it you're doing out here?"

Alison cleared her throat. "Well, like you said, Sheriff, that manhunt is of particular interest to the federal government, and we are looking for Evan Marshall just the same as you."

"How the hell do you already know his name? I just now spoke with forensics and they told me."

Mike tapped the car where the window was open with his hand. "We are federal agents, Officer Taylor. It's our job to know what you don't."

"It's Sheriff. And if you're wandering out here, you obviously don't know any more than I do. And if it's Leila Ward you're driving out here to talk to, don't bother. I just spoke with her."

"Nothing out of the ordinary?" Alison ducked down and leaned across the console to look up at the sheriff.

Sheriff Taylor looked off into the distance for a second, then back to Alison. "Nope. Nothing out of the ordinary."

"You hesitated," Alison said.

Mike looked over at her, confused.

"I'm sorry, ma'am?" the sheriff said.

"When I asked you if there was anything out of the ordinary, you paused. Like you knew there was something out of the ordinary, but you were deciding if it was something we needed to know."

Sheriff Taylor laughed. "That what you got from that pause?"

"It is," Alison said, unwavering.

"You might be overthinking that, ma'am."

"Maybe. But when we drive up and knock on Leila Ward's door, are we going to find that everything is perfectly ordinary?"

Sheriff Taylor shifted his weight and put his hands on his hips.

"You're hesitating again, Sheriff," Alison said quickly.

"Christ, you're like a mosquito on a salty neck," Sheriff Taylor said.

"I tell her the same thing," Mike said. "But it's what makes her good at reading people."

"We're just trying to find a very dangerous man, Sheriff," Alison said. "All I'm asking is that you help us do that. Or help us help you catch him."

"You have a photo of this Evan Marshall?" the sheriff said. "Somehow our department is having trouble locating one."

"There's a reason for that, Sheriff," Alison said. "And that's the reason we are here. This man is someone that powerful people don't want regular people knowing about. Catch my drift?"

"Okay then." The sheriff adjusted his belt and rested his right hand on the butt of his pistol. "I'll tell you this. There's a man I've never seen before at Leila's house right now. She says she's known him for a while. And I believe her. But when I get a break from what I have to do next, I'm going to make sure he is who he says he is."

"And who's that?"

"Tom Walker. Ring a bell?"

"Not to us," Mike answered immediately. "Like she said,

we're looking for Evan Marshall."

"Now you know everything I do," the sheriff said. "So go on and do what you have to do. Just don't get in my officers' way."

Mike started to talk, but Alison put her hand on his arm and spoke instead. "You won't even know we're here. Especially if you'll update us on anything you find."

Mike produced a card from his wallet and handed it to the sheriff.

"Will do, if you'll do the same," Sheriff Taylor said.

"Done," Alison said. "Have a nice day, Sheriff."

The sheriff tipped his hat and walked back to the cruiser. He switched off his red-and-blues, then pulled away.

"Not terrible, Alison." Mike said. "Sounds like we've got our man."

"Sounds that way. What's the play?"

"Well, this is where you sit back and let me do what I do best. We've found him. Your job is over."

"My job is to see this through to the end. And I didn't try to tell you what to do, Mike. I just asked what was next."

"We have a long night ahead of us. There's no way a man like Walker doesn't know we're coming for him. And even less of a chance that he's not ready for it."

"Why do you think he would let his real name be known?" Alison said. "And why would this Leila woman let him stay?"

"Don't know. His injury might be one reason. And maybe he told her he'd kill her if she didn't. Either way, we need to be certain of everything before we try to take him on. Now we just have to find a place to watch from." Mike turned toward her. "Then we kill the son of a bitch and get the hell back home."

16

The entire house smelled like bacon. Not only had Leila let Walker in, but she'd also whipped him up some scrambled eggs and reheated the left-over bacon she'd cooked that morning. More memories of Jim and Kim crept in. Kim would always fix a "makeup" breakfast the morning after Jim would beat up on one of the kids. It didn't soften the blow, but it was endearing the way she would squeeze the orange juice fresh.

Walker was getting tired of fifteen-year-old memories of his life. He needed modern Tom Walker recollections, or he was really going to find himself in trouble. If it wasn't already too late.

Leila set a plate down in front of him. "It's not gourmet, but it will keep your energy up."

"I told you, you don't have to feed me."

Tom was sitting at a small round table across from the sink in the kitchen. More cherrywood. There were four floral place mats at each chair and a small vase in the middle that held a few black-eyed Susans. Kim used to pick the yellow wildflowers; that's how Walker knew the name.

Leila was studying him again now as she stood over him. "Are you playing games with me?" She handed him a fork.

Walker wasn't sure the last time he'd eaten, so he stabbed at the scrambled eggs and took a large bite.

"Excuse me?" he said, mouth full.

"Is this an act? This amnesia bit?" She stepped back and folded her arms. "Did I just catch you in the barn before you could slip away and you played it like you didn't know who you are? After you killed those people? And don't lie to me. I'm not afraid of you even if you did do it. It's clear that whoever you are, or whatever you are, you aren't planning on hurting me. But did you kill them?"

Walker set down his fork and stared at Leila. He didn't know if it was her kind eyes or because of what he saw on the other side of her property, or maybe because she was the only human being on Earth that he knew at that moment, but he decided he was going to tell her everything. She was either going to kick him out or offer guidance. Walker was okay with either one.

"I think I did."

Leila's surprised look told Walker she may have wanted the truth, but she hadn't really been expecting it. She almost stumbled as her hand searched for the back of the chair opposite him.

"Well, okay," she said. "I guess that tells me you aren't playing games."

"I wish I was, Leila. It would be a lot easier."

"So you really don't remember last night?"

"No." Walker picked up a piece of bacon for a bite. It was good and salty.

"But you think you killed them. That's quite a thing to say to someone."

"You told me not to lie, and I don't see any reason to. I don't know what the hell I did or didn't do for sure, but I stumbled into your barn with a bullet wound in my leg, a bloody ink pen in my pocket, and a wad of cash sitting by a passport that has my picture on it but someone else's name."

"A bloody pen?"

"Yeah, not sure what that's about."

"So, your name isn't Tom Walker?"

"No, ma'am, it is. I remember my name. It's Tom. But the passport says Evan Marshall."

Leila laughed. "What are you, some sort of spy?"

Walker didn't laugh. He just looked her in the eye. The thought had crossed his mind.

Leila sat up and leaned forward, arms folded on the table. "You're a spy, aren't you? Or an assassin or something. I mean, you're built like one. And the way you took apart and put that gun back together . . . that was spy-like—"

"Are you . . . getting excited about this?" Walker said.

It was clear to Walker that she was; he just wanted to call it to her attention.

"What do you want from me? It's either you're a spy or a serial killer or something. I'd prefer—at least in my mind—that if you are a killer, that you'd be doing it for the right reasons. And not just for the sport of it."

"The right reasons to be a killer?"

"You know. Government said they were terrorists or something. You know what I mean."

Walker nodded as he shoveled more food into his mouth. He did understand, because he was hoping the same thing.

"I mean," Leila went on, "the passport tells us that much, that you're someone your not, like a spy, right?"

95

"I don't know . . ."

Walker believed Leila's line of thought just might be right.

"What? Was there something else in your bag? Some other clue?"

"There are some moleskin notebooks in there, but I haven't had a chance to read them. If there is even anything written in them. Your brother came in just as I was opening one."

Leila didn't respond. She just looked over at his bag sitting in the chair between them.

"What?" he said.

"I don't have a job anymore," Leila said. "And the horses are fed. Let's see what they say!"

Walker took a drink of water. "What if I don't want to know what's written in those notebooks?"

"Well, I do. And besides, you're in a lot of trouble. Would do you some good to get all the information you can get. Andy just got called back to the crash site. They found something. You don't think your DNA is in that car, do you? Do I need to remind you that your blood was all over you when I found you?"

She didn't need to remind him. He knew all too well. And he would be doing his best to run and hide right then if it wasn't for what he saw in the shed just outside her cornfield.

"I need to tell you something," Walker said.

"That doesn't sound good." Leila folded her arms. "You try to steal some money before you left or something?"

"It's not about me."

"O . . . kay . . ."

"How well do you know the guy your dad hired to keep the cornfields and do other such work on the farm?"

"Tyler? Why? That's an odd question for a stranger to be asking?"

"I have good reason. You know him well?"

"Um, no. I wouldn't say well. We all know his folks. Just like everyone else around here. Why?"

"He ever been in trouble? Been into drugs maybe?"

"Where is this coming from? Why would you be asking about him?"

"He a troublemaker or not?"

"He's had some run-ins with the law, but not for a long time. What's going on?"

"When I left the house earlier, I walked through the cornfields and popped out by the building you have back there."

"Equipment shed."

"Right. That. Well, I overheard an exchange between some guys working there. You saw them when you drove down looking for me."

"Yeah, I called Tyler to ask about that, but he didn't answer."

"Right. Someone pulled up in a police car and had a very interesting conversation with them before you got there."

"Police car? Who was it?"

"I didn't see him, but . . . well, I didn't see who it was. But the officer was asking about the accident I apparently was in."

"Makes sense. They're canvasing the area. Asking people if they saw, well, you, I guess."

Walker frowned. "Not really what I mean. He knew the men who work for you. Knows their boss too. And their boss isn't you or Tyler."

"What the hell does that mean?"

"I don't really know. He asked if their boss had anything to do with the killings, because it looks like something the cartel would do."

Leila laughed. "The cartel?" She laughed again. "You're serious?"

"Serious enough to come back here to warn you, even though I believe I am a very wanted man right now."

Leila sat back in her seat. She was staring at him blankly. Walker finished his food as he gave her a minute.

"I don't really understand what you're implying."

Walker finished his water and set down the glass. "I'm not implying anything. I'm just telling you what I heard. That, and I apparently speak Spanish. The men were speaking to each other in Spanish after the policemen left, and I could understand them. Not that it pertains to this conversation."

Leila bypassed the Spanish epiphany. "What did they say?"

"Long and short of it, I think they're running drugs from beneath your equipment shed."

"What?"

"How much I don't know. But a cop knows, and that's real bad news for you."

"Worse news than a possible drug ring in my backyard?"

"A lot worse," Walker said.

"I don't follow."

"Worse because now you can't call the police to take care of your problem. 'Cause they are part of your problem."

Leila shook her head emphatically. "Nope. No way. You just heard them wrong. Maybe your Spanish isn't what you think it is."

"Maybe not, but my English is just fine. And the cop

asked about the cartel and the car accident. It's not a coincidence that I heard the two men talking about drugs after that. The cop said clean it out now. After he left, they said they were going to finish the order they were working on."

"And you didn't see the cop?"

"I didn't. I was behind the shed."

"Damn it."

"Yeah, sorry."

Leila stood. "Well, only one way to find out what's going on."

Walker stood with her. "You can't go down there."

"The hell I can't. It's my property."

"And what if you find what I think you'll find. Then what? You'll ask them politely to leave?"

"I, well, I'll . . . I don't know. But I can't just let them make drugs, or sell drugs, or whatever they're doing."

Walker rubbed the stubble on his jaw. "That's exactly what you have to do."

"I used to date the sheriff, and my brother is on the force. I think I'll be fine."

"Yeah? And what if one of them is in on it?"

Leila put her hands on her hips. "Who the hell do you think you are?"

Walker nodded. He knew it wasn't his place. He just didn't want to see her get hurt.

"No one at all. I just don't want something bad to happen. That's all."

Now Leila folded her arms across her chest. "All right then, Mr. Maybe I'm a Spy. What are those dormant instincts telling you?" She was being sarcastic. "Huh? What do you suggest?"

"Take it for what it's worth, but I would get more information first. If you go down there and let it be known that you know what's going on, what choice are you giving the people who may be illegally using your property? They most likely aren't forgiving individuals, and they sure as hell wouldn't want you to interrupt their stream of revenue."

She was quiet for moment.

"Well damn," Leila said. "That's pretty well thought out for someone who doesn't even know who the hell he is."

"Like I said, take it for what it's worth."

Leila softened. "No . . . I-I appreciate you coming back. You could have just left me here . . . clueless."

"Least I could do."

Leila took a deep breath and sat back down. "Well . . . Now what?"

17

The house still smelled of bacon as Leila and Walker moved into the living room. It hadn't taken long to answer Leila's question of what's next. As soon as she asked it, the two of them turned their eyes to Walker's bag. In broad daylight, with the strange men still doing whatever work they were doing inside Leila's equipment shed, they couldn't investigate what was happening there. They both chose to focus on Walker and his problems for the moment.

Before moving into the living room, Walker had requested a few more ibuprofen. His leg was at a dull ache, but his head was still pounding. He'd obviously hit it hard enough to wipe his recent memory. Couple that with lack of fluids, some extreme heat on his little walk, and he was having a hard time stabilizing.

The two of them sat on the couch. As Walker went to open the bag, Leila exhaled.

"If it really is drugs, what do you think they're doing with it? And how the hell did they come to choose my property?"

Walker stopped undoing the buckles on his bag and gave Leila his full attention. "I thought about that on the way back through the cornfield. What is the talk around town about drugs? Anything the area is known for?"

"Well, yeah, they don't call it the OxyContin trail for nothing," Leila said. "And I would tell you that it isn't the problem it used to be since they cracked down on the pain clinics in Florida where all the pills were coming from, but . . ."

Walker gave Leila a minute to think.

"We were having a serious uptick in overdoses before I left the hospital. Everyone was talking about it. Saying it reminded them of a few years ago. But this time the problem was because of more fentanyl being in the pills."

"Fentanyl?"

"Fentanyl is a strong synthetic opioid. Kind of like morphine, but much more powerful. Like fifty to a hundred times more powerful. In medicine, it's used to treat pain, but the big thing right now is mixing it with oxycodone and making fake M30 pills that used to be all the rage before the crackdown. It was a real epidemic here in Eastern Kentucky. Lots of kids getting hooked and overdosing. Just like my . . ."

Leila went quiet. Walker knew she was thinking about her dad.

"Anyway," she went on, "there have been a lot more overdoses lately because the fentanyl they are lacing the pills with is too strong. It's just awful." Leila's face sank. "You don't think . . . ?"

"There's no way I can speculate. Not only am I no expert on drugs, I don't even know what I do for a living."

"Yeah, sorry. And here you are sitting with a stranger about to go through your personal things. Must be such an odd feeling."

Walker squared up to her. "Why are you helping me? You don't owe me anything. All I can do is cause you trouble. You've already lied to two police officers for me."

"One police officer," Leila said, flashing a smile. "My brother doesn't count. And to be honest, Andy doesn't really either. Trust me, he won't be coming after me with what happened between us."

That sounded like a can of worms Walker didn't want to open.

"But, to answer your question of why I'm helping you," Leila said. "I'm not really sure. My best friend and therapist would tell you it's because I couldn't save my dad, so now I'm trying to get a do-over by helping you. Maybe you should talk to her. She might have some memory tricks up her sleeve."

"I'm sure I need therapy, but . . . probably best not to involve anyone else. I have a feeling knowing about me is going to be a very complicated thing soon."

They were quiet as they considered Walker's situation. He used the silence to reach into his bag and pull out a handful of small black leather-bound notebooks. Each of them had a thin black elastic strap that held them closed. He set four of them on the end table next to the lamp, keeping one in his hands. He pulled the elastic strap over the leather, releasing the pages. The book was filled from cover to cover with black ink scribbles. Walker turned the book toward Leila and fanned the pages for her to see.

"Wow. That's a lot of writing. It's crazy to think you spent so much time logging things in there and have no memory of it. Are you nervous about what it says?"

Walker thought for a moment as he fanned the pages with his thumbs. Looking at all the documented thoughts of a stranger. Himself.

"I'm not sure nervous is the word. Afraid might be more fitting."

"Afraid? Of what you'll find?"

Walker looked up into Leila's brown eyes. "Who. Afraid of *who* I'll find."

Leila didn't need more explanation.

Walker thumbed to the first page in the notebook. At the top of the lined page was a box meant for a date. Instead of a date, all that was written was the number seven. Below that, the writing began. Walker didn't want to read it, but he didn't really have a choice.

"You don't have to read it out loud," Leila said. "And I can give you some privacy. This is personal. Feel free to keep it that way."

"Thank you. But I'm not sure I really have anything to hide from you at this point," he said, then looked back down at the page. "Just a number seven at the top. Maybe I was numbering the order of the notebooks?"

Leila shrugged. "Makes sense."

Walker cleared his throat and began reading: *After watching Omar fall to the ground, I stood over him, covered in his blood.*

Walker took a deep breath and looked up from the notebook. Leila's mouth was hanging open. They had no idea what to expect from the notebooks, but Walker felt the same on the inside as Leila looked on the outside.

Walker went back to the writing: *The room was filled with sounds—the air conditioner was running, cars passing by on the street just outside, the blood pulsing onto the floor from the opening I'd just carved in Omar's neck—but I only heard the thud of my own beating heart. It wasn't racing. It wasn't beating any faster than if I was sitting on a patio sipping a cup of coffee. And that's what scared me. It's what had always frightened me about myself. I wasn't human. How could I be? So calm in such a ferocious and violent situation. How did I get here?*

Walker was now at the end of the first page. Rather than turning over to the next, he closed the notebook. He didn't look up. Unlike the man describing himself in the notebook, Walker's heart was racing. Could he really have been writing this about himself?

"Maybe . . ." Leila broke the silence. "Maybe you just wanted to be a writer. And you are just telling a story here."

Walker didn't look up. He stared blankly at the black cover of the notebook. Maybe he did want to be a writer. When he was growing up, he often used to find a quiet place to write some poetry. He'd always voraciously read any mystery novel he could get his hands on. Walker wanted to believe this theory. But even if it were true, that he was just telling a story, he could feel in his bones that it had been written from experience.

Tom Walker was a monster.

Evan Marshall too.

And possibly many other aliases, all the same. He didn't have memory of these things . . . but he knew.

Leila's phone began ringing. Both of them jumped.

"Hello?" Leila answered. "Yes, this is she . . . what?"

Walker looked up and saw a look of horror on Leila's face.

"ICU? Is she okay?" Leila stood. "I'm on my way!"

Walker got up from the couch. Leila ended the call.

"It's my niece," she said, breathless. "She's OD'd. I have to go to the hospital."

Leila began gathering her things and throwing them into her purse.

"Thank you for all your help," Walker said. "I'll see myself out."

Leila stopped for a second. "I don't have time for this right now. Just stay and get some rest. Keep the door locked. Don't go anywhere; you'll only make things worse for yourself."

"Yeah, no, I'll be fine. Just go. I hope she's okay."

Leila stopped at the door and looked back at Walker. "Listen, I know we're strangers. But we're kind of in a mess here together. Maybe we can help each other out. So, really, don't leave."

"I won't. Go. Go take care of your family. Don't worry about me or even what's happening on your property. We'll figure it out."

Leila gave a faltering smile, then walked out the door. Walker heard her use the key to lock the door. He felt a little light-headed, so he sat back down on the couch. He glanced over at the stack of notebooks as he heard Leila pull away in her Jeep. He wasn't up for any more stories at the moment, so he decided to lie down for a bit.

But the stories came anyway. In the form of nightmares. And he caught a glimpse of Omar's face in his dreams just before he cut the man's throat, just like the notebook had said. Walker didn't know it yet, but his first memory had just come back to him. The reality he was hoping to wake up to was nothing more than a nightmare he'd been living since he left his foster home as a teenager. The question to come was, was it a nightmare for him? Or was he the nightmare for everyone else?

18

Leila's house was quiet. So much so that Walker had finally been able to relax and fall into a deep sleep. However, what awaited him in sleep was anything but relaxing.

Walker stood silent in the driving rain. Visibility was minimal. This would make it even easier to get the job done undetected. His target had been setting up for a barbecue, but the rain forced his family inside, making the assassination less messy. The clouds were dark overhead, the kind of clouds that make five in the evening look more like nine o'clock at night. Walker could see the family through the oversize window on the second story of the house. They were gathering at the dinner table that overlooked the backyard. They were waiting on Daddy to bring the food. The daddy they thought worked hard all week at his consulting job to pay for this beautiful home in the Hamptons.

Walker knew better.

This was one of the few assignments he'd had in the United States in his long career. He had considered going home to Kentucky when he'd finished, but he'd already been assigned a rogue assassin staying in Greece who needed to be dealt with.

Besides, there was nothing more than bad memories back in his home state, and enemies never sleep. From the outside looking in, as Mark Johnson flipped burgers from beneath his umbrella, he didn't look anything like an enemy. However, Andrey Sidorov, a Russian spy who'd just managed to kill a US Senator with a paring knife, was pretty good at disguises.

Walker would normally find a spot in a tree or wait to watch a neighbor's pattern to get a good shot off from their home when they left. But his boss wanted this done in a hurry, and he wanted it to look like an accident. Something about Russian-American foreign affairs. Walker didn't get involved with the politics. He was the man they sent to kill the killers, yet in comparison he would still consider the politicians to be the real down-and-dirty players.

Walker heard the car he'd been waiting for and looked back over his shoulder at the front of the house. The pizza he'd ordered for Andrey Sidorov's family had just pulled up in a maroon Nissan Altima. Walker turned back to his target. Sidorov was pulling the first burger off the grill. Over Sidorov's shoulder, Walker watched something get the family's attention. The delivery person had just rung the doorbell.

Showtime.

Walker pulled his suppressed Smith and Wesson 43 C from inside his coat. He chose the light .22 caliber round because he only wanted to penetrate the propane tank and still be able to find the round. The family had all gone to see who was at the door. It was time. Walker raised the gun, stared down the sights, and pulled the trigger when the nose was hovering over the propane tank. He knew the twenty-pound propane tank wouldn't explode from the round he fired. But he did know that when the round penetrated the tank, the propane would blow up through the fire in the grill, disguising his shot as a very unfortunate grilling accident.

The propane tank made a loud pop when hit. But it was the flame that was the star of the show. Walker hadn't expected it to flame so much and for so long. As Sidorov was blown to his back, writhing in pain, Walker bent down and picked up his shell casing from the bullet he fired and placed it in his pocket. The family would be back at the window soon, so now he needed to hurry.

Walker holstered his gun and rushed forward. The fire had finally stopped as the propane ran dry, but he could see through the rain that half of Sidorov's face had been melted. Walker reached down and grabbed the long-pronged grill fork and moved past the grill. With his right hand he pulled the only other tool he'd brought with him from his coat pocket. A handheld metal detector wand.

Judging by the angle the bullet had traveled through the tank, it should be lodged in the dirt near Sidorov's feet, who was now on his back shouting in pain. Walker toggled on the power to the wand and waved it over the ground. On his third pass, he got a blip. The ground was wet, so it was easy to fish the bullet from the mud. He picked up the propane tank and turned it to where the bullet had entered. He pounded down on it twice with the butt of the pot fork, making it too big to look like a bullet had been there. The other side of the tank was blown out, so no worries there.

That was the last of the evidence; now it was time to finish the job. His escape route was clear: he would walk right beneath the window of the dining room and around the house into the adjacent woods. Probably as the family was discovering the dead man they called Dad from the window above him. If they only knew the monster he really was.

Sidorov actually made it to a seated position, directly facing Walker. But he couldn't see his killer. The flame from the tank had made sure of that. Now it was time for Walker to make sure *nothing else was working on the Russian spy. He walked forward, and just as he was beside him, Walker reached back, then rammed the pot fork forward, both prongs sinking deep into the man's neck—*

Walker shot up from lying on the couch. He was drenched in sweat and breathing wildly. The room was pitch black, and he frantically tried to regain his wits. That's when the sound that woke him started again. A loud banging at the door.

"Leila? Leila, if you're there, open up!"

Leila.

It all came back to Walker upon hearing the man say her name. He was back in the world of strangers, where he didn't know who or what he really was. Except he did. And that dream, which he sensed was one of his memories coming back to him, told him exactly what he didn't want to know.

"Leila? You there?" The man's muffled shout came again from outside the front door. "I tried calling, but you didn't answer. It's Andy. I need to talk to your friend."

Walker stood from the couch and walked over to the door. He heard the sheriff's radio squawk. A woman's voice followed. "Sheriff, we have a report of a stranger in the Walmart parking lot. Two people have called in creeped out. Could be your guy. Want me to send a patrol car?"

"No need. I'll go check it out."

Walker was waiting for him to leave, but instead, Andy's cell phone began ringing.

"Larry, I was about to call you," Andy answered.

There was quiet for a moment. Andy didn't have the phone on speaker, so Walker couldn't hear what Leila's brother was saying.

"Wait, calm down," Andy said. "Take a breath. I can't

understand you. What are you saying happened to your daughter?"

Leila's niece. Walker knew they were talking about the overdose.

"Listen, you've got to pull it together, Larry." A pause. "Yeah, I hear what you're saying, and I'm real sorry about your daughter, but I don't have enough information to make an arrest. Much less a warrant to do so."

Andy paused to listen to Larry. Walker's mind jumped back to the police officer who was down at the equipment shed talking about the car accident and the cartel. Walker obviously didn't know what was going on inside or beneath that equipment shed, but if the cartel was involved, it had to be drugs. Walker had thought the officer speaking with the Mexican men sounded like Larry, but from the way the phone conversation was going with Andy, it sounded like Larry was trying to find out who was dealing the drugs, not in on making them himself. Larry and Andy had a similar way of speaking, same cadence, same tone; maybe it was the sheriff's car and voice he'd heard. He was mad at himself for not getting a better look. He just wasn't in position to take the chance of being seen. Being wanted for murder made him reluctant to take that risk.

"Listen . . ." Andy started talking again, but he quickly trailed off as he walked away. That was all the information Walker was going to get at that point. The car door shut, and Walker peeked out the window as the patrol car pulled away. He let out a sigh of relief. Relief that was half from the nightmare he'd had and half from wondering what the sheriff wanted with him. Both weren't good.

Before he could pull himself together, he heard another vehicle approaching the house. He checked the window again and saw a vehicle shaped like Leila's Jeep pull in from the opposite direction the sheriff had driven away in. Walker knew it was time for him to make his exit. Whatever it was the sheriff wanted could only be about what happened in that car accident. And if Walker really was in that car, and was really responsible for what happened to those men, he had to disappear.

That was his thought before he watched Leila in the yellow light of the front porch. Her figure walked around the hood of her Jeep, then hunched over it. Her head rested on her folded arms as her back repeatedly rose and fell. He could tell she was sobbing.

He would console her. Then he would leave. There was no room for anything else.

19

Walker took one more look in the direction the sheriff went, then opened the front door. Leila didn't move to look up, but he could hear her sobbing. The sticky summer night enveloped Walker like a warm, wet blanket. He walked down the porch steps and over to Leila. Walker had never been with a woman before his current memory bank stopped at fifteen, so he had no idea if he had a way with them as a man. However, he had plenty of experience comforting a suffering woman, as he did it many times with his foster mother whenever she took a solid beating.

Walker knew that less was more. Let her know you're there for her, but let her make the decision to engage. He didn't say anything when he made it to Leila; he simply rested his hand on her shoulder. She took a sharp inhale. Her lungs sputtered from the emotion. Her second breath was less shaky. She placed her hand on top of his and gave it a squeeze. Her palms were hot and sweaty.

Leila rose from her slumped position. "She's dead, Tom. My niece is dead."

Leila's face was glistening in the yellow light. Her mascara trickled with the tears from her left eye. Walker wiped away the mascara with his thumb.

"I'm sorry."

There was nothing else to say. He was a stranger in her world, but she was looking for comfort from somewhere. Leila reached up and held his wrist as he wiped her tears; she stared at him with watery eyes.

"One hell of a day, huh?" Leila deflected the awkward moment with humor.

"One for the books," Walker agreed.

Leila dropped his hand and turned away. She found the three-quarter moon hovering above the trees in her driveway. She stared for a moment.

"I went to her house after I left the hospital. My niece, Maya. She doesn't live with my brother. She lives with her mom. She never lets us see Maya. Long story for another day. Anyway, no one was home, so I let myself in."

Leila stopped herself and turned toward Walker. "I'm sorry. We literally just met, and I'm here trying to share the intimacies of my currently messed-up life."

"You're fine. I'm a good listener."

Leila shook her head. "I don't know what it is about you. I don't know you, yet I feel like I've known you for a long time."

"I know what you mean."

"That said, none of this is any of your concern, Tom. The stuff going on in the equipment shed, what happened to my niece. None of it. You have plenty of big things—massive things—to worry about yourself. I don't want to pile more on."

Walker folded his arms across his chest. "You have anyone to help you with your problems?"

Leila didn't have to think long. "No. Not with Larry losing his daughter. He'll be a wreck. So yeah. No one."

"Yeah, me neither," Walker said. He took a look up at the moon, then back at Leila. "I suppose we could help each other out. Seeing as how you like to take in strangers, and according to the police, I might have a knack when it comes to dealing with armed men, we could just be the perfect pair for the moment."

"You saying I should finish telling you what I found?"

"I suppose I am."

Leila wiped some of the wet from her cheeks. Then she took something out of her pocket and walked over to him. She handed him a small white pill bottle, the pills rattling inside as he took it. Walker looked up. Leila's expression had turned from sadness to anger.

"This is the *exact* same pill bottle I found in my dad's room after he died."

Walker turned away from Leila and held the bottle up to the light. He expected to find the hallmark branding and labeling of every other pill bottle sold in America's pharmacies, but this one was completely blank. He turned back to her.

"Counterfeit," he said.

"Yeah. Fake M30 oxycodones. The pills are pressed exactly like my dad's were and identical to the ones prescribed by pharmacies."

"But they aren't the same, are they?"

Leila shook her head and took a moment to swallow her emotion. "My niece didn't die from too many pills; she died from too much fentanyl. A deadly dose in just a couple of pills. Whoever made these didn't give a damn who they hurt and didn't pay an ounce of attention to the dose inside."

"Same thing with your father?"

"Same. Fucking. Thing."

Walker could feel Leila's fury.

"I have to know, Tom. I just have to know. Can you help me?"

He knew what she was asking, but he questioned her anyway. "Have to know what?"

"If someone is making or selling drugs on my property. I would lose it if I knew someone out in this community died from something I could have prevented."

"Leila," Walker said, measuring his words, "bad men doing bad things on your property, without your knowledge, is never something you could have prevented."

"I'll help you either way," Leila said. "But I don't know what to do here. If the police are somehow involved, and it's also the cartel as you said you heard, what the hell can I do? Where do I turn?"

Clouds rolled over the shining moon. Both of them took a second to watch it disappear.

"What time is it?" Walker said.

Leila checked her phone. "Almost ten o'clock."

"Before we get too far down the road on what to do next, let's make sure we know what we are dealing with. I'll walk down to the equipment shed tonight and have a look. Then we can assess."

"Thank you." Leila walked over and gave him a hug. "I'll see if I can find out anything about the car incident."

"Speaking of," Walker said, "Sheriff Andy was just here banging on the door. He was looking to talk to me, but I didn't answer."

"That's probably not good, but maybe not as bad as you think. If they found anything too terrible, they would have beat down the door, right?"

"You sure you weren't a detective instead of a doc in your former life?"

"Everything I know about police work, I learned from *Law and Order*," she said with a laugh.

"For what it's worth, that is currently a lot more than I know about anything, really. You realize you are asking an amnesia patient with no known skills or knowledge to help you, right?"

Leila raised an eyebrow. "You may not think you know things, but you do. Trust me when I tell you, it will all come back to you soon."

Walker's mind flashed to his dream, which he knew was more than a dream, and the image of himself shoving the pot fork through the man's neck.

"I saw you dismantle and reconfigure that pistol. And I saw your muscle memory when my brother was being a jackass." Leila smiled and wrapped her knuckles like she was knocking on a door, on top of Walker's head. "It's all still in there. We'll find it. In the meantime, thank you for helping me."

"It's you who deserves the thank-you. Not sure where I'd be right now if not for your hospitality."

Leila walked by and opened the front door. "Probably in jail, or facedown in a ditch."

She looked back and smiled as she held open the door. But Walker could still see the sadness in her eyes.

Walker smiled back. "You very well may be right. And about that handgun . . ."

"Kitchen cabinet left of the sink. I'll get the flashlights."

20

"What the hell do you think that was about?" Mike said to Alison as he put down the binoculars.

The road that ran along the front of Leila's house gradually went up a hill. Mike had found a small break in the trees and backed the car into it. Alison watched as he cleared enough branches so they could see the front of Leila's house without being exposed. Now that it was dark, it was solid cover. She'd watched as Mike mentally measured the distance from the car to the house. Though he seemed like a dumb ogre to her most of the time, it was clear he was as skilled as everyone talks about in the shadows.

"I have no idea what it could have been about, Mike. You were holding the binoculars."

"Yes, but I was explaining what I was seeing. The woman seemed upset, and he seemed to be consoling her. What the hell?"

"We don't know what we don't know, Mike. This area is

where Walker grew up, right? Till he was like a teenager or something. So, maybe she's an old friend."

Mike shook his head. "An old friend who just so happens to have property that butts up to the car accident Walker was in? No, that makes no sense."

"Okay, so maybe he was hurt and she helped him. Does it matter?"

"Everything matters now, Alison."

"The detective said she was a doctor at one point. But quit when her dad died. Maybe she just wanted another patient."

"That's so weird. No chance."

"You say no chance because you're from New York City," Alison said. "Where people would just as soon piss on you if you fell down as help you up."

"That's bullshit boonies talk that all you small-town hillbillies make up to make you feel better about not living in an actual society."

"Oh, yes, Mike . . . we envy you city folk that much."

Mike put the binoculars back to his eyes. "She let him back inside. So strange." He took the binoculars down and looked at Alison. "Say you're right, and her doctor instincts made her want to help someone who was hurt. That cop who stopped us had to have told her they were looking for a man who was hurt in an accident. He would have warned her that he killed them. That he's a murderer. After her knowing that, your idea that she just wanted to help a stranger doesn't hold water. I don't care if you're from the sweetest little town on Earth. Nobody is letting a potential wanted murderer stick around. Nobody."

"The sheriff said that Leila told him she'd known Tom Walker for a while. So maybe he dated her in middle school. Who the hell cares? She's not a threat to stopping you from doing your job tonight, is she?"

Mike laughed. "Well, that's the entire reason for the assessment, now isn't it? Will she fight for him if something goes wrong inside? That makes things more complicated if the answer is yes. Walker had to have told her by now that people would be coming after him after what he did in the car before it wrecked. They have to be prepared for us to be here."

"I don't know, Mike," Alison said with a shrug. "You were watching them just now. Did they seem at all concerned that someone could be coming for them?"

"No. That's why I'm confused. They just sat around outside the house. In plain sight. Walker would *never* do that knowing Maxwell wants him dead. Never. Something is off."

"You think he's going to stay the night?" Alison said.

"What am I, Miss Cleo? 'Call me now for your free tarot reading'?"

Alison just stared blankly.

"You don't remember Miss Cleo?" Mike said.

"I remember, Mike. I just don't find it amusing."

"Stick-in-the-mud. Anyway, I'm not a psychic. But if neither one of them leaves, I'll go in tonight while they're sleeping. Maybe I'll get lucky and they will both be as lax as they just were out front."

"Or maybe he's setting you up," Alison said. "Maybe he knows you're here and he's making you underestimate him."

"It's clear you are in the research department, darling. You learn real quick in my side of the business not to under-estimate anyone. Especially guys like me and Walker—the guys who get paid to kill the guys who kill people for a living."

"So what then? If he's going to be ready for you, how will you kill him?"

Mike was quiet for a minute. He put his binoculars to his face again and looked at the quiet driveway in front of the house.

"Something is definitely off. I can feel it. And when something feels off, I usually try to find a backup plan in case something goes wrong."

"Yeah?" Alison said. "Not sure what that could be. Not much you can pull from out here in the middle of nowhere."

Mike lowered his binoculars. "You're right, there isn't. Out here. But we just so happen to know where there is something that Tom Walker cares about, something that could be a great out for us if he would happen to get the upper hand. Which he won't. But it doesn't hurt to have a trick up your sleeve."

"What are you talking about?"

"You know exactly what I'm talking about. The lady he saved from his foster dad. The same lady he still sends money to every month. He must care about her. Therefore, he has a weakness. And I intend on exploiting that weakness if need be."

Mike started the car and put it in drive.

"What the hell are you going to do, Mike? That woman has nothing to do with Walker and why we are here for him."

"So what? She's a weakness for a man who has very few, I assure you. And we're going to use it if we have to."

"You can't do that."

"Why?"

"Because, like I said, she's innocent. Maxwell and her company might not be the most morally sound, but she's not morally bankrupt. She would not want you bringing in an innocent woman."

"Then you don't know Karen Maxwell like I do."

Mike pulled the car out into the road.

"Wait, you can't, Mike. You just can't."

"I can. And we are."

"What if—what if Walker leaves and you don't know it? Then what? Then you've lost him. For no reason."

"For good reason. Tipping the odds in our favor is massive in this game. But you make a good point."

Mike stopped the car, then reversed back into the hiding spot in the trees. Then he reached behind him and pulled his bag onto his lap. He shuffled through it for a second, then pulled out a tiny box.

"Here. Attach this to the undercarriage of her Jeep."

"What?" Alison said. "I'm not doing that."

Mike turned toward her. "What the hell are you doing then, Alison? Because all you've been good for so far is annoying the shit out of me and telling me what I should and shouldn't do. I'm not married for a reason. I don't need a woman giving me directions. *I* give the directions." Then he raised his voice. "You understand? I give the directions! Now, get your ass out of the car and go place this tracker under the Jeep. I'll pick you up when you're walking away from it. Got it? Good. Hurry the hell up."

Alison snatched the box from Mike's hand. "Just let it be known that I think this is a mistake, Mike."

"Just let it be known that I don't give a monkey shit. Hurry up. And don't let anyone see you."

Alison opened the door and walked out into the night. She was fuming. But there was nothing she could do. She hadn't told Mike the whole truth. She'd done a couple of dangerous runs during her time in the Army. But she wasn't nearly as experienced as Mike. And Mike was Maxwell's golden boy because, when she said jump, he said how high. No matter the request. That was the running talk about him anyway. So the last thing Alison wanted was a set of killers after her for doing what Tom Walker apparently had done the night before—killing other men on Maxwell's payroll.

Alison had enough problems as it was after being demoted to research. She and Tom had another thing in common: she had refused a job as well. The difference was, Alison simply refused the job; she didn't kill another one of Maxwell's assassins like Walker had. From what she'd heard, though, Mitchell had deserved it. For a secret agency working for the government, Maxwell Solutions had a couple too many loose-lipped employees.

So, here she was, having to do the bidding of the Asshole of the Year, Mike Hudson. And there was no choice. Maxwell herself had all but told her she'd already had her one strike. Everyone who worked for Maxwell knew what the second strike meant. Mike and Alison were Tom Walker's second strike. So were the men in the car with him last night. She didn't want her second-strike assassin coming for her. So she had to follow along, no matter how dirty Mike got. It just was what it was.

She hurried down the road to place the tracker. Thunder rumbled in the distance. She cursed her decision ever to join Maxwell in the first place. Even though she really was never given a choice. It was go to work for Maxwell Solutions, or be dishonorably discharged from the Army for a bullshit claim by a senior officer that she couldn't disprove. If there was any other way, she would take it. But for now, this was her life, and she had to stay alive.

Alison moved forward and slid her body beneath the Jeep. She pulled the cover off the bottom of the small tracker box, exposing the magnet, then slapped it in place beneath the Jeep. She heard Mike pull the car forward, so she rolled out from under the Jeep and rushed for the road. Mike slowed the car and opened the door. She jumped in, and they pulled away.

"All set?"

Alison didn't answer.

Mike pulled up his phone. "Okay, just sit there and pout. See if I care. Tracker is online. Nice work."

She stayed quiet.

"I like this Alison. The quiet one. Where the hell has she been hiding?"

He said it as a joke, but Alison just stared at the head-light beams out in front of her.

Mike laughed. "Perfect. Now, let's go get that insurance plan."

21

Heat lightning danced across the sky in the distance. Thunder boomed overhead. The storm had moved in quickly since Leila made it home. The dark clouds over the moon had made the sky almost pitch black as Leila stepped into the cornstalks. The air was wet and heavy, but rain had yet to fall. She clicked on her flashlight as Walker followed her in.

"There's a good chance this is a wasted trip," Walker said, stepping around a large hole in the dirt. "According to the men I overheard, they were going to be working late."

"Then we'll just catch them in the act. Maybe that's best. Not let them leave, then call the police right then. Catch them red-handed."

"Leila, we can't do that. It's too dangerous."

Leila stopped and turned around. Her face looked determined in the beam of Walker's flashlight. "Do I have to remind you that drugs killed my niece tonight, Tom? I frankly don't give a damn if it's dangerous or not."

Walker took a breath. He held up his hand, surrendering. "You asked me to help you. This is me helping—"

"I meant help me look. Help me if we find men here doing illegal things."

Walker stayed calm. "Like I said, this is me helping. You have to think this through to the point of a couple of steps ahead. If we find men here, making drugs, or organizing drugs that are ready to sell, what kind of men do you think they will be?"

"Bad men, Tom. What the hell do you mean?"

"Yeah, they might be bad men. But for sure they aren't the men in charge."

Leila shrugged her shoulders. "Okay, so?"

"So, you get them arrested and shut down the drug sales coming out of the shed on your property. Great. A wonderful short-term win. But then what?"

Leila was quiet. They both looked up when another crack of thunder sounded from the sky.

"Then they can't illegally sell tainted drugs to kids or old men anymore."

"Right. Which means the men in charge stop making money."

"Good."

"Not good. Actually, really bad for you."

Leila turned and began walking again. Walker let her work it out in her head.

"Bad for me because the men in charge have plenty more bad men to send here, right?"

"Worse men."

Leila turned again. "For a man who doesn't remember anything, you sound pretty damn sure of yourself when you talk about criminals."

Walker had thought the same thing. But what he was saying did feel like facts to him. Like he really did know what he was saying.

"But it also makes sense," Leila continued. "Maybe if I do get their operation shut down here, they would just move on. But if it's making them a lot of money, they'll want someone to pay for their losses, right? That's the way it is on TV anyway. Especially since you said they mentioned the word *cartel*. I saw the movie *Blow*. I watched *Narcos* on Netflix. I don't want any part of that. And don't get me started on *Ozark*. The cartel in that show would hunt me down for sport. You should watch that one. Real good."

Leila was rambling. Walker knew it was her nerves.

"You should go back to the house and let me handle this, Leila. This isn't a TV show. If this is really happening in your own backyard, you are in serious trouble either way."

"Either way? What does that mean?"

"Just go. I'll be back to the house in an hour. We can run a test to see if I drink whiskey or not."

Leila smiled and let out a soft laugh. A warm breeze rustled the cornstalks around them. She took a step closer to Walker. "Why did we have to meet under literally the weirdest circumstances of all time?"

"They really are strange."

"I just wish you could remember who you are so you could tell me more about yourself."

"I think that part of the odd way we met is probably a good thing. I don't think you want to know the real me."

"I think you're wrong. And if—*when*—you do get your memories back, if you like the man you are right now, just know that it is never too late to change."

"I'm not sure that's true," Walker said.

Leila reached up and caressed his cheek with her thumb. "Well, the good thing is, it's up to you, Tom. And whatever the circumstances were that brought you here, no matter how bad, I see a good man."

Walker didn't know what to say. He liked the way she was looking at him, but it made him uncomfortable. That's why he was happy when they heard an engine roar to life at the other end of the cornfield.

Leila whipped her head around. "Sounds like they're leaving. We can go ahead now."

"*I* can go ahead now. If any of these men see you, there is no putting that rabbit back in the hat. They see me, I have no affiliation to you anyway. Go back to the house. I'll be there shortly."

A raindrop hit Leila on the forehead. She wiped it away as she contemplated. More began to follow, and she glanced up at the sky.

"Don't put yourself in any danger," she said. "See what needs to be seen and get the hell out of there. Got it? I'll pull one of my special bottles to jog your bourbon memories."

"I won't be long."

Walker moved past her. She captured his arm before he could get away.

"Thank you."

She wanted to say more. Maybe even wanted something else from him. But the rain began to fall harder on the two of them. Walker moved his flashlight to the ground and disappeared into the corn. Both of them had enough on their plates. They didn't need to add another side of complication to it.

"Be careful!" Leila whisper-shouted one last time.

Walker didn't stop. He moved toward the unknown. They both had a lot of separate questions about their lives, and he was determined that one of them was going to get some answers. Even if it wasn't him.

22

As best as he could in the coal-black night, shrouded in steady rain, Walker determined the vehicles were gone. He moved to the side of the equipment shed. There were no lights. If he hadn't known the building was sitting where the cornstalks stopped, he would've walked right into it.

The night was warm, but the rain wasn't. He was already soaked through. Walker listened for any sounds that could let him know the occupancy level of the shed, but he couldn't hear a thing above the rain beating on the metal roof above him. The crackling thunder didn't help either. He waited for lightning to flash before he moved. When it finally did, it showed him the vehicles had indeed vacated the premises.

He took a look around the corner, and with another flash of lightning, he could see the gravel road going up the hill was also empty. When he walked around the corner, there was an oversize garage door, painted white. It was stark against the brown of the shed, even in the low light. He moved along the garage, his hand dragging against it, until he came to another door. This one the size of any front or back door to a home. He tried the handle, and to his surprise it turned.

Walker waited in the rain for a moment. Even though he wasn't sure of his own identity, he couldn't help but think that some of the feelings and thoughts running through his mind were messages from his subconscious. And right now that subconscious was telling him there was no way in the world that, if someone were hiding some sort of drug operation in that shed, they would leave the door unlocked.

The biggest problem he was having with his real self being suppressed wasn't that his instincts weren't working. He could tell they were still intact. The issue was that whoever he was at the moment—the brain-dead him— didn't know what to do with those instinctual cues. And he couldn't help but think, as he stood with the door handle in his hand, that it would be better not to have the instincts at all than to have them and have no idea what to do next.

The bottom line remained, instincts or not, he had to go in, and that is why he decided to go ahead and push open the door—he wanted to find out exactly what was going on. For Leila's sake, but also for his. He was tired of everything being a question, and for once that day, regardless of the danger, he was going to get an answer.

The door creaked as he pushed inside. The scent of spilled oil and a bit of something burning met him there. Maybe it was burning, he wasn't sure. There was a lot going on with his senses. It felt nice to no longer be pelted by the rain, but he couldn't help feel his situation was a bit of "out of the frying pan, into the fire." It was dark. He couldn't hear a thing other than the rain driving into the roof. Before he pulled the door shut, a bolt of lightning showed a mostly empty shed. Only a large tractor along the far wall.

With the quick glance, he saw no signs of a person, so he shut the door behind him and flipped on his flashlight. The area closest to the door was empty. The flooring below was poured concrete. Toward the back of the shed was the tractor Leila had mentioned. Beyond it a wall full of tools and other such things useful for farming. Hay and feed were stacked up along the side walls, but he saw no sign of any other room or an entrance to any spaces beneath the floor. If there was a drug operation in or around there, it was fairly well hidden, at least in his darkened glance. He imagined it would be in the daylight too.

But Walker knew better. He heard the conversation earlier, so now it was just a matter of finding how they were getting to the secret area of the shed. The tractor at the back was huge. The kind used for tilling, planting, and more. Eight massive tires. A real professional model. He noticed that there was enough room to move it backward in the shed without having to open the garage door. That, he figured, was for a reason. It was the only place that made sense to hide the cellar door.

He walked over to the giant green John Deere. He could smell the cut grass in the blades. The rain was still thumping steadily on the roof above. It occurred to him that it would be incredibly difficult to hear someone coming because of the rain. However, he had no other choice but to continue searching. He bent down to kneel beside the over-size tire and shined his flashlight beneath the tractor. There was some lose hay there, but he could also see that there was a difference in the smoothness of the concrete under it. That was the way down.

It had been a while—long ago in his childhood anyway —since Walker had manned a tractor, but seeing as how most of the memories he'd made in his life were missing, the ones driving a tractor were still pretty solid. Until he climbed into the cockpit. It was immediately clear that tractors had changed completely. There was a flat screen monitor with all kinds of buttons on it. Luckily for him, below that was the manual shifter. It showed P for park, R for reverse, F for forward, and, at the bottom, N for neutral. However, there was so much going on in front of him that he had no idea how to turn on the machine. He looked around and saw a lot of switches and buttons. Starting it wasn't going to happen. So he grabbed the shift knob, pressed the brake at his feet, slid the knob right and down toward the N. He was going to have to push that beast.

He hopped out of the tractor to a searing pain in his thigh when he landed. The pain pills had taken away the dull ache for the most part, but the jarring of slamming his feet on concrete reminded him of his injury. Walker moved around to the front and put both hands on the front of the tractor. He squatted at the knees and began pushing forward. Flexing his leg hurt, but the pounding it caused in his head from the pressure he was exerting was much worse. He had to let go.

He stepped back as much as he could, placing his back against the wall. Then he shot forward, slamming his hands against the front, and dug in with his feet, pumping his legs forward like a sprinter. Finally, the tractor began edging backward. He continued to drive forward until he could fully see the door in the floor at his feet. Only problem was, the tractor had momentum and he couldn't stop it. It kept rolling back until it ran into the garage door. The metal and plastic made a bending sound, but it didn't break. The tractor stopped, and he hadn't *completely* ruined the door.

Rain was still pelting the building. Other than nearly smashing Leila's garage door, there hadn't been another sound since he'd been in the equipment shed. So, when he bent down and pulled open the two doors that had stairs leading beneath the floor, he felt confident he was alone. He descended into the darkness, his curiosity overshadowing any dormant instincts he might have had from his unknown life.

23

Walker decided it was best, at least for the moment, to descend the stairs without the flashlight. He was fairly certain he was alone, but until he got below the surface, he was going to keep it dark. As he stepped down, there were no lights coming up to greet him. For no good reason at all, his imagination flashed a horrific scene of what was not likely in the room below him—a grizzly scene of dead bodies and tortured souls. When the lights go out, the darkest crevices of the mind make way for the worst imaginings. He shook the image from his mind and continued down the stairs.

When he got low enough, he felt for the walls around him. They helped guide him to a left turn at the landing to find the last five steps. Then the floor leveled out. The smell of gasoline subsided a bit, but it still felt like he was in the garage. It was near total black. There wasn't a sound to be heard other than the faint noise of the rain dancing on the roof above. His wet clothes gave him a chill. He felt along the wall on his right. It felt rough, like cinder blocks. Then he felt along the wall on his left, and his hand found a switch.

"Anybody down here?" he called out. He figured it better to announce his presence instead of surprising anyone who might be down there. However, if anyone were down there, they were most likely either asleep or dead, because there wasn't any ability to see even as much as a foot in front of him.

Walker shut his eyes and flipped the switch. He blinked away the pain of the light in his concussed eyes. It was intense enough to make them water. What he saw wasn't anything like his horrible flash of imagination a moment ago. Instead, it was almost exactly like what he'd expected.

The room was a long, open area. There were rectangular tables lined up end to end in the center of the room, all the way from one side to the other. Shelves on both side walls were filled with boxes, probably full of pill bottles ready for sale. The only other noticeable feature of the room was a door on the far wall. Each table had a different setup, stations for what could only be explained as the different steps in manufacturing drugs. One had scales, beakers, and a couple of burners. Even an exhaust pipe that ran up into the ceiling. The next looked like a sorting station. Then maybe packaging. Walker strolled alongside them until he reached the last table at the end. The money-counting station. There were a couple of cash counters and a box of rubber bands. But the dealers were at least smart enough not to leave any cash lying around.

The door right in front of him swung open.

Walker was so caught off guard that he froze entirely— even as the Mexican man reached for the pistol on his hip.

"Alguien está aquí!" the man shouted, alerting someone else that Walker was there.

Walker did the only thing he could think of and threw the flashlight at the man's head. He knew he wasn't going to be able to pull the pistol quick enough to shoot, so that was all he had. When the man ducked, Walker reached over to his right and grabbed the tall shelving with both hands, gave it a hard yank, and sent it toppling over in front of him. This gave him a small barrier between the gunman and himself. The gunman's partner then came walking out of the other room, but unlike the first gunman, he was prepared. He was firing rounds from a handgun with each step he took toward Walker.

If Walker's instincts had been at full go, like the man he probably was before the memory lapse, he wouldn't have been stupid enough to walk through the room without clearing the adjacent room first. And he also wouldn't have done it without having his own pistol out and ready. Now his head trauma, leaving him unprepared for what he'd stepped into here on Leila's farm, was likely going to get him killed. Instead of being on offense and taking the fight to these men, he was just going to have to figure out how to survive. And for now, that meant putting enough things in between him and the men firing at him so he'd have a chance to fight back.

Walker sped backward, grabbed the next shelf in line and pulled it over too. He ducked down and tried to cover his left ear as he pulled his pistol. The sound of the gunshots in that enclosed room were deafening. But the state his brain was in after the accident tripled the effect on him, and it nearly rendered him helpless, the pain was so severe. He would probably be dead either way, but if he didn't at least try to defend himself, he was on his last stand for sure.

Before he fired back, he decided to try a different approach.

"Wait! Please! Por favor, deja de disparar! Stop shooting! Please!" Walker pleaded.

A couple more shots rang out; then they stopped.

"Habla inglés?" Walker said. "This is a mistake. I'll leave now!"

"Who are you?" one of the men said in a heavy Mexican accent.

"Just a drifter. Trying to get out of the rain. I was being nosy when I saw the door in the floor. I'm sorry. I'll leave now."

The man told his partner in Spanish to call the boss and tell him to send more men.

"No! That's not necessary," Walker said. "You don't need more men. I'm leaving right now."

"How many of you are there?" the man said.

"Just me, I swear," Walker said. "I'm telling you the truth. I was just passing by and saw the shed. The storm is crazy out there. I made a mistake."

The other man was already on the phone. Not only had Walker not helped Leila with this situation; he had just made it eminently worse. One small step at a time, he began backing his way toward the stairs behind him.

"No!" the man shouted. "Stop. Just stay right there."

Walker stopped for a moment. He tried to figure out the best approach, but he had no idea. The sound of more men possibly on their way was bad. But he had to keep this contained to the equipment shed at all costs. Even if there were more men coming. He could not let them know that Leila knew anything. They would almost certainly kill her. For the moment, all he could do was wish for the man who did the writing in his notebooks in his bag. Or the man who took out the terrorist in his dream. *That* Tom Walker would know what to do here. But that man was nowhere to be found inside his own mind.

He was going to have to find a way out of this himself.

24

"Put down your weapon, gringo!" one of the men shouted at Walker.

That wasn't an option. He had to get out from beneath that shed, and even though he didn't like it, he was going to have to get out of there without those two drug dealers leaving as well. Because if they walked out, they would just follow him to Leila's house. He thought for a moment about just leaving entirely, but not only could he not leave Leila alone after seeing what was happening in her own backyard, he couldn't leave his bag. If he ever wanted to have a chance at living a normal life, what was in that bag needed to remain a secret.

"Drop it now!" the gunman shouted again.

Time was up. Walker had to make a move. He scanned his surroundings. Nothing but toppled shelves, boxes, and pill supplies. He was going to have to shoot his way out. He peered through the boxes on the half-toppled shelf in front of him. Both men had been smart enough to duck behind the table for cover. So, Walker did the same.

Once his stomach hit the floor, he brought his hands together around the pistol he now held out in front of him. The man on the right was blocked entirely by the other fallen shelves. But the man on the left, Walker could see his left leg bent.

"There is no way out of here," one of the gunmen said. "More men will be here soon. If you don't put the gun down now, I'm going to kill you. It's not worth it, ese."

Walker shot twice instead of answering the man. The first bullet ricocheted off the wall behind the crouching gunman, at least a foot off to the left. The second shot wasn't any better.

"That's it! Get him!"

The crouched gunman made the unfortunate error of moving to his left as he stood to go after Walker. Right in line with the errant shots Walker had just fired. Walker pulled the trigger twice more and hit the gunman's legs. The man dropped flat to the floor, and Walker fired until the slide on his pistol locked back and stopped firing.

"Carlos!" the other gunman shouted. "Carlos! Estás bien?"

Carlos didn't answer. Walker had lucked out and hit the man in a critical area.

"You son of a bitch!" the other gunman shouted.

Walker bounced back up to his feet as gunshots rang out. He ducked behind the overturned shelves and stayed low as he moved around the back of them, keeping the shelves between himself and the man firing at him. He was lucky these men were no more than drug dealers—leaving a lot to be desired in their shooting ability—because he couldn't seem to fire any better himself.

As quiet as he could, he rushed his crouched walk forward to situate himself behind the first shelf he'd pulled down. The gunman had been shooting in Walker's general direction, but he was about a foot behind Walker's progress. Walker's ears were buzzing from the echoing shots, but it was like music to those ears when he heard the faint sound of the man's pistol click, having fired its last round. It was now or never.

Walker ran around the shelf as fast as his injured leg would let him. With the adrenaline flowing, it really didn't slow him much. The light fixture was shining straight down on the gunman who was loading a new magazine into his pistol. Just as he hammered it into the pistol and was able to charge the weapon, Walker leaped forward and made contact with the man's waist. Walker's momentum carried both of them crashing into a shelf on the opposite wall.

Boxes fell on top of them as the shelving unit teetered back and forth. Walker didn't know if he'd be capable of besting the man in hand-to-hand combat, so he reached up, pulled the shelf above him as hard as he could, and rolled to his right. The man attempted to get up, but the metal unit caught him when he was halfway standing, taking him down. The man grunted in pain as the shelving unit slammed on top of him.

Walker realized he'd dropped his gun in the scuffle. He looked down at his feet but didn't see it. The gunman began writhing beneath the shelves. Walker started kicking away the boxes, searching for the gun. He didn't want to shoot the man, but he knew there was no other option. But then he noticed the zip ties lying on the table where the money counting machines sat. He knew somewhere in his heart that if he had his normal wits about him, there would be no question in his mind that killing the man was the only way forward. There really was no good reason to leave him alive.

But he wasn't that Tom Walker right then. And though

he had just shot and killed the other man, that felt different. More self-defense. He knew if the man struggling beneath the shelves made it to his gun first, there was no question he would kill Walker. But Walker couldn't kill him first. Not like that. He couldn't execute a man. Instead, he moved to the table, stuffed the zip ties in his pocket, and grabbed one of the rectangular money counters. When he turned around, the man was just squeezing his way out from under the shelves. Walker hated the look in the man's eyes as he swung the metal and plastic money counter down on his forehead. At least he didn't kill him.

The man slumped onto the floor. The machine had opened up a pretty good slice on his forehead, and blood began running down and pooling at his head. There was no time to waste. More of these men had been summoned, and the last place Walker wanted to be was huddled over one of their own, one dead and one unconscious. He supposed he wouldn't be able to talk or fight his way out of that one.

Walker took a knee beside the man he'd just knocked down and pulled his arms behind his back. He wrapped the zip tie around both wrists, along with the metal leg of the shelving. He did the same to the man's ankles. He was still out cold. Walker was thankful for that. He didn't want to hear the man plead for his own life or threaten Walker's. So he stood, grabbed the gun of the dead man as he stepped over him, and waded through the boxes and pill bottles until he reached the stairs.

Once he made it to the top of the stairs, the sound of the rain splattering on the roof once again greeted him. But so, too, did the sound of tires sliding over top of gravel. The men the gunmen had called for had made it to the equipment shed before Walker made it out. The shed door slammed against the wall after being thrown open. Without Walker's flashlight, it was nearly completely dark in the room. His only saving grace.

Just before the lights flipped on, Walker dove across the floor and scooted over behind the industrial mower. He cringed when the bright lights shined. He squeezed his eyes shut as he tightened his grip on the gun in his hand. For the first time, he noticed he was shaking. He thought it was from being wet in the cool underground room, but it could very well have been the aftereffects of the adrenaline dump he'd just experienced.

He heard the footsteps of men moving into the shed. Walker frantically blinked away the sting of the light so he could see if he needed to shoot anyone. His breathing was rapid, but he was doing his best to keep the sound of it below the decibel level of the driving rain. With squinted eyes, he held the gun out in front of him, ready to shoot the first thing that moved. Then he saw the pocket of a pair of jeans moving down the stairs to the cellar. Then another pair followed. Then nothing but the sound of the rain again.

Walker raised from his crouched position, careful not to brush against something on the mower that might make noise. With deliberate steps, he walked toward the opening in the floor. It was the only way out of the shed after he'd backed the mower into the garage door.

"José?" a man's voice said from beneath the floor.

They'd found their men. It was time to run for it. Walker jumped over the opening in the floor and sprinted for the door. He turned right as the rain began soaking him. The men had left the truck's headlights on, so Walker could see the path around the shed, but then he saw only darkness as he ran into the cornstalks. The cold wet from the leaves of the growing corn were slapping him as he went through the field. It was uncomfortable, but it was far better than facing what he'd left behind in that shed.

As he maneuvered his way through the cornfield, working his way back to the house, all he could think about was what he'd left behind. Problems. Problems for the one person who'd been trying to help him in this world. Now he had made her bad situation far worse. The only hope he was holding on to was the story he gave the two gunmen—that he was a drifter—if they bought that, maybe they would leave Leila alone. Maybe they would think that she was still clueless and they could continue, business as usual.

Maybe.

However, something buried deep inside Walker's lizard brain told him there wasn't much chance of that happening. He needed to convince Leila that it was time to go. That staying only invited more trouble. Unfortunately, his would just be the words of a stranger, someone she didn't even know, pleading with her to move away from the only memories left of her father. Those words probably weren't going to be greeted with an open mind. But he had to try. Since he couldn't remember enough to help her fight the drug-dealing thugs, they would lose if they tried, so he was going to have to convince her to run from them. Otherwise, he was going to have to leave altogether. He had his own unopened box of problems that needed tending. It would be ridiculous to wait around and watch Leila get herself killed.

As he moved through the corn, the rain drowning him, he also knew he couldn't leave her alone. Whether or not he ever got his memory back, he knew he would never be able to forgive himself if he left someone good to be hurt by someone bad. He didn't know his old self at the moment, but he knew enough about that Tom Walker to know that he would never let something like that happen.

25

The windshield wipers on Mike and Alison's rental car couldn't keep up with the torrential downpour. They had been sitting across the street from Kim Kidwell's home for at least fifteen minutes waiting to see if it would die down. It hadn't, and Mike was growing more and more frustrated by the second.

"So what's the plan here, Mike?" Alison said. "Take an innocent woman hostage? To what end? I thought killing is what you do, so why do we need Walker's old foster mom?"

"I told you, insurance. I know you've heard like I have that Walker is damn good. He's not Mike Hudson good, but still, can never be too careful. If something goes wrong and I need Mommy here to gain an edge, it's better than having nothing."

"I think it's wrong."

"I don't give a damn what you think. I'm the one going in to take Walker out. I'm the one who'll make the decisions on how best to get it done. Are you with me or not, Alison? Because it sounds an awful lot like you're not here lately. Do

I need to subdue you and call Maxwell? Tell her you aren't cooperating?"

"I just need you to know that I think taking this woman is bullshit. And I think it's unnecessary for you if you are as good at your job as you say you are. Call whoever you want, but make sure you tell them you can't get it done without involving innocent people."

Mike reached over and smacked Alison right in the mouth. She immediately jumped at him, getting a punch in on his face, but that only made him angrier. He grabbed both of her arms and pinned her back against the door.

"That's enough out of you! I can't take your mouth any-damn-more!"

Mike switched to one hand around Alison's throat. He was squeezing just enough so that she couldn't move. He reached over the console to the floor of the backseat. When he brought his hand back up, he had a handful of zip ties. Alison tried to protest, but she couldn't get her voice past the squeeze of his hand. Mike set the zip ties on the console between them, then reached down and pulled out his pistol. Alison's eyes were as wide as saucers.

"You realize you've made me do this. I'm not even sure whose side you're on, the way you've been talking. So, I'm going to remove my hand from around your neck. When I do, if you make a move at me again, I shoot you. Do you understand me?"

Alison nodded frantically. She could see in Mike's eyes that he absolutely wouldn't hesitate to kill her right then and there. Mike let go, and Alison gasped for air. When he took her hands, she didn't fight him. He moved both of her wrists together and zipped them up. Then he reached down below her seat, squeezed her ankles together, and zip-tied her legs.

"Next comes the gag if you think you still have some smart-ass things to say," Mike said.

Alison just shook her head.

"Good. Now that we understand each other, I'm going to get this old bag, tie her up, and then I am going back to that farm to finish this job. Are we on the same page?"

Alison nodded as she was still trying to normalize her breathing.

"Good girl. I'd say don't go anywhere," Mike said as he laughed and pointed with his pistol at her hands, "but you already have that down pat."

Mike holstered his gun. He took out his leather gloves from his bag so he could avoid leaving a fingerprint trail. Then he opened the door and stepped out into the rain. It was coming down in sheets. He jogged across the street, trying to pull his leather jacket over his head, but it was no use. He was soaked. He didn't waste time knocking, or even to see if the front door was unlocked; he just kicked it in and moved inside out of the rain. He shook the water from his jacket as he put it back down on his shoulders. He smoothed his hair back and wiped his wet gloves on his jeans.

There wasn't a light on in the house. No sounds either. He thought the old lady must be dead, or deaf, because it would've been hard to sleep through the noise he'd made upon entering. As Mike walked down the hall, the floor creaked beneath him. He remembered that if he walked all the way in he'd be in the kitchen and living room area, so he tried the first door he came to. It was unlocked, so he opened it slowly. He pulled out his phone and used it as a flashlight. It was a mostly empty room except for shelves all along every wall. They were filled with old dolls.

"Creepy," slipped from Mike's lips.

He turned and moved to the door across the hall. It was a small half-bathroom. There was only one more door; he knew she had to be in there. He moved to it and turned the handle. It moaned as he pushed it inward. His light showed him a bed at the far end of the room. The woman was fast asleep beneath the covers. Her ability to sleep through a lot of noise was admirable, but it also made it real easy for someone to sneak up on her.

Mike moved for the bed. He knew he was taking a chance by leaving Walker at the house and not keeping an eye on him. But it was a calculated risk. Kidnapping maybe the only person Walker cared about would certainly tip any wavering scales in Mike's favor. Any advantage was a good one. He reached down for the blanket and ripped it off the woman.

"Time to wake—"

Beneath the covers was a row of pillows. The woman was nowhere to be found.

Behind him Mike heard the unmistakable sound of a shotgun slide, racking a round into the chamber.

"Hands up, slimeball," a woman's voice said. Mike instantly recognized her as Kim Kidwell. She'd gotten the jump on him.

"This is going to get you killed, lady," Mike said.

"Says the man with a loaded twelve-gauge shotgun pointed at his back."

Mike was quiet for a moment. He was trying to assess the situation for his next move.

"You know how I knew you wasn't FBI?"

"My leather jacket?"

"No. That was a poor choice of garment in mid-ninety-degree heat, but not the giveaway."

"Enlighten me, Granny," Mike said.

"Tommy," she said.

"Tom Walker? What about him?"

"He told me this day might come. Said that one day if somebody came around looking for him, they more than likely wouldn't be who they said they were. So he bought me this gun and taught me how to use it. It's been several years, but I kept practicing. I let that poor boy endure hell when he lived at my house, and I swore if I ever got the chance to even halfway make it up to him, I'd be ready. So, I never forgot what he told me. Tommy's a tough guy, but where he beats morons like you is with his brain."

"Yeah, real smart killing three people involved in a government program with a roster of trained killers. Then not disappearing after doing it? A real genius you've got there, lady."

"Again, says the *trained killer* in an old lady's room with a gun to his back after she got the drop on him."

"Yeah? You're the smart one? What about my partner? You don't think she's watching? Waiting for her moment to strike?"

"I know she isn't," Kim said. "One, because she can't stand you. That was clear in the five minutes we met earlier. Two, she never got out of the car. You think just because you turned your headlights off down the road that I wouldn't see you? Tommy says the number one way to get yourself hurt is by underestimating someone. Apparently you weren't trained by the same people."

Mike whipped himself around and smacked the nose of Kim's shotgun just as she pulled the trigger. The blast was deafening. The contact knocked Kim back against the wall, and as she brought the shotgun around to fire again, Mike stepped in, caught the barrel in his hand and yanked it from Kim's grasp.

"No!" Kim shouted.

It was too late; Mike was already halfway into his right cross when she shouted. When his fist connected with her cheek, her head bounced off the wall behind her. She fell to the floor like a sack of potatoes.

"Who got the drop on who, bitch?" Mike said to the room. Then he bent over, picked up Kim, threw her over his shoulder, grabbed the shotgun, and walked out into the hallway.

The rain had subsided a bit on his way out the front door, but it was still hanging around. He was so wet from his walk into the house that it couldn't make things worse. He opened the back door of the car and threw Kim onto the backseat. He took a couple more zip ties and secured Kim's wrists and ankles as she lay facedown. Then he got in the car.

"Really coming down out there," Mike said, nonchalant.

"Since you tied her up, I'm assuming the gunshots didn't kill her," Alison said.

"That was her gun," Mike said as he started the car. "Clever old lady. She actually had me fooled. But she was too damn slow, and too proud of herself for pulling one over on me. I can't hear much out of my left ear, but I'm okay otherwise. Thanks for asking."

"I didn't ask."

"Well, that's not very nice, now is it?"

Alison looked down at her tied hands. "Not really feeling nice at the moment for some reason."

"You're a real smart-ass, aren't you? Real pain in my ass, too, the entire time we've been unhappily paired together. I've reached my limit. I'm sick of your mouth. The rest of this thing is being done by me and me alone. My way. One more word out of you and I tell Maxwell how you tried to help Tom Walker escape."

"You're a real prick, you know that?"

Mike threw his fist sideways and pounded Alison in the forehead. Knocking her out cold.

"There. That's better. Just take you a little nap."

Mike flipped on his headlights and turned on the radio. As he pulled away from Kim's farm, he was humming along to "Free Bird" by Skynyrd as it came through the speakers. He turned it up and tuned out everything but the goal ahead.

Kill Tom Walker.

26

The rain was just beginning to subside as Walker stepped up to Leila's front door. Too little too late, because he was already soaked to the bone. Before he could knock, the door swung open and Leila rushed out, throwing her arms around him.

"You're okay!"

Walker gave her a squeeze; then she pulled away.

"It took you so long I was sure something bad had happened to you."

She looked him over, deciding he looked like a wet dog, then grabbed his hand and pulled him inside.

"My God, you are drenched. Let me get you a towel."

Leila bounced away and disappeared to the hallway. Walker bent down and undid the laces on his boots. As he pulled them off, water dripped from every part of him. It was also the first time he'd felt the tinge of pain in his leg. The adrenaline rush from the equipment shed must have been wearing off.

Leila hurried back into the room. "Well, tell me some good news. You found nothing in there, right?" She tossed him one of the towels, and he immediately wiped away the water from his face and hair.

"Leila, we need to go."

Leila's smile turned to a frown. "What? You found something?"

"Pack a bag. I'll tell you on our way out."

"Tom, I'm not leaving here. This is *my* home. Now tell me what happened out there that has you all shaken up?"

"Unfortunately, I was right. There's a full-scale drug operation going on down there. Work stations, equipment, pills, and best of all, armed workers."

Leila stopped drying him off and wore a stunned look.

"Exactly. And I ran into the armed gunmen and was lucky enough to make it back here. So, now we have to leave. It's not worth dying over. You'd have to fight a cartel to get back full control over your farm."

Leila put her hands on her hips. "Then that's exactly what I'll have to do."

Her resolve surprised Walker. Most women, and even men, would be running for the hills with information like this. Or going to the police, of course. But seeing as how there was a police officer involved, there was only one option for her.

Leila began drying him again. "I mean, you said it yourself, I can't go to the police. And I'm sure as hell not going to just leave the only thing I have left in the world behind. The land, my father's memories . . . the horses. You expect me just to leave them?"

"What are those horses going to do out in that barn when you're dead?" Walker needed to take a harder approach. "Because that's what comes next here, Leila. I had to kill one of theirs just to make it out of that shed alive."

She was stunned once again. "You telling me you shot someone? There's a dead man on my property right now?"

"There is. And a couple more men showed up as I was leaving. I barely got away."

"So, they saw you? Alive?"

"One of the men did. I told him I was just a drifter trying to get in out of the rain. So they would still think you were in the dark about all of this."

"Smart. Thank you."

They heard something out in the driveway. Walker leaned over and pulled aside the curtain covering the window. "Pickup truck. Dark color."

Leila rushed over. "That's Tyler's truck. What do I do?"

"You're about to find out if Tyler is in on this little drug business or not."

"What do I say?"

"Let him do the talking. If he tells you anything other than what I just told you happened down there, you know you can't trust him."

Leila nodded. There was a knock at the door.

"Go on," Leila whispered. "Can't let him see you. They see you, they'll know you told me what is happening out there, right?"

Walker nodded, then walked over into the kitchen. He wanted to be out of sight, but close enough in case something went wrong. He still had the gunman's pistol on him, so he pulled it out and stood at the ready.

Leila opened the door. "Awfully late for you to be out here, Tyler. Everything all right?"

"Sorry, ma'am. Just wanted to come and check on you."

"On me? Why would I need checked on?"

"Well, there was a drifter who came through your property. I had some guys working late in the shed. Organizing things and such. And well, he tried to, um, rob them."

"Oh my God," Leila said. "Is everyone all right?"

"No, but my guy who got hurt already went to the hospital. Just make sure you keep your place locked up. The guy got away. I'm sorry, ma'am."

"Okay. I definitely will. You called the police, right?"

"Yes, ma'am," Tyler said. "Spoke with the sheriff actually. He's sending a car out."

"Well, thank you, Tyler. I'll lock up. You get home and be safe okay?"

"Will do. Night, ma'am."

Leila shut the door. She was quiet for a moment until she heard Tyler pull away. "Well . . . shit."

Walker came back into the room. "Sorry, Leila. But at least you know now whose side he's on."

"Did I do okay? Did I seem surprised?"

"I'm not sure he would really care, since he's lying to you, but yeah, you did just fine."

"You think we're in the clear now?"

"No," Walker said. "I think you should leave and never look back. But . . . I understand why you feel like you can't. It's just dangerous."

"You should go then, Tom. You have enough problems of your own. And you have no reason to worry yourself further with mine."

"I agree with you. I should. I had this very conversation with myself on the walk back up here."

"And?" Leila said.

"And . . . I decided I can't. Maybe it's some instinct buried inside me to stay and fight. Maybe it's that I've seen enough good women lose something to bad men." Walker let a smirk grow across his face. "Or maybe it's just the caveman instincts in me that can't leave a pretty woman in distress."

Leila smiled and twirled her hair with her finger. "I knew you thought I was pretty."

Walker laughed. "Good thing, because you sure come with a lot of baggage."

Leila frowned and punched playfully at his shoulder. Then her mood sobered. "I can't believe all of this is happening. It's so much. My dad, then my niece, and now this whole drug thing on my family property . . . I really, I-I just don't know what I would do if you weren't here, Tom."

"I actually haven't done anything but confirm your troubles."

"Yeah, and then you said you weren't going to leave. Even after what you had to do in that shed. I didn't know what to think about you when I found you lying in my barn unconscious. But I'm glad I went with *my* instincts. I don't care what brought you here. I don't care what you do for a living in that unknown part of your life. Here, with me, you are a decent man. No matter what happens when everything comes back to you, don't forget that."

Leila moved close and ran her fingers through his wet hair. He took a step back.

"I don't think that's a good idea," Walker said.

"There needs to be something good that happens today. For both of us. We both need it."

Walker was going to fight it, but he wanted to kiss her. He decided she was right. Something needed to go right that night, before what he was afraid was going to be a very bad night.

So he let her in.

He was glad he did.

27

W alker stared at the ceiling as he lay under the sheets next to Leila. The room was dark, just a hint of yellow light seeping in beneath the door from the lamp in the living room and the filtered glow of the moon shining through the sheer curtains on his right. The rain had stopped at some point during their little bedtime escapade.

Leila was sound asleep, her head resting in the nook of his arm. Her light, hypnotic breathing tempted to lull him back to sleep, but there were too many questions floating in his head to give in. Even after an hour full of rigorous yet pleasurable exercise. So passionate that at one point he nearly popped his stitches.

As he lay with his other arm resting beneath his head, his thoughts swirled in and out of the ups and downs of the day. One minute he'd get a flash of the dream he'd had where he put the grill fork through the man's neck; the next he'd see Leila staring into his eyes as she moved on top of him; then on to the man he'd shot dead in the underground drug room. He imagined that few humans had seen a more roller-coaster day than his.

A shadow moved past the window beside him.

Walker slid his arm out from under Leila's neck, slinked out of bed, and quickly pulled on his jeans. He picked up the nine-millimeter he'd left on the dresser and moved over to the door. He glanced back at the window where he'd seen the figure go by, but now he saw only moonlight. In between Leila's soft breaths, he listened closely for any sign of movement. He didn't hear anything yet.

Holding the gun in his left hand he turned the doorknob with his right, one centimeter at a time. Once the latch cleared the latch strike, Walker eased the door open a slit. He could see half the hallway wall, then the opening into the living room. The lamp light showed him the curtain-covered window overlooking the driveway and the right half of the front door.

Everything was still.

Walker pulled the door open a little further, listening intently as he went. His mind was flashing to the basement of the equipment shed. To the second gunmen he'd tied up instead of killing. That was probably going to come back to haunt him. No doubt an error caused by the amnesia that kept him from being himself. He stepped out into the hallway. He heard the faint whinny of a horse from the back of the property and the ticking of the old-school cuckoo clock in the kitchen. Nothing else.

Walker's breath quickened as his adrenaline began rising. He inhaled through his nose and gave a long exhale through his mouth to try to even himself out. If he was a pro at this, his subconscious mind didn't know it at the moment. He stepped down the hallway toward the opening to the living room. No one was inside. He could see through all the way to the kitchen.

He made his way over to the window by the front door. He pulled back the right edge of the curtain just a smidge. Enough to see that no one was standing outside the door. The driveway only had Leila's Jeep, but when he moved the curtain a little more, down the road to the right, he saw a pickup truck parked just off the pavement. That jangled Walker's nerves. The figure passing by outside hadn't just been a figment of his imagination. Someone or multiple someones were definitely there.

Walker let go of the curtain and moved into the kitchen. He passed the table and went over to the sink. He didn't have to move the curtain that overlooked the backyard because another shadowy figure, or maybe the same one, walked right by. Walker raised the gun to shoulder height. He shuffled over to the door that led out to the deck. He turned the lock, flung open the door, and held the gun on the back of the man who was walking away from him.

"Don't move," Walker said.

The man stopped and turned around. He was holding a shotgun in his right hand. He wore a Miller Lite trucker cap, a flannel button-down with the sleeves cut off, along with blue jeans and a pair of work boots. Nothing about this man said cartel. Walker was confused.

"Drop the gun," Walker said.

The man did as asked.

"Who are you?" Walker said. "And what are you doing creeping around out here?"

"I have the same question." The man had a thick country accent. "Who the hell are you? This is Leila Ward's property. You ain't the sheriff, who she used to date. You her new man?"

Walker poked forward with his pistol. "I'm the one asking the questions."

"Yeah? Not for long."

Walker felt something solid slam down on his arms. Even if it hadn't caught him off guard, it would have been hard enough to send his gun sliding across the wooden deck. As he turned he felt two big arms wrap around him, and before he knew it, he crashed through the back door, sliding to a stop on the kitchen floor. A man twice the size of the one wearing the trucker hat, and at least twice as ugly, came stalking into the house.

Walker scrambled to his feet, but the man with the round body, round face, and red shaggy beard already had both hands under Walker's armpits, pinning him to the wall. The man smiled, showing a couple of missing teeth, then slid his forearm onto Walker's throat. Trucker Hat walked in behind him, wearing the same satisfied grin. He was once again holding his shotgun.

"Now, this can go one of two ways, Mr. . . . ."

The man waited for Walker to say his name, but even if Walker wanted to divulge such information, the meaty and hairy forearm blocking his windpipe wouldn't allow it.

"Let up a little so he can talk," Trucker Hat said. "We ain't savages."

The bear of a man lowered his arm from Walker's throat, but he still applied the same amount of pressure, pinning him in place.

"There, now, I'm Tim, and that there big man is Hank. And you are?"

"Walker," he managed. He noticed Leila peeking around the corner of the hallway wall.

"Ah, Mr. Walker," Tim said, taking a couple of steps forward. "Mr. Walker, as I was sayin', this can go one of two ways. You point us to the little business that the cartel has been running out of Ms. Leila Ward's property right now, and I'll let you get out of here without getting hurt. The second way is, you don't tell us, and I let Hank here have a little fun with you. And just so you know before you make your decision, ole Hank here has some anger issues. He rather likes takin' said issues out on other people with his fists. Do we understand each other?"

"I have no idea what you're talking about," Walker said.

Tim winced as he shook his head and took another step closer. "See, now, that's not what I asked you. Hank."

On command, Hank pulled his right arm back, then violently brought it forward, slamming his fist into Walker's stomach. Every last bit of air in Walker pushed from his lungs, and he nearly vomited from the force of the impact. Walker coughed away the punishing blow, gasping for air to refill his lungs. There was a shock wave of pain from his stomach, all the way down his legs. Another man walked in behind Tim. Similar athletic build as Tim, but even rougher around the edges.

"This here is my brother, Jason."

Jason tipped the bill of his own trucker hat. He was holding a baseball bat in his right hand.

"Jason here used to hit a lot of home runs with that there bat. If you don't tell me what I want to know, he's gonna use his hitting prowess on Ms. Leila Ward until she gives me what I want. Seeing as how you are walkin' around her house at night, with your shirt off, you're probably friendly enough with her to not want to see her pretty face get all twisted up. Am I right?"

"You can deal with me," Walker said. "Just leave her alone."

"Riiiight, that's what I thought," Tim said. Then he looked over at Jason. "He's sweet on her, ain't he?"

"Sounds like he might be," Jason said. Though it was a little hard to understand him because his accent was so thick.

"I'm a little disappointed, Mr. Walker," Tim said. "When you told me not to move outside, and I turned around and saw how you was built, like a brick shithouse, all cut and muscled, I thought you'd put up more of a fight. Maybe give Hank here a little workout. His fat ass needs it."

Walker's mind was running, but he felt like a student who'd forgotten everything he studied before the big exam. He could feel that inside him somewhere the knowledge of how to fight his way out of this kind of situation was there, but he just couldn't manage to retrieve it. He felt helpless. And he knew in that moment that it was going to get him and Leila either badly hurt or worse.

28

"I'll tell you what you want to know if you promise to let Leila go."

Walker didn't know what else to say. They had him dead to rights, so at the very least he could try to make a play so they wouldn't hurt Leila. He was finally able to get back to normal breathing after being punched in the gut, but the sick feeling of being hit so hard in the stomach still lingered.

"Aw, wouldya look at that, Jason," Tim said, smiling. "Chivalry ain't dead after all."

"Chiva-what?" Jason said.

Tim laughed. "You'll have to excuse my brothers, Mr. Walker. If you haven't figured it out, I'm the brains of the operation. Tell you what. You tell me what I want to know and I'll let you go. As for Ms. Ward, I'm not sure I can be as nice. When I find the drug operation that has been steadily taking away my customers, and take it from the cartel tonight, you don't think she'll ask her cartel partners to come up here to Kentucky and retaliate against me?"

"She's not involved," Walker said.

"No? If she ain't involved, then just how in the hell do you know about it?"

Walker knew he had to be careful. If he told Tim—who clearly had some sort of local drug trade going of his own— where the cartel's shop was beneath the equipment shed, he would go and take all the inventory, then destroy the shed and any way of continuing the cartel's business. That would blow back on Leila, one way or another. Walker didn't know anything about the cartel involved in this, but he imagined their countermeasures for such a thing would be far more pragmatic, and unstoppable, than these country boys and their little operation. At least that's what he'd read about the cocaine cartels in the eighties when he was a teenager. Walker had to assume a Mexican cartel would operate in much the same ruthless way.

Though he had no idea how he would get himself out of trouble with Tim, he thought it was the best decision to keep them in the dark instead of inviting the wrath of the cartel. No decision was going to bring a favorable short-term outcome, but all he could do was make the best of the situation and hope he, or Leila, didn't die in the process.

"I'm here on behalf of the cartel," Walker said. "My job is to get close to her, like you can see that I have, and see just how much she knows. I can tell you that she knows nothing about it. She's just here to tend to her dead father's farm until she can get the place sold. Which, obviously, we're going to buy."

Tim's demeanor changed. He squinted his eyes and stepped closer. "I'm afraid that's not going to work for me, Mr. Walker."

It was time for Walker to go all in. "I'm afraid it has to, Tim."

Tim didn't like that answer. "Hank, give Mr. Walker a

preview of what happens when I don't get what I want, would you?"

Hank pulled back his right hand and then brought it forward. Walker ducked, and Hank's hand went right through the drywall behind him. Walker tried to move to his right, but the big man caught his arm with one of his oversize paws, yanked him back, then threw another punch. Walker was able to move just enough so Hank slammed his shoulder, instead of his face, as intended. He hit Walker so hard that it knocked him off his feet and he skidded across the kitchen tile.

"Boy, the cartel must not be teaching you guys how to fight," Tim said. "What good is it to be in the shape you're in and not be able to handle yourself?"

Walker scrambled to his feet. As Hank lumbered forward, Walker picked up the chair beside him and busted Hank on the shoulder with it. The chair shattered into a dozen wood pieces and fell to the floor. Hank, however, did not. He was still moving toward Walker. Walker backpedaled around the table and toward the front door. Jason and his bat had moved to cover the entrance to the hallway. The front door behind him was Walker's only escape hatch. But he couldn't take it. He couldn't leave Leila alone with these guys. Hard telling what they would do to her.

"Hold on," Walker said, holding up his finger to Hank who was rounding the kitchen table. "Wait just a minute."

Hank kept coming. Just before he got to Walker, Tim spoke up.

"Hang on a second, Hank. Sounds like he might already be in a better frame of mind for negotiating." Tim looked at Walker. "Hank has that effect."

Hank stopped as he was told.

"Go on," Tim said. "I'm listening, but I have a short attention span for bullshit."

"You're a smart man, Tim."

"Flattery will get you everywhere."

"Being as that is the case, I know you've already thought through what my boss will do if you hurt me, much less what he'll do if you stunt the growth of his business. So let's find a way to resolve this where we both can win. And Leila can safely walk away from this entire thing."

"You think I'm worried about some Mexican drug dealers coming here onto my land?"

"I think you should be. These guys aren't just drug dealers, Tim. They have their hands in a lot of pots. And there are a lot more of them than there are of you."

"The hell you say. You don't know how many boys I've got workin' for me. I've been doing this a long time. And these pills they're making are just a small part of what we do."

"Then just let it go, Tim," Walker said.

"You threatenin' me, boy?" Tim looked at Hank. "Is he threatenin' me?"

"I'm not. I'm just trying to lay all the cards out on the table."

"Well then, how 'bout these cards, Mr. Walker. Since you work for this cartel, how's about I just hold you and Leila here hostage until your boss talks to me himself?"

Walker knew when he threw the scent off Leila by posing as one of the cartel that it would come to this. He would have to fight all three of them with all he had, because if they took him hostage, they would kill him. His only hope now was that he could convince them to leave Leila out of it.

"I don't want to go with you, Tim. I'll be honest. But I'll

go without a fight if you just leave Leila out of it. She's one of you. Just a farm girl trying to keep her daddy's legacy alive."

Tim laughed and started shaking his head. "Shew-wee, boys. She must be awfully good in bed to turn a hardened criminal like Mr. Walker here into a knight in shining armor." He walked over to Walker. "Once I've got you tied up, I just might have to see for myself."

As if a reflex had been triggered, Walker punched Tim right in the mouth. As Hank wrapped his arms around Walker, a gun went off in the hallway. Everyone looked over just in time to watch Jason fall to the floor. Leila was standing in the doorway, a pistol in her hand. Jason began moaning in pain on the floor.

"She shot me!" Jason shouted. "She shot my leg!"

"Drop it," Leila said to Tim as he started to raise his shotgun. "Drop it right now or I'll shoot him again. This time it will be much worse for him."

Tim tossed his shotgun toward the back door. "Woman, you are making a mighty big mistake right now," he said.

"Yeah? Looks pretty good from my view," Leila said. Then she looked at Hank. "Let him go. Right now."

Tim looked over at Hank and nodded. Walker felt Hank's massive arms relax and let go. Walker stepped away over to Leila.

"You all right?" she said.

Walker nodded.

Leila waved her pistol toward the front door. "Over by the door. Right now."

Tim pulled Jason to his feet and helped him limp over in front of the door.

"This ain't gonna end well for you, Leila." Tim said.

"Unless you let us walk out of here right now, I ain't gonna let this go."

Leila circled away from the three of them and made her way over by the ruined back door. "And you think I'm dumb enough to think you're going to let this go, if I let you go tonight? I don't know who the hell you are, or why you are here at my house because you think some kind of drug dealing is going on, but it isn't. You've got the wrong place."

Tim smiled. "Well, your boyfriend here tells a different story. Says he works for the cartel that's dealing out of your property. Is he lying? Or are you? 'Cause I'm gonna find out."

Leila bent down and picked up Tim's shotgun.

"He's lying," Leila said as she looked over at Walker. "He made a mistake and thought telling you what you wanted to hear would keep me safe. I'm not with him for his brains. And we haven't been together long enough for him to know anything about what goes on, on my daddy's farm. But I do. And unless you're talking about corn, it isn't being made here."

"That right?" Tim said. "Well, I believe you when you say he's lying. I'm sure you think he is. But I believe him. That's why he's got to come with me. You've just been caught in the middle of something that needs settlin'. I'm sorry for the inconvenience, but it just is what it is."

Leila set the shotgun down on the chair beside her. "Yeah, well, I'll just let the police sort it out for me since you all are trespassing on my property. I called them from the bedroom. They'll be here any minute. If you're right and Tom is lying, well, they'll find that out too. Not my job. I just want my peace and quiet back."

"Like I said," Tim said, "you've made a big mistake."

Walker saw movement from outside the back door, but

it was too late to warn Leila. A man moved through the broken door as Walker shouted Leila's name. He had already hit her over the head with the butt of a shotgun before she could turn around. As she fell to the floor, Tim rushed Walker. He drove him backward and slammed Walker against the wall. When he pulled back his arm to throw a punch, Walker ducked and Tim hit the wall behind him. The man with the shotgun stepped over Leila as Walker pushed Tim to the ground. But Hank had already moved over and picked up Jason's baseball bat.

Walker had time to throw a punch at Jason as he limped at him. But it didn't land. However, Hank's swing did hit home, and the bat coming right at his head was the last thing Walker saw before his lights went out.

29

Alison's head was still hurting from the blow she'd taken from Mike a while ago. She'd regained consciousness shortly after, but she hadn't said a word. Not even when Mike had been addressing her directly. She had nothing to say to him. Kim had woken up in the backseat a while back too. After Mike had hit her a couple of times, she decided it was in her best interest to keep her mouth shut as well.

"What the hell is going on at this house?" Mike said. "Was that Walker they were carrying?"

Alison leaned forward. She strained her eyes to see the men Mike was talking about. It did look like they were carrying a man who was unconscious and a woman right behind him. Alison didn't answer Mike. They had been waiting from the hiding spot where Mike once again parked the car to watch the front of the house where they last saw Tom Walker. The Jeep was still out front, and the tracker had shown that it hadn't moved from its spot.

There hadn't been any movement at the house for over an hour, but just when Mike was about to get out and "end his shitty assignment," as he said out loud, they watched a man in a hat go walking across the road toward the house. He looked like he was holding a baseball bat, but it was dark so they weren't sure. Then two more men came walking around behind him, and one of them was definitely holding a shotgun.

Mike turned toward her. "Was that Walker they were carrying out of there?"

Alison just looked him in the eye and didn't say a word.

"Answer me, or I'll knock your ass out again."

She didn't answer.

"Hell, what do I care anyway?" Mike said. "Soon as this is done, I'll just drive back to the airport and leave your ass in the car. Once I tell Maxwell you were plotting to help Walker escape, she'll send someone to kill you anyway. I don't even have to worry about it. And I probably wouldn't even be lying to her. The way you've been since we made it to Kentucky sure does feel like you've been trying to sabotage this entire thing. So just sit there and say nothing. Your ass will be dead soon anyway."

Mike took his bag from the back floorboard. He pulled out his phone and showed Alison that he was pressing Maxwell's contact, calling her. They watched the men put the woman, probably Leila, in the Jeep. Then they carried Walker to the pickup truck. After the Jeep pulled away and the pickup turned around in the driveway and left, Mike opened the door and got out. While the phone was ringing, he reminded Alison that, even if she made it out of the car, her legs were bound, so it wouldn't do her any good.

"Mrs. Maxwell, we have a problem," Mike said as he waited to shut the door. Then he ducked back down so Alison could see his face. "No, it's Alison. She tried to help Walker escape."

As he listened to Maxwell speak, he gave Alison a devilish grin. She lunged at him, but with her hands tied, there was nothing she could do. Mike winked at her, then shut the door and walked across the street. As he walked, he hit the lock on the car doors. Then he disappeared around the back of the house.

"Shit!" Alison shouted as she stomped her feet on the floor. "Shit, shit, shit!" Her breathing was heavy. Her adrenaline was pumping, and she had no way to release it but to throw a mini tantrum. "I'm dead. That bitch is going to kill me."

Alison heard Kim mumble through her gag from the backseat. She turned around as best she could while being bound. "I can't understand you, ma'am. There's nothing I can do for you anyway. I'm just as tied up as you are."

Alison watched as Kim's head looked around the back area of the car. Alison couldn't see quite well enough to make out if Kim was in pain or not from the expression on her face. It was too dark in the car where they were tucked between the trees.

"I'd ask you what you are looking for, but you can't talk. I'm assuming either a way to pull down your gag or cut your zip ties . . . good luck with that."

Though Alison didn't think Kim would find anything, it did prompt her to take a look around herself. It was dark up front as well, but there were streaks of moonlight. She knew nothing was lying around in the rental car. And she'd watched Mike take the keys, so driving away wasn't an option.

"Looks like we might be stuck here."

Then Kim's ass plopped down on the console between the front seats. Alison jumped back, not sure what the hell was going on. Kim's hands were tied behind her back and her mouth was gagged, so Alison just looked at her like she was crazy.

"Mm mm mm mm-mm mm mm-mm." Kim hummed like she was trying to say something.

"I don't know what you're saying. Literally, no clue."

Kim tried again, more emphatic this time. ""Mm mm mm mm-mm mm mm-mm!"

"Just because you put more oomph into it doesn't mean it's any clearer, Kim. I don't know what you are saying."

Kim sighed loudly. Then she started putting her shoulder to her cheek. After watching her do that a few times, Alison realized she was motioning to the gag.

"I can't get the gag off you. My hands are tied."

Kim sighed again, then laid her back down on the console. "Mm mm mm."

"Did you just say try it now?" Alison said.

Kim's eyes went wide, and she nodded emphatically. "Hmm mm!"

"All right, let me turn around. Don't move." Alison shifted in her seat and turned her backside toward Kim's face. "Excuse the booty, but it's the only way I can get close."

Kim edged her head closer, and Alison lowered her hands down to Kim's face. She managed to hook her finger between the gag and Kim's cheek. "Sorry if I scratch you. I've got it. If you just push out with your tongue, and thrust yourself forward, toward the dashboard, I think I can—"

Kim pushed with her tongue, and just like that, the gag was out. Kim sucked in and out a couple deep breaths. "Oh, thank God. That was awful."

"Well, we can talk about how we can't get out of here now, I guess. Too bad removing your gag doesn't get us any closer to escaping."

"I've got a knife in my panties," Kim blurted.

"What? Why the hell would you have a knife down there? Is that what you were trying to tell me."

"Yes, and I didn't mean for it to slide down that far. I had it tucked at the waistband of my jeans so he wouldn't find it in the event I didn't blow his head off. It fell down in my underwear when he threw me in the backseat. I've been trying to dig for it, but I need my jeans unbuttoned to give my hands enough room to get down that far."

"I knew I liked you, Kim. How'd you know we'd come back?"

"Tommy has taught me a few things about being prepared over the years."

"So you two are closer than you were letting on?" Alison said.

"I'm not sure I should tell you anything else. You are trying to kill Tommy, and you did come back to kill me."

Alison smiled. Kim leaned in.

"Is that a smile?" Kim said. "Are you smiling?"

"Tom and I are—were—closer than I've been letting on too."

Kim gasped. "I knew it! I knew you weren't like that Mike fella. You and Tommy, you were a thing?"

"Listen . . ." Alison's tone became more serious. "Do you really have a knife?"

"I do. In my panties, as I said."

"Then we have to get it now. Mike won't be much longer in that house."

"Was that really my Tommy they were carrying out of there?"

"It looked like it."

Kim nodded. "Well here," she said as she turned her belly toward Alison. "Unbutton my pants and I'll get it."

Kim turned her back again and searched Kim's jeans

until her fingers found the button. She undid it, and Kim flopped herself back into the backseat. Alison turned back around so she could try to see. All she could make out was Kim writhing her body around.

"Any luck?" Kim said.

"Almost. The damn thing wiggled all the way down to my crack!"

Alison began to feel like time was running out. "Please hurry. And how did the knife not cut you?"

"It's a—oh, I almost got it—pocket knife. It's closed. Can't . . . get . . . cut—I got it!"

Alison felt her first drop of hope ripple over her. "Sit back around on the console. Hand me the knife and I'll cut you free."

"No offense," Kim said, "but have you ever even owned a pocket knife?"

Alison had to think about it. "No. But—"

"I've had one my entire life. I've already got the blade out. Just give me a second to cut myself free."

"Then you'll cut mine too, right?" Alison said.

"Ain't sure I should. You both are here to kill my Tommy, right?"

Alison turned toward her. "I would not have let Mike kill him. I promise." She wanted to be able to look Kim in the eye, to show her that she meant it, but it was too dark.

"Let me just get myself undone here first."

"How's it coming?"

"Had to situate the blade first. I'm sawin' on it now. I've had this knife a while though, kinda dull. But it's comin'."

Alison looked out the windshield. Her stomach dropped when she saw movement coming around the house. Mike was coming.

"Shit, he's coming! Cut the tie! He's coming!"

"You panickin' ain't gonna make this go any faster," Kim said.

"He's going to kill us both if you don't cut me loose. Does that make it faster?"

"I'm doin' all I can!"

Mike started across the road. It was too late.

"If you don't cut yourself free right now, we're dead. Please hurry!"

"I'm almost there!"

He was across the street. Their time was up. The car doors unlocked as Mike approached.

"We're dead. Just make sure he doesn't see that your gag is down. Turn your head or something. Not that it matters."

Mike opened the door. He had two bags now, and he set both of them on the console; then he sat down and shut the car door. Alison put her back to the passenger door, as far away from Mike as she could get.

"Well, it must have been Walker and the owner of the farm those guys took with them. Quite the fight inside. No sign of where they could have been taking him. But I did find his bag. Evan Marshall passport inside. Bunch of cash and, get this, several notebooks. Full of writing. Son of a bitch thinks he's an author or something. I guess I can call that detective and see what he knows about some redneck gang or whatever the hell is going on. Hand me his card."

Mike looked over at Alison. She wore a blank face. He laughed.

"That's right, you can't move."

Mike reached over and began feeling around her pockets. Alison squirmed as he was extra handsy.

"It's in my back left pocket," she said, to help avoid any more of his groping.

"Ah, she speaks!" Mike pulled the card from her pocket. Then he set it down and pulled out his gun.

"You don't need that," she said. "I promise, you don't need that."

"Boss says I do. And I don't need you hearing the detective tell who might have taken Walker and where he might be." Mike held the gun out in front of him, pointing it right at Alison's head.

"Please! Please don't!"

"Wish I could say I'll miss you," Mike said.

Alison closed her eyes. Waiting to hear the gunshot blast. Instead, she heard a thud and Kim letting out a grunt. When Alison opened her eyes, she watched Kim plunge the knife into Mike's neck, over and over again. Much faster than an older woman should be able to move. So much so that he never had a chance to fight it. Kim had hit an artery and blood was splashing all over both Kim and Alison. But Mike dropped his gun . . . and his life. That was worth a blood shower any day.

30

Walker could feel rumbling and cool wind blowing all around him. He was aware that he was alive, but nothing else. He pulled and pulled with his forehead to open his eyes, but they wouldn't budge. The rumble was met with bouncing. He was fairly certain he was lying down, but nothing was working properly in his brain. He had zero motor functions. He let the rumble continue for a few seconds longer; then he gave opening his eyes another shot.

Walker felt like he was moving his forehead up to try to peel his eyes apart, but he really wasn't sure if he was moving anything at all. Then his left eyelid finally popped open. His senses overloaded. He could smell blood, gasoline, and vomit. He was lying facedown in the bed of a pickup truck. As soon as he felt his left index finger move, a pain like he had never felt before shocked his brain, and the back of that truck turned back into nothingness.

. . .

THE SMELL of blood came to him first this time. There was no rumble accompanying it. No wind. No noise at all. Before he attempted to open his eyes, he took a moment to affix himself to his current situation. He was sitting up, leaning his back against a wall, though his head was slumped forward. His hands were under his bent legs, tied to his ankles. Then there was the pain.

The pain was indescribable.

Walker hadn't felt pain like that since number three, Santiago Pérez, when he'd fallen out of the three-story window on top of a black Ford Crown Victoria in Mexico City.

Walker's eyes shot open, and he lifted his head.

He remembered.

Not only did he remember the incredible chase of his third assassination, which led to him falling out of the three-story window, but he remembered that he had numbered them all and that was always how he referred to the people he was hired to kill. He also now knew that he was back, the real Tom Walker, not the imposter who'd woken up in the barn, void of all the skills that had taken years and years to acquire.

No, he was himself again, and all of his memories were entirely intact. But more importantly, all that he knew about getting out of situations like the one he was currently in came back as well. No more weak-minded, confused, and hesitant self. He was back. And if he could just get rid of the intense pain at the base of his skull, he could start to think of a way out of there and properly introduce himself to the redneck thugs who had so easily put him in that place. Then he could find . . .

Leila.

Walker's mind flashed back to Leila's house before the

baseball bat knocked him unconscious. Leila had been hit first. That's right. They must have taken her too. His mind was racing, and he began pulling at the ropes that bound his arms to his ankles. His brain was hurting, his memories were swirling, and he just had to—

Walker stopped moving everything all at once and closed his eyes. He inhaled long and slow through his nose, then with the same tempo released it out through his mouth. He followed this procedure three more times until the only thing on his mind was the pain that wouldn't be leaving his head anytime soon. He was quiet. He was still. He was ready to focus.

Walker opened his eyes and assessed the room. The only light he saw shined through the gap at the bottom of a door to his left. Stairs. He was in a basement. The musty smell and the poured concrete beneath his feet confirmed this assessment. He was leaning against the back wall of the room. He was still shirtless, and his back could feel the rough texture of cinder-block walls. It also could have been brick. It was too dark to know. And it didn't matter. Step one was get free of the ropes.

Whoever had bound him was good with knots. They'd taken their time and made sure he was secured tight. It was smart to tie his hands to his ankles to allow minimal move-ment, but their first misstep had been to neglect tying him to something fixed. Though it would be awkward, tied up as he was, he could still move around, and that was their mistake. All he had to do was find a turn in the wall. A lot of times in basements, when walls meet, the edges of the cinder block or brick could come to a semi-sharp edge. That would be all he needed.

Walker toppled over onto his side. Using his feet to push, he moved along like an inchworm. He did this for about a minute until his head bumped against the cinder block of another wall. He barely grazed it, but it was enough to send a lightning bolt surge of pain down his entire spine. His head had seen a lot of trauma since the car accident. The car accident that he now remembered. A visual of jabbing the pen into Trevor's jugular in the seat beside him flashed across his mind. Then he got back to work.

He inched along the new wall. He grew closer to the stairs with each push. If someone came down at that moment, it would most likely mean death. Or at least another beating if they still fell for the whole "I work for the cartel" thing. But he couldn't worry about things he couldn't control. That is how people drive themselves crazy. Instead, he focused on inching his way along, hoping for a hallway to the left that would give him that edge he needed. About six feet from the bottom of the stairs, he felt the wall behind him disappear.

Luck be a lady.

Walker craned his neck, and when the top of his back rubbed the corner, it was sharp enough. He scooted out a little farther, then pulled his legs and hands up into the air. Shimmying his ass to the right, he finally caught the corner of the wall near his feet. Then he began to saw. Up and down, his arms and legs worked together as he pressed forward against the cinder block. He could hear the rough edges of the blocks fraying the rope. The hard part was that with each push and pull, he was moving farther away from the wall. The sweat began beading on his brow almost instantly. Scoot, pull, push. Scoot, pull, push. Over and over.

The rope at his feet gave in first. His legs separated, and he was able to sit up properly. Sweat dripped from his skin as he got to his feet. He immediately placed his hands around the corner of the wall and raked them up and down.

This went much faster as he was able to apply constant forward pressure. His head pounded as he ripped away the last of the rope. The concussion mixed with all the exertion began to make him dizzy. Then the rope around his wrists gave way.

His hands were free.

Walker immediately put them to use as he let them wander along the wall for a light switch. He found one and flipped it on. He shielded his eyes as soon as the light hit them. They would have needed to adjust after being in such darkness anyway, but after the hits his head had taken, the light coming in felt like the blade of a sword. He buried his face in the bend of his arm, but it was too late. He should have protected his eyes first. His stomach lurched, and he lost it on the floor.

Bending over with hands on knees, he used one hand to wipe away the vomit. He took a few deep breaths to try to bring himself somewhere near normal. He didn't have time to be hurt or to be sick. He only had time to save Leila from these hillbillies and maybe even save himself. He stood up straight with another long deep breath. He didn't feel dizzy.

Small victories.

He was about to need a lot of those. And as the man put in charge of Walker when he was just fifteen, John Sparks, used to tell him whenever Walker said he wanted to skip the little lessons and get straight to the big ones, "Son, there's only one way to eat an elephant. One small bite at a time." Walker used to hate that saying. He was too young to understand the concept that at first everything in life seems daunting, overwhelming, and sometimes even impossible. But as you get older and achieve certain things, you realize that even the impossible can be accomplished if you take it just a little bit at a time.

Walker knew he had the impossible staring him right in the face as he stood there alone in that basement, hurting, weaponless, and severely outnumbered. But now that he had his memories, he could pull from all the times he'd been in positions just like this one and worked his way out of them.

One thing at a time.

First thing: get out of wherever the hell he was being held—alive. No matter what it took. Then he would worry about the rest.

31

W alker slowly regained his composure. Amazing what a little vomiting and a few deep breaths will do. He looked around the room, and much to his chagrin, there wasn't a weapon in sight. He didn't know a lot about his situation, but one thing was certain: without a weapon, he wasn't going to make it. He turned to the small hallway behind him. There was a white door on the wall to his right, tucked into the gray cinder block.

He moved over and opened it. A tiny unfinished room. The pipes suggested it had been plumbed for a future bathroom. Walker imagined that a man cave built by these guys would be chock-full of deer heads, Confederate flags, beer funnels, and all the cans of wintergreen long cut a man could chew. Unfortunately, he saw nothing he could shoot them, hit them, or stab them with. He'd better stop assuming they were as dumb as they looked. He knew Tim wasn't, but the rest of them––gravel for brains.

Walker left the future bathroom, turned left, and started up the stairs. He was still sweating from his battle against the ropes. Shirtless and shoeless, he figured he probably looked like he would fit right in with his enemy at the moment. When he reached the top, he got on his knees so he could detect if there was any movement. He hadn't heard anything from above since the moment he regained consciousness. He hoped that didn't mean they were busy with Leila, but the mind always goes to the worst place first.

He peered under the door leading to the basement he was in but saw nothing. Still no noise either. He was going to have to bring them to him. Walking out that door with nothing but his good looks wasn't going to be enough to stay alive. He turned away from the door, coned his hands around his mouth and shouted, "Someone help me! Please! I'm down here!"

Then he waited.

Nothing.

So he repeated. "Please! I'm down here! Please help me!"

Finally he heard movement, and it sounded like one set of feet. Perfect. He would be able to get a weapon from whoever was coming without anyone getting the chance to shout. He bent down again to look beneath the door, but this time not resting on his knees. Now he was coiled up like a cobra. His legs ready to spring him forward, his arm ready to strike.

A worn pair of chocolate-brown work boots appeared in the slot beneath the door. The door handle shook, and Walker pushed up with his legs and snapped his arm upward. The man in the doorway didn't even have the chance to put one foot forward before Walker's hand bounced off his throat. The man involuntarily reeled backward, hands on his neck, but Walker caught the bat he dropped with his left hand and a fistful of the man's shirt with his right. He yanked the man toward the stairs, watching him surf on his back all the way down to the concrete below. Walker quietly shut the door and walked down the stairs.

"If you scream, I'll crush your windpipe," Walker said in a cold but calm voice as he pointed with the bat toward the man who was scooting away on his back. "You'll still be alive to answer my questions, but you won't be able to make any noise. Either way, I'll get what I want. So it's up to you whether you answer me in more pain than you've ever felt in your life or with just the pain you're feeling now."

The man held out his hand, then pointed at his throat.

Walker stepped over right in front of him. "You have ten seconds to answer me."

The man pointed more emphatically at his throat again. Walker knew he meant that he still wasn't ready to talk from the first blow to his throat, but Walker knew he could work through it if he was motivated enough. At five seconds, Walker pulled back with the bat, ready to swing.

"Okay," the man said. It came out hoarse but intelligible. He cleared his throat and gave it another try. "Tim . . . ," he started but had to cough away the last of the hoarse. "Tim will kill me and you if I tell you anything."

Walker already knew Tim was the leader of the pack, but confirmation is always nice.

"Okay. Well, I'm going to kill you if you don't tell me everything. Let me worry about what Tim does to me."

"All right, man. But I'm tellin' ya. You're a dead man."

"Noted," Walker said. "Can we move this along? I haven't killed anyone in a day or two. Sometimes it starts to itch."

The man's eyes widened. "Just relax. Please. You-You're on Tim Riggins and his brothers' farm."

"Working farm?"

"Yeah, it's workin'."

"Working as in full go?" Walker said. "Or bare minimum to hide the drug trade? Friendly reminder, wrong answers mean broken bones."

The man pulled himself up and propped his back against the wall. "I-I don't know what you're talking about."

"Take off your shirt and stuff it in your mouth," Walker said.

"What? Why?"

"If you don't do it, you're dead."

The man looked into Walker's eyes and found truth. He took off his shirt and stuffed as much of it in his mouth as he could. Walker lifted the bat and swung down hard, smashing the man's ankle. The man screamed into the shirt. Walker let the pain marinate. The man didn't know it, but Walker was showing him mercy. When the conversation was over, Walker couldn't afford to have to fight the man later. So he either had to kill him or maim him. Walker felt generous, even though the situation didn't really warrant such kindness.

"Now remove the shirt. If you scream, you'll leave me no choice but to silence you. I think you know me well enough by now to know what that means."

The man had tears of pain running down his face. He was breathing heavily, but he managed a nod and spit out the shirt.

"The real answer now, please," Walker said.

"Yes. Bare minimum just to cover the drug trade."

"Good. Now, where's Leila, the woman who was brought here with me?"

"She . . . she's out in the barn. Couple hundred yards out the back door. But I'm tellin' ya, man, you don't wanna go out there. Tim called everybody in when he was bringin' you two back. You won't make it."

"I will if you don't lie to me," Walker said. "And remember, you lie, you die." Walker laughed. "Look at that, I'm a poet."

The man didn't laugh. "I'll tell you anything. Just please don't kill me."

"Deal," Walker said. "How many men?"

The man held up his hand defensively. "Now I can't know that for sure. But there's gotta be at least twelve."

His answer was acceptable. "All armed?"

"I imagine so. The only other time I can remember Tim calling everyone in like this was when we had to go take down an up-and-coming drug business. Weapons were a must then."

That made sense to Walker as well, because he knew from what Tim said in Leila's house that taking down the drug operation on Leila's property was his goal, regardless of whether it was being run by a Mexican cartel or not. Shortsighted from Walker's perspective, but he was only an expert in killing highly skilled and high-value targeted humans, not drug selling operations.

"What will they do with Leila?" Walker said.

"Honestly?"

"Yeah, let's stick with honesty," Walker said.

"They'll probably do what they want with her, then kill her."

Walker appreciated the honesty, but those words stung.

The man continued. "If Tim were to let her go now, she could bring down his whole operation. It's unlikely he'll take that chance."

Walker nodded. "So I'm assuming since you think Tim would be willing to kill Leila, that he's killed before?"

"I think he'll kill her. Is it really important what he's done before?"

"It is to me. Therefore, it is to you."

The distinction was paramount for the way Walker would be handling the next couple of hours. If Tim was just a hard-nosed drug dealer, Walker would take the more difficult yet softer approach. But if Tim had already proven to be a cold-blooded killer, Walker didn't mind fighting fire with fire.

"All right. Yes. I've seen him kill, and he's had people kill for him. That good enough? Will you let me live?"

Walker bent down and used the ropes that had bound him early and wrapped them around the man's ankles. The man yelped in pain. The ankle was shattered—he wasn't going to be walking on it anytime soon—but Walker couldn't take the chance that he could drag himself up the stairs and alert someone that Walker had escaped.

"Stop making noise," Walker said. "It's either this or I kill you."

The man nodded through the pain. Walker wasn't going to make the mistake his captors had and not tie this guy to something, so he dragged him over and tied him to the first post on the railing going up the stairs. It wasn't something that couldn't be pulled apart, but at least this made the man's job harder. Then Walker dug his hand into the man's jeans, pulling out his phone.

"Check in with Tim. Tell him all is good with the sexy, bare-chested man in the basement. Feel free to ad-lib."

The man looked at him as if he had no idea what ad-lib meant.

"Just check in and tell him all is good."

Walker used the man's face to unlock the phone.

"Press that one there at the top," the man said about the contact list.

Walker pressed "BOSS"—how imaginative—and the phone began ringing.

"You mess this up, you're dead," Walker said as he pressed speaker.

The man nodded.

"Everything all right?" Tim answered.

"All good here," the man said. "He's still tied up. Anything you need me to do?"

"Just make sure it stays that way," Tim said. "I'll be down to get him in about a half an hour."

"You got it."

Walker ended the call and pocketed the phone. He had just enough rope left to tie it as a bit of a gag in the man's mouth. The man protested with grunts and moans. Walker finished and didn't say another word. He walked over and picked up the man's Skoal hat. Then he put on the man's black Dale Earnhardt T-shirt. It was skintight on Walker because he was a lot bigger than this guy. He then squeezed his feet into the man's boots. He pulled the hat low and readied the baseball bat in his hands. There was nothing left to do but get things done. And he knew where he had to go and what he had to do.

He just hoped he wasn't too late.

lison and Kim watched as, beneath the dome light inside the car, Mike's blood continued to leak from his neck.

"That was a close one," Kim said.

Alison wasn't ready to speak. She was five seconds away from being dead just then. Now all the consequences of Mike being dead were swirling about in her mind. Maxwell would hunt her to the ends of the earth. And the only thing that might be worse than being dead was living a life on the run, constantly looking over your shoulder. But at least she had options.

"He sure does have a lot of that stuff in him, don't he?" Kim said.

Alison shook from her trance and took a deep breath. "What? You mean blood?"

"Well, I don't mean shit. But I suppose he's probably chock-full of that too."

Kim was smiling, blood still running down her arm.

Alison shook her head. "You're awfully calm for what just about happened. After what *did* just happen."

"I'm just glad it ain't one of us leakin' all that oil. Ain't you?"

Alison laughed as she shook her head. "You know what, Kim. I like your attitude. I am glad it isn't one of us too. You mind using that knife to cut me loose?"

Kim scooted forward with her hands over the bloody console. Alison turned her back and extended her tied wrists backward.

"I cut you loose, what happens then?" Kim said.

"I'll drive you home. Where you should have been in the first place."

"I ain't goin home, Alison. I owe Tommy everything in the world for what he did for me. He sacrificed his entire life to kill my deadbeat husband. Hell, it's the only reason he's in this spot right now. He was smart. Loved his books. He woulda been somethin' special. Now he's just a tool of the government, who just uses him to make sure they keep getting more and more powerful, making more and more money. No offense."

Alison didn't take any. She was surprised by Kim. Not because she didn't think people who were from "the hollers" weren't smart—because she'd known a few growing up—but just how spot-on Kim's assessment of Walker and even Alison were. Alison hadn't spent a lot of time with Walker. Really just a couple of one-night stands when their schedules aligned. But she did hear Walker say once that he didn't like being a rich man's weapon. It had stuck with her, because Alison had never felt right about it either.

"No offense taken. And I understand, Kim. I do. But where I have to go to try to help Walker is very dangerous. Not fit for you."

"That what you're gonna do? Go try to help Tommy?

Thought you was here to kill him."

"Mike was here to kill him. I was never going to let that happen."

Kim studied Alison for a moment as she was turned enough to look her in the eyes. Then she nodded. "Okay. I believe you. But I cut you loose on one condition."

"I can see where this is going," Alison said, "but go ahead."

"You take me with you."

"I'm telling you, Kim. It's too—"

"I don't give a possum's butthole how dangerous it is. I owe Tommy my life. I'll gladly give it back just for the chance to help him like he helped me. You understand that?"

Alison nodded. "I do. But you've been warned."

Kim began cutting at the zip tie around Alison's wrists. After just a few seconds, Alison was free. Kim handed her the knife, and she cut her ankles free as well. She rubbed at her wrists as she turned in her seat to face Kim.

"Better?" Kim said.

"Better. Thank you."

Kim pointed at Mike. "So of the two of you, I assume you were the smart one?"

"He was definitely 'the muscle,' if that's what you mean."

"It is. So you are here 'cause you're good at research and lookin' into stuff?"

"You could say that," Alison said.

"So you have an idea how to track those guys down and find Tommy?"

Alison smiled. Then she reached down and picked up Mike's phone. She held it to his face, and it unlocked. Then she moved through the phone to the tracking app. She held it up and showed Kim.

"And that is?"

"That . . . is where your Tommy is."

"What? You already know?"

Alison nodded. "We put a tracker on Leila Ward's Jeep just in case they left and we weren't there to see it. The guys who took the two of them took the Jeep with them. Now we know where they are."

"Hot damn!" Kim said. "What are we waiting for? We got my shotgun, this dead guy's pistol, that's enough for me!"

"I have a pistol in my purse too. But we are going to have to call the police in on this one. Hard telling how many men will be where they are. And clearly, they aren't all friends."

"We can't call the police," Kim said. "Didn't you say Tommy was wanted? What happened on that anyway? Why are you all really looking for him?"

"Long story short, Mike here isn't the first person the company sent after Walker."

"Let me guess," Kim said. "It didn't go so good for the last guy either?"

"It did not."

Kim giggled. "Good boy. So, what's he doing at this woman's farm?"

"When he killed the other men—"

"Men?" Kim said. "As in plural?"

"Three, to be exact."

"Sheesh all mighty. What the hell did he do to get himself in that much trouble?"

"The right thing."

Kim nodded. "Yep. That sounds like Tommy."

"Now," Alison said, thinking out loud, "what that has to do with sticking around at this house, and whoever in the hell just took him—I mean, do you know what it would take to knock Walker out and take him hostage? That's what I'm saying. We have no choice but to call the police. Because I sure as hell can't call for backup. I've had some combat experience, but I'm not like Walker or even Mike here. They are lifers. Trained by all the best the military's ever had."

"Right. But Tommy is there. We get him loose from these guys, and all we have to do is just help him find a way out as he does his thing."

Alison sat back in her seat. She looked over at Mike's lifeless body. As morbid as it sounded, she was glad the son of a bitch was dead. What to do with his body and how to get out of her new pickle with Maxwell was another massive problem yet to be solved.

"He'll help you, you know," Kim said.

Alison looked up at her.

Kim nodded to Mike. "You're in real trouble now, ain't ya?"

Alison nodded.

"Same people who want Tommy dead, right?"

Alison nodded again.

"You help him tonight, y'all can work together and get shed of the problems the people you work for might be havin'."

"I'm afraid it isn't that simple," Alison said.

"Ain't it? You got another choice?"

Alison let out a sigh. Then she opened her door and got out.

"Where ya goin'?" Kim said.

Alison walked around and pulled the driver-side door the rest of the way open. She gripped Mike's jacket and began tugging at him. Then she leaned in and looked at Kim. "It was your idea to go help Walker. So you going to help me with this or not?"

Alison watched a smile grow across Kim's face beneath the yellow interior car light.

"Hell yeah!" Kim shouted as she popped open her door.

The two of them pulled away at the large dead man, finally yanking him out of the car and onto the ground. They each took an arm and dragged him over by a thick set of bushes.

Alison clapped her hands together like she was ridding herself of a dirty task. "This will do right here until we get back and figure out a more permanent resting place."

"So we off to get Tommy back then?"

"We are. But we're still going to need some help. I think I know a detective I can call who just might help us out."

33

At the top of the basement stairs, Walker eased open the door. So far the man in the basement was staying quiet. Walker didn't see anyone, so he took a step out into the kitchen. An island sink sat just in front of him, and the entry to a living room just beyond that. The wood floors were old but well kept. The white textured wallpaper had a hunter-green border with roosters filling the empty space. A Coca-Cola sign hung on the wall just beneath a telephone sitting in its cradle. He hadn't seen one of those in a while.

A television blared somewhere in the house. He could hear the laugh track to a sitcom. Then he heard the unmistakable voice of Archie Bunker popping off at Edith. *All in the Family*. Jim and Kim used to watch that one when Jim enjoyed one of his few sober days. He would always make fun of Walker for reading instead of watching the show. "There's a whole life goin' on out here that you're missin' with that damn nose o' yours buried in that stupid book," he would say.

Walker's grip tightened around the baseball bat. He

nearly laughed out loud that all of his recent memories were back in stock, yet there he was, remembering that asshole again from when he was fifteen. The past rules every decision you make if you let it. That was especially true when you murder the past and they use you to murder everyone else's problems thereafter.

To his right was a hallway, his left, a dining room. He walked past the stove, then the oven, and looked around the hallway wall. It was a straight shot to the front door. The quickest exit would be the smartest. The faster he got out into the dark of night, the sooner he could become the shadow, back where he belonged. His head was pounding, so he took a few extra seconds in the kitchen. On the third cabinet door he opened, there was a bottle of ibuprofen. He popped open the bottle, dry-swallowed four, and moved back to the edge of the hallway.

He stepped out into the hallway and moved past the pictures of family hanging on both sides. Just as he reached for the front door, a man's voice stopped him in his tracks.

"Cutty? Ain't you s'posed to be watchin' the basement?"

It was fairly dark in the foyer, and Walker had "Cutty's" hat pulled low and his T-shirt on. He could see out of the corner of his eye that the man was sitting in front of a computer in a room that was fairly far away. So he gave nonviolence a chance.

"Forgot my dip," Walker said, opening the front door. "Be right back."

"Shit, man can't be without that," the man said. "Hurry up!"

Walker left and shut the door behind him. He thought putting on the man's redneck uniform would help; he just didn't think it would help him get outside that quick. He stepped out onto the front porch. There was a swing on his left, couple of rockers on the right. And about seven pickup trucks pulled into various places across the front lawn. The baseball bat in his hand wasn't a bad weapon, but its range was lacking. Surely one of those trucks had some sort of firearm inside.

He walked down the porch steps and tried the first truck. Locked. He moved on to the second, and it, too, wouldn't open.

"You lookin' for somethin' there, Hoss?" a man said from behind him.

"Actually, yes," Walker said as he turned around, taking a step right toward the man. "I misplaced my gun, can I borrow yours?"

Walker was already swinging the bat before the man could pull his pistol from his hip holster. The bat bounced off the man's head, and he dropped to the ground. Walker bent down and took the pistol for himself, then patted the man on the chest and said, "Appreciate ya." His keys were in his pocket. Walker took the fob in his hand and pressed the lock button. Headlights flashed two trucks down. Walker dragged the man by his arm over to his truck. He unlocked the door, pulled the man up inside, laying him on the floorboard. If he'd had a knife, Walker would have killed him. As it were, the chance of drawing attention by expending a round was the greater of the two evils. He performed a quick press check. The moonlight glinted off the brass round in the chamber. The gun was hot.

Walker checked the back of the truck for a rope but saw none. He took the man's phone, smashed it on the ground with his bat, and moved on. He tucked the pistol in his waistband and held onto the bat. Time to move toward the back of the house and get on to the barn. He could only imagine what Leila was going through, and his imagination went to dark places. So that's where he would go.

He moved around the truck and up to the left side of the house. Positioned on top of a hill, there wasn't much in the way of cover. He stopped at the back corner. In the distance he could see the light on in front of the barn. A couple more trucks were parked near the entrance. To the right looked to be nothing but pasture. Down about a hundred yards on his left were cornstalks. That would be the way in. After all of this was said and done, he wasn't sure he'd ever eat another ear of corn again.

After a glance at the back porch revealed it empty, Walker jogged out to his left toward the head-high corn. His leg felt pretty good considering the wound. It wouldn't interfere with what would happen next. Judging by the position of the moon, it was going on one or two o'clock in the morning. He had too much adrenaline to feel tired. The nap earlier didn't hurt. The rain clouds were gone, leaving behind the warm damp air of summer in the South. Muddy ground beneath his boots.

As he drew parallel with the barn, he moved toward the edge of the stalks. One man stood guard at the barn's front entrance. Squinting, Walker could make out a shotgun in the man's hand. Not ideal. The barn itself was tall and wide. Walker imagined lofts on both ends filled with hay. He moved left through the stalks to where he could see the back of the barn. There was another man posted there.

The two men weren't a problem. The issue was his weapons. The gun could only be used in an emergency, because as soon as he fired a round, everyone nearby would know his location. A real problem when he's a one-man team. The bat was fine, but if he was off with his swing even by a little, one of the men would be able to shout, thus rendering the silent weapon useless.

He was just going to have to be exact with his swing.

The man at the back wasn't being quite as attentive as the man out front. He was smoking a cigarette and playing with his phone. Walker figured redneck security probably never was highly trained, but just paying attention can go a long way when you have a gun in your hand. These men were no more trained than what was required to hunt a deer. That, and maybe a few bar fights. Close combat with a man like Walker would be like Michael Jordan going one-on-one with a grade schooler. But numbers matter. And they had plenty. Guns level the playing field, too, so his main goal would be to fight one-on-one for as long as he could.

A woman's scream echoed over the farm.

Adrenaline crackled through Walker's bloodstream like a bolt of lightning through a tree.

He was finally ready to use his regained memory bank full of the deadliest skills in the game. His hard-earned killer instinct. And he was going to start with the man at the back door.

Until he found Leila, there would be no more mercy.

34

W alker could see the man's face at the back entrance to the barn glowing in the light of his iPhone screen. He focused intently. Probably sucked in by some Tikgram or InstaTok app or whatever was the latest fad. So Walker went to work.

He plucked an ear of corn from the last stalk in front of him, then sprinted for the side of the barn. Unseen. He walked to the corner, peeked, and found the man still oblivious. He chucked the ear of corn as far as he could. It sailed over the man's head and landed on the other side of him. When he looked up from his phone in the opposite direction from where Walker was hiding, Walker moved in.

As he ran, Walker pulled back his bat. The man heard his footfalls, but it was too late. Walker swung forward, and the meat of the bat met skull bone at the man's forehead. A sickening thud. Walker pulled the bat up over his head and slammed down one more time to make sure.

No mercy.

He bent over the dead man and went through his pockets. Nothing there. However, fortune favored Walker and he found a horizontal-carry, fixed-blade knife running along the back of his belt. He removed the man's belt, undid his own, then slipped the knife, which was tucked in a stiff sheath, inside his own belt loop, all the way to his back. Then he reached over and picked up the man's phone. There was a half-naked woman dancing in front of the camera in her bedroom on loop. At least the man died happy.

Walker stood and practiced pulling the blade from the sheath three times fast. It wasn't much practice, but a quick acclimation to new equipment can help in an intense moment. He left the bat behind and moved over to the open door. At first glance inside the barn, he saw no one. He strained to hear faint voices. This gave Walker hope that they could be on ground level with Leila. The barn stretched a good distance out in front of him. Plenty of room for offices and other rooms beyond the open area in front of him now. There were no sounds or smells of animals. Which made sense. If they were making or cooking drugs in this building, they wouldn't want a possible explosion to kill their horses too. If they even had any.

Walker stepped inside. There was a yellow light shining down from one of the beams up in the loft. There was a blue tractor, a highlighter-green Dodge Challenger, two white vans, and a late model Chevy pickup truck. Obviously, it was the garage portion of the building for Tim. Walker slid right, keeping his back to the wall. He moved past the van to the outside wall that the other man keeping guard at the front entrance had been leaning against. He inched up to the open door, moved his head in and out just fast enough to gauge the man's distance from the opening. It was too far to slip around unseen. He would have to catch him off guard.

Walker pulled the knife and held it down by his side as he prepared his voice with the best country twang he could muster. Then he walked outside. "Tim said go take ya a break."

When the man looked up, Walker jammed the blade of the knife—in, then out—an inch to the left of his Adam's apple. No way to scream, no way to keep too much blood from spilling out. Then Walker turned back inside the barn. What little he could hear was all coming from the opposite end of the barn. The cicadas had really sparked up conversation outside, making it all the more difficult to tune in.

Before moving toward the voices, Walker moved back beside the first van. Methodically, he went from vehicle to vehicle, stabbing the knife through every single tire so there were no nearby getaway cars.

The wall in front of him that led to the rest of what the massive barn had to offer was completely closed up. One door on the right, and one door on the left. He was transported back to Kim and Jim's house when the next day, after a good beating from Jim, Kim would sit around and lick her wounds into the afternoon. *The Price Is Right* would always be playing, and Bob Barker always asked which door they would like to pick.

Walker went with door number two on his right. He put his ear to the oak wood. Once again he could hear muffled words. One lower voice would speak; then a higher pitch followed. He imagined they were questioning Leila. They must have been planning on questioning Walker last. Did that mean they didn't really buy his story about being a cartel member? Probably. It wasn't all that well thought out by Walker before his memory returned. Not only would he never have said that if he'd had all of his wits about him, but Tim and his men would never have gotten the drop on him and Leila in the first place.

And he never would have slept with Leila.

Some mistakes, he figured, could be forgiven.

A high-pitch scream came muffled through the door to Walker's ear. Leila wasn't giving Tim the answers he wanted. Walker twisted the doorknob and inched the door open. A long hallway greeted him, along with a door halfway down to his left and another door at the very end. This part of the barn was drywalled in, much more like a regular office would be. He swapped out the knife for the pistol. The hallway was too long to take chances with only a blade in hand.

He stepped inside the door, listening close for which direction her voice might come from. He closed the door and locked it behind him. At the very least, slowing someone down who may come up behind him was always a good idea. There was still no one in the hallway with him. He heard the voices again, and as he approached the door on his left, he could tell they were coming from a room much farther away than that one. But as much as he wanted to rush in and save Leila, he had to save her the smart way. Clearing each room as he went would help him know where he could and couldn't go in the event of a quick exit.

He eased open the door. There was no light. A good sign there were no people as well, but he had to check. He found the light switch and flipped it on. There were no men inside, but the large room definitely wasn't empty. Boxes were everywhere. It looked like a business that had just got a supply shipment, but the crew had yet to organize it and put it away.

Walker pulled his knife and cut the tape on the box

206

closest to him. When he opened the top and peeked inside, he saw envelopes. Odd. He pulled a few stacks of the envelopes and found a false bottom about three quarters of the way down the box. He cut there, and beneath the cardboard were pill-sized bottles. When he pulled one out, it was empty. There were dozens more in the box. Tim was hiding his supplies in plain sight, in case anyone came snooping around. Interesting, but not what Walker was worried about.

He moved back out into the hallway and hurried down toward the door at the end. The voices grew closer, and he sensed it was time for the showdown. The first of many in the coming days, if he knew the company he worked for. There was sure to be someone else closing in on him after the first three couldn't handle the job.

One thing at a time. Life-and-death situations are a bad time to get ahead of yourself. Another, more bone-rattling scream reached his ears. They were hurting her. And for that, they were going to pay. All his other troubles would just have to wait.

35

"We're getting close," Alison said. "Looks like it's just up here on the left."

Alison was staring at the tracker on her phone. Leila Ward's Jeep was their only connection to where Walker had been taken.

"I don't see how you can tell a damn thing on those little doohickies," Kim said as she steered around a turn. "I still have me a flip phone from 'bout twenty years ago."

"Yeah?" Alison laughed. "Well, I don't see how you can tell what is what on these damn backroads without a smartphone. Everything looks the same. Trees, winding road, pasture, repeat."

"This? Hell, this ain't nothin'. There's some hollers 'round here make you think you're turning circles."

"So, just like this one, then?" Alison said.

"I'm tellin' ya, this ain't bad at all."

"I'll take your word for it."

Alison's phone began ringing. "Finally! Slow down. It's that detective calling me back."

Earlier, before Kim had pulled the car out of the hiding

spot across the street from Leila Ward's house, Alison called Detective Pelfrey. She had to dance a bit, because she still needed him to think that she was FBI, and it hadn't been any easier when he asked about her partner, Mike, but she made it work.

Alison told Pelfrey that while they were staking out Leila Ward's house, where they believed Evan Marshall to be, because an officer they'd spoken with had tipped her off, they saw men dressed in country-ish attire carrying Evan and Leila Ward out against their will. When she told him where the tracker they'd put on Leila's Jeep had stopped, he let her know it was a property that had been under surveillance for a while. And that some really rough people were living there, possibly into some very dangerous activities. Alison thought it sounded like he was putting on for her—the FBI agent she was posing as—but nevertheless, she requested a squad car join them just in case. And if Detective Pelfrey could make it, she'd be happy to have him since her partner had flown off on other business.

"Agent Brookins, it's me, Detective Pelfrey—"

"Detective," Alison said, sounding overly happy to hear from him. "Thank goodness you called. We are almost there, and, well, you made me a little nervous how you were talking about who lived at this property. Especially since I watched them take Evan and Leila with my own eyes."

"Well, you should be nervous. Listen, without your partner, I have to advise that you not go anywhere near there until I get a warrant."

"Warrant?" Alison said. Kim was shaking her head in the driver's seat as she rolled the car slowly along. "Evan Marshall is a high-value target, Detective. He may be caught up in whatever underground business these people are doing here, as you alluded to earlier. I have no choice but to go in. Do you have some backup for me or not?"

"Ma'am, all due respect, but we can't just charge onto this property without a warrant. We have a history of attempting such things, and, well, let's just say it has not gone too good. So we are just—"

"I'm not waiting," Alison said. "But I'll be sure to let your superiors know how unwilling to help a federal agent you were. I'm sure that will go over well with my bosses too."

"Now wait. Just hang on a dang minute. How close to the Riggins property did you say you are?"

"Not far at all. If you can get me someone out here, I can pull over and wait. But not long."

"I have already reached out, as I supposed you would insist on going in regardless. The only officer I have close to you is too close to the situation. Leila Ward is his sister. So I can't involve him."

"So you're hanging me out to dry?" Alison said.

Detective Pelfrey let out a long sigh. "I normally wouldn't even hesitate to send officers. If this was any other property, I'd . . ." Pelfrey trailed off.

Alison covered the phone. "Pull over for just a minute, okay?"

Kim shook her head no, then whispered, "Tommy is in trouble. I'm going to help him."

"Just one minute, I promise."

Kim rolled her eyes and shooed Alison away with her hand. Then, reluctantly, she pulled the car to the side of the road.

Pelfrey cleared his throat. "You sure you saw them physically take your target and Leila Ward from her property?"

"With my own eyes."

"You're positive that the tracker you placed on her vehicle, which these men drove away in, is now sitting at the property you showed me?"

"It hasn't moved since I sent you a screenshot of the tracker blip."

"All right, Agent Brookins. That's probable cause enough for me. I'll get some squad cars out to you, but I can't help that you are twenty minutes from the station here. I might be able to find some closer patrol cars, but I can't promise anything faster."

"Just knowing they are coming is enough for me. Thank you, Detective."

"Just don't go in until my officers get there. Please."

"Can't promise that, but I appreciate the warning."

Alison ended the call.

"Sounds like the cops don't really want to mess with these fellas," Kim said.

"Yeah, they have a lot more red tape and bureaucracy to deal with than we do. But he's not wrong. I have some shooting skills, Kim, but I'm not an assassin. I don't have the years of training that Walker does from the very best military tacticians in the world. If there's a lot of men with guns up here, we'll just end up sitting beside your Tommy, being absolutely no help to him at all."

Kim took a moment. She looked to her left out the driver-side window into the darkness.

"You know I'm right. I mean, sure, you can probably shoot, Kim, but you've got no combat skills."

Kim looked back over at Alison. "And you think these country boys out here do? All they do is shoot beer cans and bucks. Hell, I can do that."

"But there will be far more of them."

Kim looked away again.

"You know I'm—"

"Oh, just hush for a second now," Kim snapped at her. "I'm trying to figure out what Tommy would want me to do."

"That's easy, Kim. He'd want you to wait for the police. Even if he was dying. That's how these guys are wired."

Kim made air quotes with her hands. "Yeah, but Tommy ain't 'these guys.' He's the reason me and the three girls he and I was livin' with at the time have lives of our own at all."

"Right. And he wouldn't want you wasting it trying to play Annie Oakley and getting yourself killed."

Kim was about to speak when a car went flying by them on the road.

"Was that a police car?" Kim said.

"I think I saw lights on top of the car."

"Well, hell, let's go!" Kim said as she put the car in drive and slammed on the gas.

"Why would he not be flashing his red-and-blues?" Alison said.

"Who cares! You wanted backup, now we got it!"

The car sped forward.

Alison remembered the cop Detective Pelfrey mentioned. "Wait, that must have been the cop Pelfrey mentioned. It's his sister they took with Walker. That's why he didn't have his lights on. He's going in rogue!"

Kim was speeding down the road. "Sounds like the perfect person to help us. 'Cause we're all goin' rogue."

"There!" Alison shouted as she pointed at the road in between the trees on their left. "Take that road!"

Kim jerked the steering wheel left, and the back end of the car drifted out to the right. She managed to straighten the car just in time to make the road Alison had pointed to. Alison pulled out her pistol, press-checked, making sure it was ready to go. They couldn't see any houses or barns yet, but they were closing in on the dot on her phone.

"Slow down!" Alison shouted. "There's the cop."

Kim laid on the brakes, but she had been going too fast. She had to steer off the road when the officer came into view with a shotgun in his hand. They bumped a little into the grass, then came to a stop. A second later, the cop was tapping on Alison's window with the nose of his shotgun.

"Hands up as you step out," he said. "Both of you."

Alison rolled down her window instead and held up her credentials. "FBI. I think we're working toward the same goal."

The officer pointed his gun away from the window and took a step back. "Yeah? What goal is that?"

Alison got out of the car. "You're Leila Ward's brother, right?"

"Why?"

"We're after the man she was taken with, Tom Walker. Ring a bell?"

"I met him earlier. What does the FBI want with him?"

"Not sure what he or your sister told you about him when you met him, but I'm pretty sure it was a lie."

"I knew it," Larry said. "He was the man in the car accident behind my father's property, wasn't he? Killed those guys?"

"Yes, Officer Ward. And now he's in the custody of the same people who took your sister. How'd you know she was here?"

"Small town. Word got to me fast from Detective Pelfrey. Sheriff told me to stand down, but I already lost my daughter tonight. I ain't losing my sister too. Not to these redneck pricks."

"I'm so sorry about your daughter. I—"

"I don't have time to talk about this. Don't have time for you to tell me to wait for backup or that this is your investigation now, or whatever the hell they say on TV. I'm going in to get my sister. If you want to pick up your fugitive while I'm at it, that's on you. Just stay out of my way, because I'm shooting whatever gets in it that ain't my sister."

"Noted. Walker isn't a fugitive, but I get what you mean. Like I said, we want the same thing. If you know this property, or these people, feel free to lead the way."

"Just don't shoot me, or try to stop me from shooting, and we'll be okay."

Kim joined Alison by the car. Larry just shook his head and walked away. Alison looked at Kim.

"You ready for this?"

"I'm ready to help Tommy. Whatever that means."

"Just stay behind me, and stay alert," Alison said. "And like the officer said, please don't shoot me."

Kim nodded, and the two of them followed behind Larry toward the house off in the distance. They weren't exactly the crew Alison would have liked to have with her, but it sure beat going in alone.

She hoped.

36

Walker made it to the door at the end of the hallway. He slapped away a mosquito at the back of his neck with the hand not holding a gun. Even though the voices were close, they weren't just on the other side of the door. Could mean it was a large room and they were at the other end. Or there could be a subterranean room. The room beneath Leila's equipment shed came to mind.

Only one way to find out.

Walker turned the knob and pushed open the door. Through the small crack, he saw a small square room. The room was empty except for a door in the middle of the far wall. But it wasn't an ordinary "house" door as the others had been to that point. It was a grey, industrial-type door with a metal handle and a keypad just above it. Walker approached it, but just as he suspected, it was locked. A demoralizing end to his positive momentum. He was going to have to go back outside, walk to the far end of the barn, and try to find a way in on the opposite side.

Just as he turned to head back out to the hallway, he heard beeping from the other side of the door. Someone was entering the code and coming his way. He swapped his gun for the knife and backed up against the wall so he could hide behind the door when it opened. The door handle turned downward, and Walker tightened his grip on the knife.

One man walked into the room. As he stepped forward, Walker took a step toward him, raising the knife to strike. Then the man's walkie-talkie made a blip, and he stopped in the middle of the room. The door closed behind him. Walker hesitated; he felt good about one-on-one, even if he was seen, so instead of killing him, he waited to hear what information might be radioed in front of him. He held his breath.

"This is Cody. Go ahead." The man's voice echoed in the empty room.

The radio squawked. "You need to tell Tim we've got a problem. We just caught some people outside the house."

"So what?" Cody said. "Tim is busy with that woman, and I'm headed to get the dude that said he was cartel. Figure it out on your own."

"One is a cop, and one had an FBI badge on her. You think Tim might want to hear that?"

"FBI? And a cop? At the farm? We don't have time for jokes, man. You better stay off the channel and hope Tim didn't just hear this."

Cody's radio beeped again, but this time it was a voice Walker had heard before. "Tim did just hear this. Greg, what the hell are you talking about?"

It was Tim.

"Sorry, Tim," Greg replied.

Now Cody was listening to Greg and Tim talk, all while Walker stood behind him with a blade ready for his neck. "I didn't want to bother you, but there's a real problem. A cop, an FBI agent, and some old lady. I don't know. The cop must be the brother of the woman you took from the farm 'cause I can hear him screamin' about her in the next room where Carter has 'em at gunpoint."

"Shit," Tim responded. "Where there's one cop, there's a bunch of them. They're like cockroaches. And the FBI must be watching the cartel or something. Don't matter. This bitch just told us that the Walker guy we're holding in the basement really is with the cartel and that he told her they were using a facility they built beneath her equipment shed for the drugs that have been eating into all our profits. We're going to take the back road there now to shut this thing down tonight. Cops will be coming, so we want no trace of that cop and the other two on our property. Greg, you get Walker and bring him to the Ward property so he can watch us shut his shit down. Then we'll kill him on video and send it back to his bosses from his phone."

Greg clicked in. "You got it boss."

"Cody," Tim came back, "you kill the three trespassers and bring their bodies to the Wards' farm. We'll burn them with the equipment shed along with Leila. Tie this thing off. The police can draw their own conclusions, and none of them will point back to us."

Cody pressed the button on his radio. "Copy that, boss."

"And Cody," Tim said, "don't leave any trace of them here. None. The police will be snooping around."

"You got it, boss."

Cody clipped his radio back to his belt, then moved forward. Walker jabbed a hole in his neck before Cody could get the doorknob turned. As he bled out, Walker wiped his blade clean on the man's jeans, sheathed it, borrowed his radio, then took out his pistol as he went running out into the hallway. He jogged past the vehicles with all the deflated tires, hoping they were the automobiles Tim needed to get to Leila's house. But he didn't have time to wait and see. Tim was taking Leila back to her farm. Alive. For now. But the others would be killed as soon as Greg found Cutty in the basement tied up where Walker was supposed to be.

Walker stepped over the guard he'd put down earlier, then ran for the back of the house. He heard an engine or two roaring in the distance. His hope that he'd hobbled Tim's transportation died with those echoes. There was no movement at the back of the house as he approached, so he ran right up the back porch and through the back door. The time for covertly slinking around was over.

He moved through the living room, pistol out in front. He could see all the way down where he had walked out the front door earlier. The kitchen would be on his right. He poked his gun inside but saw no movement. But he knew from Tim's request of a man named Greg that Greg was supposed to be checking on Walker.

Right before Walker was about to move across the kitchen to the basement door, the radio he stole beeped.

"Tim, can you hear me?"

"Yeah, _ can _ you," Tim said, but his words were cutting out. He was moving out of the radio's range.

"He's gone!" Walker could hear Greg shouting into the radio, but he could also hear Greg's voice bellowing from the basement. "Cutty said he cut his ropes, and the Walker guy is gone!"

The radio beeped. Tim came back in, but it was so choppy that not a single word could be understood.

"Tim?" Greg said. "What's that? What do I do?"

Tim came in again, but it was almost entirely static.

"Never mind!" Greg shouted. "I'll call your cell!"

Walker rushed down the steps of the basement and caught Greg off guard as he was pulling out his cell phone. Walker held his gun on him, but he didn't shoot.

"Let's hit the pause button on that phone call, you mind?" Walker said.

The man stared at Walker's gun for a second. "I, uh, yeah, I can do that."

"Cutty, good to see you again." Walker motioned toward Cutty's ankle. "How's the wheel holding up?"

Cutty didn't say anything.

"Here's how this is going to go, Greg. You don't mind if I call you Greg, do you?"

The lanky, dark-haired man with a goatee covered in tobacco spit seemed a bit baffled by Walker's polite demeanor. He shook his head.

"Good. Greg, you know your buddy Cody, the guy who was supposed to come back here and kill my three friends you have trapped somewhere in this house? He's not gonna be able to make it. He started leaking blood from his neck and couldn't figure out a way to make it stop."

"O-Okay," Greg said.

"Whatever it is that caused it," Walker said, "seems to be going around. So, if you like your blood staying on the inside where it belongs, you're going to do exactly what I say."

"Yeah, man. Say the words, I'll do it."

"Good man, Greg. I knew I could count on you. Ready?"

"R-ready."

"Call Tim like you were going to. Only this time, I want you to say what I tell you to say."

"I want to," Greg said, "but you don't know Tim. He won't just bust my ankle like you did Cutty's, he'll kill me."

Walker moved the end of his pistol down to Greg's leg, gently pulled back his finger, and shot Greg on the outside of his right thigh. Greg dropped to the ground and began wailing in pain. Walker went over to him and took his gun, placing it at the small of his back.

"Greg," Walker said, then he waited a few seconds. Greg was wheezing and moaning in pain. "Excuse me, Greg? If I could just get your attention for just a second. Otherwise, Cutty here will be happy to make the call to Tim for me, won't you, brother?"

"Damn right," Cutty said. Zero hesitation.

"But Greg, if he does that for me, then I won't need you."

Greg sobered and pulled himself up to where he was leaning his back against the wall.

"Last chance, Greg. Because I have to get going."

While Walker was dealing with Greg, he kept one eye back up the stairs. There were a lot of men running around that farm, and he didn't want to lose momentum to someone getting lucky and catching him off guard.

"I'm ready," Greg said.

Walker nodded. "Start by telling Tim that Cody took care of the three trespassers. You're calling him about it because Cody is loading up the bodies. You with me so far?"

"I'm with you," Greg said.

"Next, tell him you're real sorry, but when you came downstairs to get that Walker fella, he had gotten loose and broken Cutty's ankle. He shot you in the leg, so you had no choice but to shoot him. You didn't mean to kill Walker, because you know that wasn't what Tim wanted, but at least he's dead. Now, repeat it back to me."

"Wait," Greg said, "so you knew you were going to shoot me no matter what? Just to make the story work better?"

"It's called a plan, Greg. Not really rocket science."

Greg's phone started ringing. "Shit! It's Tim!"

"Why are you so worked up, Greg?" Walker said. "Deep breath, and repeat what I just told you to Tim."

"What if I mess up?"

"Then I'll kill you. Trial by fire, my friend. But I have faith in you. Oh, and put the call on speakerphone."

Greg answered the phone. "Hey, boss."

"Radio went out," Tim said. "Everything get done?"

Greg looked up at Walker, nervous. Walker showed him to take a breath by exaggerating a deep one of his own. Gregg mimicked him.

"Greg, you there?" Tim said.

"Yeah, sorry. Just trying to . . . the three people that showed up? Cody took care of 'em. Putting their bodies in his truck now. He told me to tell you."

"Good. What about Walker?"

Walker made sure Greg was still keenly aware of the situation by taking a step toward him and leveling his pistol on Greg's head.

Greg nodded. "I came down to get him like you asked, and, well, the fucker shot me."

"What?" Tim said.

"He smashed Cutty's ankle real good. Shot me as I was coming down the stairs. I had no choice but to fire on him. You understand?"

"No, Greg, I don't. You best not be telling me he got away."

"Oh, no boss. I shot him. Didn't mean to kill him, but

he's dead. I was just defending myself, I swear I didn't mean to—"

"So, he's for sure dead?"

"Yeah. Yes. He's dead."

"Okay, fine. Didn't give a damn about him anyway. We're about to light up this cartel drug lab over here. I want those three people Cody killed and Walker in the fire with Leila over here so we don't have to answer for any of this shit. Got it?"

Greg looked at Walker. Walker nodded.

"Yeah. Yep. Be there shortly."

"Hurry the hell up," Tim said. "There's too many cops around as it is. Don't want to wait longer than I have to."

"Be right there, boss."

Greg ended the call. "There, I did what you asked. We're good now, right?"

Walker laughed. "Good? You were coming down here to kill me. No, we're not *good*. We're just getting started. Now tell me where my three friends are being held, then hobble your ass upstairs. You're driving me to Tim."

Greg's eyes widened. "I can't . . . he'll—"

"Greg, if you haven't realized it by now, I'll kill you first if you don't do what I say." Walker looked at Cutty and tossed him his hat that he'd borrowed earlier. "Thanks for the clothes. Mind if I keep the shirt and boots a while longer? No offense, but I don't think you're gonna want to put this boot on that foot anytime soon anyway."

"Keep 'em. And the people you're looking for are in the office. Right of the front door when you head that way down the hallway. I heard Greg say that Nate is watching them."

Walker looked back at Greg and smiled. "See? Cutty gets it. Act like him and you might get to see tomorrow after all."

Then back to Cutty. "On second thought, toss me that hat back. Better for the surprise."

Walker caught the hat, pulled it low, and made his way up the stairs. He was feeling good about his renewed abilities that having all his faculties again brought. But he still had a long way to go. Leila was currently smack dab in the middle of the belly of the beast. Walker was ready to go to any length necessary to get her back. He just hoped he could get there in time.

37

W alker looked both ways before entering the hallway. When he saw it was clear, he moved toward the front door. When he scanned the pictures on the wall, one stopped him dead in his tracks. But he didn't have time to ponder Tim and his family tree at the moment. He could hear a man's voice at the other end of the house. When he reached the end of the hallway, this time the door to the office was closed. He noticed a pretty good gap between the bottom of the door and the floor, so he hurried over, slid down to his stomach, and had a look.

At first he just saw a set of brown boots standing toward the right side of the room. They were facing three other sets of shoes, toward the back of the room. Walker lowered his head as much as he could and saw a mirror on the wall, and he could just make out a beard above an extended gun.

Walker stood, lined his pistol up with where the boots were positioned on the other side of the door, and fired twice. As screams erupted inside the room, he kicked in the door and watched the man holding the gun fall to the floor. He was holding his neck as blood ran between his fingers.

"Tommy?" a woman said.

Walker looked over and was nearly floored to see his foster mother, Kim, standing there with an elated look on her face. He was even more shocked when he noticed to Kim's left that Alison Brookins was standing there. Quite a few things flashed across his mind. First, she was employed by the company that had been trying to kill him, which is why he moved his gun and positioned it toward her chest. After all, the reason she was there had to be because they sent her after him. The second flash was the first passionate night they'd shared together in Iran, just after he'd carried out a political assassination. The juxtaposition of a former lover now trying to kill him had him rattled. So much so that he didn't see the man move in from the hallway.

"Tommy!" Kim shouted.

But it was too late. The baseball bat bounced off Walker's left shoulder, then grazed the nose of his pistol. As the man pulled the bat back for another swing, Walker's gun dropped to the floor. He turned to see a short, stalky, blond-haired man who couldn't have been a day over twenty-one. When the bat came back his way, Walker jumped back and sucked in his stomach so the bat would miss his midsection. The swing was so violent that it threw the man's weight off balance, and as he stumbled forward, Walker kicked down on the outside of his knee, bending it the wrong way, then helped him to the floor with a hard overhand right to the jaw.

He was out cold.

"Tom, I know what you're thinking, but I'm only here to help you," Alison said from behind him.

Walker turned around, working the shoulder that had been hit by the wooden bat. "Yeah? And where's the assassin they sent with you? Because I know you didn't come alone."

Alison shook her head. Her dark ponytail weaved along with it. "No. They sent me with Mike," Alison said with a nervous laugh. "Funny story, your foster mom here killed him in the car about an hour or so ago."

Kim came forward and wrapped her arms around Walker, then stepped back. "It's good to see you, Tommy. You look good, considering. And don't you listen to Alison here, I couldn't have got rid of that Mike asshole if she hadn't cut me loose and trusted me to do so."

"You killed Mike Hudson?"

"What?" Kim said. "That a big deal?"

"A story for a different day. Just like the one that led you to being here tonight. But right now, we have to go."

"Before we do," Alison said. "You have to know. They killed John Sparks. Well, Karen Maxwell had him killed. I'm sorry."

Walker's world spun. John Sparks was the man who'd taken responsibility for Walker when he came in fresh from jail at fifteen years old. He'd been the closest thing Walker had ever had to a father. Just about everything he knew, he knew because of that man. But now wasn't the time for anger, and it wasn't the time for grieving. It was time to go.

Walker looked over at Larry. "I know where they took Leila."

Larry looked rattled. He couldn't understand how Walker, who could barely hold his own in a fight a few hours ago, who was just supposed to be a hospital friend of Leila's, was now talking about men hunting him down, easily dispatching a man with a baseball bat, and acting like he was running the show.

Walker spoke again in place of Larry's inability to form a

sentence. "I can catch you up in the car. I have a plan. Right now you just need to follow me."

"Who the hell are *you* anyway?" Larry said, finding his voice. "This is *my* sister. What the hell do you know about how to get her out of trouble?"

"We don't have time for this, Larry. You'll just have to trust me."

Larry moved forward. "You're the reason she's in this mess to begin with, aren't you?"

"Larry, don't," Walker said.

But Larry did. He grabbed two handfuls of Walker's T-shirt and tried to move him. Walker raked his arm down, ripping Larry's grip from his shirt, then stepped in with his right leg and hip-tossed him to the ground.

"Larry," Walker said as Larry tried to get up, "I know how things look, but we're on the same team. And I need your help."

"Get your hands off me!" Larry pulled away and got back up to his feet. Walker stepped back and picked up his pistol.

Alison stepped in. "Larry, I don't know the details of how and why all this is happening with your sister, and why Walker even cares enough to try to help her, but I'm telling you, if he wants to help her, he will. And you couldn't have a better person on your side than him."

"We need the police is what we need!" Larry said.

"No," Walker said, remaining calm. "We need to go. I don't have time to walk you through this. I can on the way there. But this guy Tim is going to kill Leila. He already ordered one of his men to kill all of you, but I was able to stop him. Just know this . . . you can't call the police. One of the officers on your force is involved. We have to do this ourselves."

"Involved in what? What the hell is going on?"

Walker saw movement in the hallway, over Larry's shoulder. He raised his gun as he pulled Alison to the ground and fired twice. Right in front of Larry. A man dropped to the ground just outside the office door. Larry looked at Walker, then down at the body, then back to Walker.

"I told you," Walker said, "I'm on your side. But we have to go. Now. Either you're with me, or I leave you here. But we are out of time."

Walker helped Alison back to her feet. Larry looked down at the body again, then gave Walker a nod as he collected himself.

"All right," Walker said. "Tim thinks all of us are dead, courtesy of some fortunate timing on my part in finding one of his men. He wants us all brought to your father's farm. Larry—"

"What? My dad's farm?"

"I told you, I'll explain more on the way. Larry, Tim will be expecting three or four dead bodies in the back of a pickup truck. So we need two bodies, you and I will be the other two."

"What? I'm a cop, I ain't no spy assassin or whatever you are. I can't—"

"Larry, you're either with me on this or not. I can do it myself. And if you're going to panic out there, then I'd rather go it alone. But real talk? You're going to have to kill some men tonight if you go with me to save your sister. If you can't do that, fine. I just need to know now. Because they are going to kill her."

Larry bowed up his chest. "I've lost enough today. I'm not losing my sister too."

Walker thought of sharing his condolences for Larry's

daughter, but they needed to focus. He turned to Alison.

"Alison, will you help Larry get two bodies in the back of a truck? Then I need you to get Kim to safety. Got it?"

"I'm not leaving you. Kim can take the car back to her place, but I'll help you take care of whatever mess you've got yourself into here."

"It's not your fight," Walker said.

"No, but you and I both have a fight of our own against another common enemy if we can make it out of this one alive."

Walker stared at her for a moment. She was right. He had already been fighting it when he got in the car at the airport. He knew for Alison that Maxwell wouldn't let Mike's death and Walker's escape go unpunished.

"Okay. Go help Larry. I've got to make sure our driver is going to play his part. Just get two bodies to the trucks outside. We'll load them up when I get Greg's keys."

Alison nodded and started to leave the room with Larry.

"You two keep your guard up," Walker said. "And Larry?"

"Yeah?"

"Find something else to wear. You're not an officer of the law tonight. And put your uniform on one of the dead men. They're going to be expecting a cop in the body pile. Let's at least give them that illusion as long as they'll buy it."

Larry glanced down at his beacon of law and order that was his khaki-and-brown police uniform, then nodded. He and Alison left the room.

"I ain't leavin' now, Tommy," Kim said from behind him. He turned to face her. "If that's what you're thinkin'."

"I don't have time for this, Kim. I didn't train you to go and fight. I trained you to fight only to protect yourself. At home. Out here you're only going to slow me down."

Kim's face drooped. "But I want to see with my own eyes what they did to you when they took you from me."

"No," Walker said. "I promise you, you don't."

"But it's my fault that you're like this. That you have to do all these things. I just—"

"Kim." Walker was stern. "I'm not doing this. And I'm not asking you. Go home. Right now."

Walker turned and left the room. He walked down the hall toward the kitchen. A week ago, when he stopped Maxwell's favorite assassin from murdering the daughter of a senator, just so Maxwell's choice for the Senate would have a clearer shot at the seat, he knew it was the end of his life sentence as the tip of the government's secret sword. But he never thought it would all go down like this—where he grew up—having to worry about someone like Leila whom he didn't even know before yesterday. Tack on the temporary memory loss—if that hadn't happened, he wouldn't be in any of his current mess; he'd be on a beach somewhere, listening to the ocean waves from his open hotel window. Not to mention Karen Maxwell and all the problems that came along with her and her company.

But all of those things did happen. He did end up here, where he grew up, fighting a fight that wasn't his, just like he'd been doing his entire adult life. Only this time, the reason he was fighting was actually a good one. A *real* reason to be who they trained him to be. Because Leila was definitely real. She took him in when he was injured and lost. And he wasn't about to leave her when she was in the same position now.

It was time to return a favor, something he wasn't sure he'd ever done before since no one had ever paid him any favors that he could recall.

It was time to save Leila.

38

After Walker finished tying the man who'd hit him with the bat to the wall rail of the basement stairs, opposite of Cutty, he walked Greg out the front door to meet up with Larry and Alison. They were waiting with the two bodies Walker had requested. Kim had chosen to leave without a fight. She didn't want Walker to have to worry about her while he tried to help Leila.

"The navy-blue one over there," Greg said as he pointed over Larry's shoulder. Greg limped down the front porch as he took his keys from his pocket.

Walker stepped over to Larry and Alison. Larry had done as he'd asked and changed out of his police uniform. He was in a T-shirt that was too tight, showing his dad-bod belly pooching over the front of his black sweatpants.

"Much better," Walker said, nodding to Larry's attire.

"Had some gym clothes in my trunk."

Walker passed on the chance to poke fun at his belly and lack of exercise. He cut to the chase. "I'll get this guy," he said, pointing to the smaller of the two dead bodies at his feet. "You two get the one in Larry's police uniform. And turn them facedown so we can conceal their identity for as long as possible. It will be dark out there, and if we give them a bit of what they're expecting to see at first, it might buy me more time."

Walker bent down to a knee, took the body in his arms like a groom carrying his bride over the threshold, then walked over and tossed it in Greg's truck bed. Larry and Alison were right behind him with decoy number two. They tossed him beside the other dead man, and Walker proceeded to cover them all with a tarp.

"I'll tell you the plan on the ride over. Spoiler alert, you all aren't going to like it."

"Glad to see you haven't changed a bit," Alison said.

Walker hopped down from the truck bed. The jarring landing reminded him of the wound in his leg. "Yeah?"

"Yeah," she said. "You still think you're funny, even though you're really not."

She didn't smile, but Walker remembered her sarcastic nature. They'd go back and forth a lot before they would take their frustrations out in bed. Odd form of foreplay, but Walker knew he was an odd guy. Alison never seemed to mind.

Walker moved around to the passenger-side back door of the Chevy Silverado and opened it for her. Even managed a wry smile. "Opinions are like assholes and all of that," he said.

Alison rolled her eyes as she and Larry climbed into the rear bench seat. Walker got in front and made sure that Greg could see the pistol lying in his lap.

"We're not going to have a problem, are we, Greg?"

"No sir. I'll do what you ask. And just for the record, I

wouldn't have killed you down in that basement. I've never killed anyone before. Cutty would have been the one to do it."

Walker believed Greg, but he ignored him.

"All right. To Leila Ward's farm then. But you're going to drop me off away from where Tim is. I'll be coming in by myself."

"You want to catch us up now?" Larry said. "And let us in on what you have planned so that I can poke holes in it and tell you the right way to go about it? I am the law, you know. I've got experience in these types of situations."

Walker turned in his seat so he could see Larry. "Larry, neither one of us has time for bullshit, and we certainly don't have time for a pissing contest. Just answer me one question. If the answer is no, then you will keep your mouth shut and do everything I say."

"Okay." Larry laughed. "And if it's yes?"

"Then you'll still keep your mouth shut. I'll just have more respect for your ability to help me."

Larry looked over and smiled at Alison, unconvinced.

"Don't look at me," she said. "I'm going to do everything he says to the letter. Because I know what he's capable of."

"What, you some kind of soldier or something?" Larry said.

"Something like that. But that is my question to you. You ever serve?"

"Military?"

"Yeah."

"No," Larry said, but his chest pumped proudly like a peacock. "But I'm third-generation police. And we take it seriously in my family."

"That's good," Walker said. "But it's not the same. So just

233

let me fill you in. If you do what I ask, our little mission impossible that we're about to attempt will have a much better chance of succeeding."

"Okay, but you ain't military either or you would have said so."

"What he is, Larry, is classified," Alison said.

"Just spit out the plan already," Larry said.

Walker jumped right in as Greg turned onto the county road. "Greg here is going to drop me off at Leila's house. You all will wait till I text you that I'm in position. I'm going to come up behind them from the cornstalks."

"How do you know these boys won't be at the house? Ain't a thing beyond the corn but an old equipment shed my daddy fixed up for some reason a couple of years ago after he retired from the force."

Walker had a sinister thought about the renovation of the shed, but he didn't want to confuse the situation.

"I know they're going to be there, because beneath the shed is where a Mexican cartel is operating a sophisticated pill mill and maybe more."

"A pill mill? Under my daddy's shed? What the hell are you talking about? You've lost your damn mind."

"Long story short," Walker said, "when I injured myself after I killed the three men in the car wreck—"

"Damn it, I knew it was you! Why would my sister cover for you like that? Pull the damn car over and let me out!"

"Larry," Walker said, "calm down. I'm the only chance you've got of saving your sister. Just let me finish."

Larry shook his head, but he didn't say anything else.

"As I was saying," Walker went on, "after I took out the three men who were there to kill me . . ." Walker let that sink in for effect. "I was shot. I passed out in Leila's barn, and she found me there, but I didn't remember who the hell I was."

"What?" Alison said. "Like not at all?"

"Nothing past when I strangled my foster father when I was fifteen."

"You hearing this?" Larry said to Alison. "We're in a truck with a damn serial killer." Then he looked at Walker. "How am I supposed to trust you're not the cartel yourself? Or that you want to help my sister at all?"

"Because she helped me," Walker said. "Like no one ever has. She took care of me when I was hurt and didn't know who the hell I was. But the more we talked, the more we started to understand that what I was, was something scary. I tried to leave after you showed up, Larry. So I wouldn't cause Leila any trouble. But when I was making my way off the property, the cornstalks led me to the back of the shed. Where I watched a police car pull down the road. I don't know who it was, but he got out and started talking about the cartel with the two Mexican men working in the shed.

"I went back to warn Leila, and she convinced me to take a closer look for her. Because, like you, she didn't believe it was possible that could be going on, on her property, right under her nose. When I did go have a look, I found a full-scale pill production facility beneath your father's shed. And I had to shoot my way out just so I could be here now."

Larry continued shaking his head in disbelief. "There just ain't no way."

"When I went back to tell Leila about it," Walker went on, "as we started strategizing what she could do about all of it, that's when Tim and his redneck crew showed up. When his brother knocked me unconscious, it knocked the sense back into me, because when I woke up in the basement back there, I remembered who I was, and that's how I was able to escape."

"This guy for real?" Larry asked Alison.

Alison ignored him and asked Walker a question of her own. "So that's why you stuck around after you killed Maxwell's men in that car. You didn't remember, and you had no idea that more like them would be coming after you."

"I thought you were FBI?" Larry was dumbfounded.

"Yeah, something like that," Alison said.

"Something like that," Larry said. "You all sound like some sort of deranged TV show."

Alison shrugged. "It does seem like that some days."

"Can I pull this together for you guys now?" Walker said. "Great. To answer your question, Alison, yes. That is why I stayed around. If I hadn't temporarily lost my memory, I would have been long gone. But Leila patched me up." Walker looked over at Larry. "And even lied to the police for me. I can't just bail now. Plus, I think we can use this situation to both of our advantage when it comes to permanently exiting Maxwell Solutions."

"Well, I'm all ears," Alison said. "Because as it stands, I'm the next in line for one of our own to come and kill me."

"We're close," Greg said.

Walker held up his finger to Alison. "Hold that thought." Then to Greg. "Call Tim. Tell him you are on your way, and ask him exactly where he wants you to go. That's all I need from you."

"Right now?"

"Right now," Walker said. "And put it on speaker. I don't want anything lost in translation."

"You're the boss," Greg said as he took his phone from Walker.

Walker turned back to Alison and Larry. "We can get Leila back safely, and put ourselves in a good position to take down Maxwell. But it's not going to be easy. I can do this myself if you all aren't up for it. I realize it's going to be out of your comfort zones."

"Hell with that," Larry said. "These assholes took my sister. And probably the reason my dad and daughter both died from pills. These assholes have been lacing the shit they sell with fentanyl. Can you believe that? Just a little bit of that shit and . . ."

Larry trailed off. Walker knew he was thinking of his daughter. Death meant something different to Walker than it did most people. He'd been around it so much that it frankly had lost its meaning. Could be, too, that he never had anyone he cared enough about losing. Family and black ops assassins go together like peanut butter and salsa. But he could feel the pain coming from Larry in that moment. It was so thick in the air that it seemed to infiltrate Walker's system too. He was angry for Larry. And he wanted to make it right.

"Larry," Walker said. "I know we got off on the wrong foot, but I'm telling you right now, I'm going to make these men pay for what they've done. I've been the tip of the spear in some of the most unforgiving situations a man can be in since I was eighteen years old. And I'm still here to tell you about it."

Larry wiped away a tear.

"I'll get this done too. And I'll tell you how you can help as soon as Greg finishes his call."

Alison gave Walker a nod; then Walker saw her give Larry a pat on the shoulder. This was the oddest mission

Walker had ever been a part of, but somehow it had also become the most important.

For once he wasn't fighting for what a bunch of politicians believed in.

Walker was fighting for something *he* believed in.

Failure was not an option.

39

Greg drove the truck past the gravel road entrance that Tim had told him to take to get down to the equipment shed. It was going on three in the morning, but high adrenaline levels kept the weariness at bay for Walker. He felt like a sprinter waiting for the gunshot at the starter line. He just wanted to get in the mix and ruin Tim's plans.

Alison had mentioned Mike's hiding spot in the trees where they'd parked to watch Leila's house across the street earlier. As they drove past the house, Alison pointed to it, and Greg pulled the truck into the shadows. The clock was ticking. Tim had already texted Greg since they'd hung up. He was getting anxious.

When Greg put the truck in park, Walker reached over and grabbed the keys. "Everybody out."

Everyone exited the truck and followed Walker around to the back where he was lowering the gate to the truck bed. The cicadas were dueling with the crickets, and the humidity from the rain earlier made the air around them feel wet.

"First things first, Greg, let me see your wallet."

The four of them were aglow in the light of Greg's cell phone that Walker had opened so they could see. Greg passed the wallet as asked. Walker checked inside, but there were no photos. Walker handed the wallet back.

Next, Walker thumbed to Greg's photo app on his phone. He opened it, scrolled past the pictures of him skinning a buck, and stopped when he saw Greg in a photo eating ice cream with a little boy and a woman who looked to be roughly Greg's age.

"This your family?" Walker said.

"Man, what the hell? They got nothing to do with all of this."

Walker held the phone up, ensuring that Greg could see the picture. "We agree on that, Greg. But the next part of what you have to do for me requires me either to trust you or to threaten you. And Greg, I don't trust you. Do I need to elaborate, or do we understand each other?"

"No. I understand."

"And just so we are crystal clear," Walker said. Then he motioned between himself, Alison, and Larry. "Have the conversations you've heard the three of us having on the way over led you to understand exactly what it is I do for a living?"

"No, well, not exactly," Greg said with a shake in his voice.

"I kill people."

The song of the surrounding insects filled in the silence.

"This is important, Greg," Walker said as he moved the picture of Greg and his family closer to Greg's face. "Do we fully understand each other about what happens if you don't do what I need you to do?"

Greg nodded. "Yeah. I may look dumb, but I ain't. I'll do exactly what you ask. Just don't hurt them."

Walker would never actually hurt a man's family for a man's own sins. So much so that it was the very reason he was on the run from his organization now. But Greg needed to believe it. Because if Greg got a mind of his own or decided to be loyal to Tim during what was about to happen, Alison and Larry would most likely be the ones to pay with their lives. And Walker didn't take endangering people's lives lightly.

"Good. Now, Larry, the only way this works is if you know your dad's property like I hope you do."

"Like the back of my hand."

"Perfect. Because I've rethought things. You're going to take Alison with you down the back of the property, through the cornfield, and out behind the equipment shed. Tim is only expecting to see Greg with his truck full of dead bodies coming down the gravel road. You should be pretty clear to wait behind the shed." Walker pulled a nine-millimeter pistol from the back of his belt line and handed it to Larry. "It's locked and loaded. Don't flip that safety off until you're ready to fire."

"Okay," Larry said.

"Okay," Alison said. "But where the hell are you going to be?"

"Dead," Walker said. Then he turned the light of the phone toward the dead bodies lying beneath the tarp in the truck bed. "With them. Where I'm supposed to be."

"I don't get it," Larry said. "You're the one who should be out shooting from behind them right? I mean, you're the better shooter, aren't you?"

"Yes, but we are going to be outgunned and outnumbered. By how many? I don't know. So the only thing we really have going for us is the element of surprise. Greg, tell Alison your phone number. Alison, when you two get down near the shed, text me the lay of the land. How many are out there and where they are, if you can. If not, just let me know you're there, ready to get my back. It's going to get pretty hairy, so just stay covered and shoot who you can."

"So," Alison said, "you're just going to have Greg drive you up to them, and then what?"

"I'll just take it as it comes. My goal is to surprise, without making a lot of noise. But if I can only shoot, that's what I'll do."

"You're insane," Larry said.

"To you, I can see how it looks insane," Walker said. "For me? It's the only thing I know. It would be like you doing a traffic stop. That's how many times I've done this. Difference is, there were far more better trained people around than there are now. But my experience doesn't mean this will be easy. If you see an opportunity, get your sister out of there. Otherwise, hang back and let me work."

Larry shook his head in disbelief. "Whatever you say, man. Just know . . . I appreciate you trying to help her. You could just run and leave us with our problems."

"I really can't. Alison and I have problems of our own. I'm going to try to tie it all off in a nice bow right here, tonight." Walker looked at Alison while Greg put his number in her phone. "Which leads me to our part of this adventure. Where's Mike's body?"

Alison stepped off to her right and pointed beyond the truck. "Kim and I dragged him over there."

"Okay. You two get going. And be careful. We'll be ready to drive down as soon as you text."

Greg's phone dinged in Walker's pocket. He pulled it out; it was a test text from Alison.

"We're good," Walker said.

Alison began backpedaling away with Larry. "You be careful too, Tom. See you when this is over."

The two of them ran off across the street. Walker watched them until they disappeared behind Leila's house. Then he looked over at Greg.

Walker pointed. "How's the leg?"

"It's got a hole in it, so pretty much as expected."

"How'd you get mixed up in all this drug shit with Tim?" Walker said. "You seem like a decent guy."

"How'd you become a killer, Mr. Walker? Life has a way of tossin' a man around. Sometimes you don't land exactly where you want to."

"Amen to that. I know the feeling. Help me with this body back here."

"Your wish is my command," Greg said as he limped behind Walker around the truck.

Walker headed over to the place Alison had pointed to. Sure enough, tucked beneath the leaves of some wild brush was a body. Walker hit the light on the iPhone and handed it to Greg to shine over him. Then he grabbed the leather sleeve and pulled the body into the clear.

"Mike Hudson," Walker said.

Walker had never met Mike, but he'd heard through the grapevine that he was a real miserable SOB. Of course, that was almost a requirement of the job. Walker had always tried to maintain his sense of humor throughout his career. Mostly because if they hadn't come and gotten him that day when he was fifteen, he'd still be in prison for the murder of his sorry-ass foster parent, Jim. It's not that he liked traveling the world, throwing himself into dangerous situations, and hunting human beings, but the perks sure beat jail. When he wasn't ending the lives of powerful and dangerous men, he was able to fit in some fine dining, the occasional company of a beautiful woman, and a few sunsets over places most people only dreamed of visiting. His dark life wasn't all bad.

However, as he looked down at Mike's dead body, he always knew this was the inevitable ending to a life doing deeds such as he did. Dead young. No one to celebrate his life because he never stuck around long enough to have any sort of real relationships—friends or otherwise. But he always held the opinion that it was better to die on the outside rather than in a cell. Walker never knew all the circumstances of his missions, but he was sure that at least a few of the people he'd sent to the afterlife probably made the world a better place after they were gone.

That was probably his only regret to date. He had all the skills of a super soldier, but the only impact he could have on the world came from the musings of powerful men and women who moved him around like a chess piece. If he did make it out of his current situation alive, and somehow a "free" man, that's what he was going to change. He was going to find a way to do more things like he was doing right then—helping someone whom *he* felt needed it. He wanted to make his own decisions on how to make an impact—and make sure it was a positive one.

The odds of achieving that sort of freedom from where he knelt over Mike Hudson's body at the moment were somewhere around the level of, well, nil. But since the day he went into training, Walker had accomplished many things the people who took him in said he never would. So there was still a chance.

"You knew him?" Greg said.

Walker snapped out of his internal dialogue and looked up at Greg behind the light of the phone. "No. You don't meet a lot of guys like us and live to tell about it. That was the reason he was out here."

"To get rid of you?" Greg said.

"Yep."

"Why? You kill somebody you wasn't supposed to?"

Walker's mind flashed back to the mission that set all of what was happening to him in motion. To the decision to stop Maxwell's other top assassin, Collin Mitchell, from killing an innocent woman and the baby growing inside her. If he'd killed her, his life would have been a lot different than it was right now, but he wouldn't have been able to live with himself if he'd let her and her baby die. Maxwell had gone too far. And though it wasn't Walker's place to question elite government officials and their actions, at some point you have to draw a line in the sand and figure out just what kind of man you really are. And Walker had had enough.

"Something like that," Walker said. "Help me get him over to the truck."

Walker took the phone back, then moved around so he could scoop Mike up from under his arms. Greg lifted at his feet.

"Big son of a bitch," Greg said. "They couldn't have sent someone smaller?"

Walker laughed as they heaved, then walked the body over to the open tailgate of the truck. "They did. Alison was supposed to help."

"Well, damn," Greg said. "You pay her so she wouldn't or something?"

They laid Mike's body in the truck bed.

"No. I slept with her."

"Dang," Greg said with a laugh. "Every girl I sleep with

ends up wanting to kill me, not save me. You must have done somethin' right."

"Yeah?" Walker said. "That, or she just has really low standards."

"Ha ha. Yeah. Probably that."

Walker handed Greg the cell phone light again; then he took out his knife. He opened Mike's jacket, pulled up his shirt, and cut a long, deep gash into Mike's stomach. Blood gushed out onto the truck.

"Jesus, man, I think he was already dead," Greg said.

Walker put away the knife, plunged his hands into Mike's blood, and began wiping it all over his own shirt.

"What in the hell is wrong with you?" Greg said.

Walker went back for more blood and kept applying. "You told Tim you killed me, right?"

"Well, yeah, but—"

"Well, I'm making it look like you actually did."

"You're a crazy son of a bitch," Greg said as he shook his head. "But you ain't stupid, I guess."

Walker jumped up into the truck bed and pulled Mike's body up under the tarp. Greg's phone buzzed.

"It's your girl, Alison," Greg said.

"Read it."

Walker watched Greg squint at the phone's screen. "It says, '*At shed. I see four men outside. No sign of Leila.*' Want me to text her back?"

Walker figured they'd have Leila inside. He wiped his hands on the back of his jeans to clear away as much of Mike's blood as he could. "Tell her, 'On our way. Stay back and let me work. If Greg signals anyone, shoot him and I'll improvise.'"

Greg looked from his screen to Walker. "Really?"

"Yeah, really."

"What happens to me if I don't signal him."

"I'll let you go home to your family," Walker said.

Greg went back to finishing the text. Walker sat down on the three dead bodies. Greg walked over and handed him the phone. Walker looked back over his shoulder at the back window of the truck, where he made out the outline of a hunting rifle.

Walker looked back at Greg. "You any good with that thing? Or is it just for decoration?"

Greg looked over Walker's shoulder. "That? Been huntin' since I could walk. Very few things I can't hit inside of a hundred yards."

"Do what I ask of you tonight and you can teach your son too. Got it?"

"I'll do it."

Walker turned the phone light on Greg. "Now, cover me with this tarp, shut the tailgate, and drive me down to them. Say as little as possible. And don't get in my way."

"You got it."

Walker tossed him the keys, made sure his pistol was well positioned just above the knife in its sheath at his back, then he laid down. The tarp fell into place over him. Just Walker and his dead friends. Though the copper-like scent of blood was heavy, the bodies were still fresh enough not to smell. Small victories. Walker closed his eyes as he heard the truck start up. He focused his mind on the task at hand and readied himself for the fight.

Time once again to go toward the danger. This time, at least it was the danger he'd chosen.

40

The truck's engine revved as Greg put it in reverse. The uneven ground just off the road jostled Walker back and forth alongside his other dead truck-bed mates. Even in the middle of the night, the summer air was warm. But lying beneath the polyethylene tarp was like being trapped in a sauna. Walker could feel the sweat running down his face.

He closed his eyes and focused forward. The jostling stopped as the truck backed onto the pavement. He pictured Larry and Alison hiding behind the shed. He imagined them looking at a scene of a few cars and trucks parked on the other side of the shed. Maybe a few men out front leaning against their trucks, waiting for Greg to arrive.

There were probably a few more men down in the drug room with Leila. He could see her brown hair matted to her sweat and tear-filled face. Probably gagged, chomping at it nervously, wondering if anyone would be able to save her. She probably heard Greg telling Tim that Walker was dead. This would have left her without a lot of hope.

Tim was probably pacing the subterranean room.

Ready to get the place lit on fire so he could get back to the comforts of his own operation. A couple of the men had probably been busy carrying boxes of pills out to their trucks. No sense wasting good product that could kill more innocent kids like Larry's daughter. Probably those very pills, or at least the ones Tim was selling, were the same ones that killed her. Her and Leila's dad, no less.

There was one thing about the entire situation that was bothering Walker, now that he was of sound mind. If Leila had to come and keep the farm running, it must have been under too much debt to sell. The thought crossed Walker's mind that maybe Leila's father had not only known about the drug operation but used it to keep the farm a lot longer than he could have otherwise. It would explain, at least a little, how the operation had gotten started without Leila knowing. Because it would have started while she was still a practicing ER doc—before she ever had to take over for her father after he passed.

None of it really mattered. The situation was what it was. It was just curious how the farm hand, Tyler, got in on it as well. Maybe he was the one who brought the prospect to Leila's father in the beginning. Could it be that the very drugs he allowed to be made on his property were also the ones that killed him?

Walker felt the truck make a right turn. The smooth roll of the tires turned into the bump of gravel. He could hear it kicking up off the tires. It was showtime. He took in a couple of stale deep breaths, all he could manage beneath that tarp. He was supposed to be dead, so as the truck came to a stop and the engine shut off, he forced himself to relax, ready to hold his breath when his "*dead*" *body* was revealed.

The cicadas came back in tune. He heard Greg's door open and shut. Walker didn't like that a man he had just shot not more than an hour ago somewhat held his fate in his hands, but he had to trust that the threat of hurting the man's family, and hearing of Walker's full-time profession, would be enough to keep Greg on track.

"Got the bodies Tim asked for," Greg said. Walker could tell he was standing to the right, parallel to where he was lying in the truck bed.

"I'll go get him," a man said. "He's been waitin' for ya."

Greg didn't speak. Good boy.

Walker imagined the men walking into the shed, then down into the pill mill. While he'd never been in a situation where he was lying in the back of a truck, surrounded by dead people, acting as one of those dead himself, he had been in just about every other, it seemed. From assassinating a prime minister of the Democratic party in the Congo to killing a commander in chief of the Chilean Army, Walker was no stranger to uncomfortable and dangerous situations.

One of the ways he kept his head in moments like this was visualization. While the real moment of truth never played out exactly as it did in his mind beforehand, he found that the routine of visualizing what was about to happen offered him peace of mind. Like studying gives someone more confidence for an exam, envisioning how the attack might play out helped him act with more confidence when things got real. Sort of like a violent meditation.

As Walker pictured the men getting Tim now, his vision started with Tim opening the tailgate and ripping away the tarp. Walker would look dead to Tim, especially with the blood he'd covered himself in and the rest of his current surroundings. Tim would also have his guard down, thinking that his men had already taken care of any and all threats. This was good.

Walker wanted to be able to make his way to Leila without gunshots. There was no telling how many men Tim had brought, so avoiding gunshots would at least keep him from having to fight all of them in one area. Every little bit would help the underdog trying to save the innocent woman in her distress. And Walker would use every advantage to its fullest. If there were any advantages at all.

"Took you long enough, Greg."

Walker heard Tim's voice to the south, in the direction of the shed. Once again, Greg didn't speak.

"Didn't figure dead men would give you so much trouble," Tim said. He was at the back of the truck now.

"Lots of dead weight," Greg said.

Tim laughed. "Glad to hear the gunshot wound didn't steal that sharp wit, Greg."

The tailgate screeched to a thud as Tim opened it. The truck bed dipped as Tim stepped up. Walker took in a long breath. The tarp flapped open. Nothing happened until Walker heard a click. He could tell a flashlight had been switched on. Tim was eyeing the situation.

"Guy in the leather jacket. He FBI?"

"That's what his wallet said," Greg answered.

"Cop put up a fight?"

"Not as much as he should have."

Tim laughed. "You're on a roll, aren't you?"

Walker felt Tim's foot kick his leg. "This one here shot you, did he?"

Walker didn't like all the assessment Tim was giving the body pile. He'd hoped he could wait to kill him so he could have a better view of how many men there were, and where they all were. But he knew he had to take what he was given. For now he stayed quiet.

"Right in the damn leg," Greg said. "He paid for it, though."

Walker heard the sound a camera makes when a picture is taken.

"Might need this evidence that he's dead, just in case he really was cartel," Tim said.

Walker felt the truck lift back up as Tim jumped down. He slowly let the rest of his breath release, then inhaled just as slowly.

"Well, don't just stand there, bring them in. Been a long night. I'm ready to light this candle and get home. I'm gonna give this bitch one last chance to tell me who her contact is in the cartel before I kill her. Set those bodies on the hay and corn pile we made in the shed. I want her to see her future if she doesn't talk."

"You got it," Greg said.

Walker heard footsteps and some unintelligible conversation between the men as they approached the truck. One or two of them stepped up into the truck bed. Walker first felt hands wrap around his ankles. He went as dead as he could, letting all of his body go limp. He felt a pull at his legs and Walker slid off the dead man he was piled on, his head bouncing off the bottom of the truck bed, then on to the tailgate. He felt another set of hands then wrap beneath his underarms. As he moved, the tailgate disappeared beneath him.

"Shit this one's heavy," a man said.

"Momma says muscle weighs more than fat. Maybe that's why he's heavier than he looks," the other man holding Walker offered.

"Billy, the only thing your momma knows about

muscles is the one every single dude in Boyd County has put inside her."

"Fuck you, Terry."

They both laughed.

Walker appreciated good, classless humor. He just wasn't really in the laughing mood, so he stayed dead. His body bounced and bobbed as they walked him toward the shed. It was when the scent of gasoline hit his nose that he decided it was probably about time he did something about his current situation. But the timing had to be just right. He was the first body out of the truck, so that meant more men would be walking behind the men carrying him. How far back they were, a quick glance would show.

As they bounced him once more, Walker helped his head slump back toward the direction of the truck behind them. Greg was still overseeing the project from beside the truck, as two more men were pulling another body from its bed. They were moving slowly. Nothing Walker loved seeing more.

"We s'posed to throw him right on the pile? Or beside it?"

"Don't you listen to anything, fatso?"

"I do, and don't call me fatso. I just didn't hear if he said on it or beside it, asshole."

"Watch how you talk to me, or I'll cook you on that pile with these bodies."

Walker heard the change in the way their voices reverberated once they stepped inside the shed.

The sight line the men back at the truck had on him was now blocked.

The moment had finally arrived.

It was time for Walker to make his move.

41

The entire world outside Leila's equipment shed ceased to exist. No worrying about the police searching for his alternate identity, Evan Marshall, after murdering three men in the car accident. No thoughts on Maxwell's next hitman coming for him. No energy into a next move the cartel might make on Leila once this night was through. There was only the right now, and it was time for him to turn it on.

Walker slipped his hand back to the knife sheathed at his back. He got a solid grip around the bone handle and pulled it loose.

"So did he say on top of the damn pile or not, Terry?" one of Tim's cronies said to the other.

"On top, good God. Let's just toss him on top."

Walker felt his body sway back as they were gaining momentum to toss him forward. The smell of gasoline was even heavier now.

"One, two . . ."

As they took his body back the last time, Walker brought the knife around, slammed the blade down into the man's bicep who was holding his ankles, and yanked the knife hard, straight down his arm. The vertical wound was deep inside the brachial artery. The man would be dead in a matter of seconds.

As the man he stabbed dropped Walker's legs, Walker flipped the knife in his hand and swung straight back, stabbing Fatso in the Adam's apple. When he pulled the knife out, hot blood shot onto him. When the man grabbed at his neck, Walker dropped to the ground, jumped to his feet, and jammed the knife in the neck of the first man to stifle the scream that had already slipped out.

Walker shoved him to the ground, spun around to his right, and hit the carotid artery in Fatso's neck to speed the dying process. As he dropped to his knees, one of the men getting another body shouted from outside.

"You all right in there, Terry?"

"Yeah," Walker shouted with a twang. "Fatso just hurt his back carryin' this dude."

Walker stood motionless as he waited for a response, hoping the jig wasn't up just yet.

"What a puss," the man called back. "Nut up, Billy. You still got another body to carry."

Walker slid Terry to the far corner of the shed. He was already dead. Billy had just face-planted onto the ground. He was a lot harder to slide across the floor than Terry, living up to his Fatso nickname, but Walker got him there. Then he hustled over to the edge of the open shed door, awaiting his next victim.

The men carrying the next dead body had plodding footfalls as they all but stumbled toward the large opening into the shed. This made it easy for Walker to know when to strike. Speed would be the key here. While he could easily keep the first man from making noise with a precision strike to the neck, it would be silencing the man on the other end of the body that would be tricky. However, if fast enough, he could do it.

The men were at the open garage door.

Walker stepped forward with his left foot and jabbed violently in the same direction with his left arm. The blade of the knife sank into the man's skin near the front of his neck, giving his vocal cords no chance to do their job. For Walker, the key to quiet this time was leaving the blade in, twisting his hips to the left, and whipping an overhand right to the man's jaw across from him with everything he had.

The man dropped to the ground, somehow staying conscious, so Walker dove over to him, bringing a heavy elbow down with him. The man's head bounced off the concrete, and the lights went out. Walker spun back to his feet and helped the stabbed man down to the ground, removing the blade and allowing his life force to flow out onto the ground.

That's when Walker heard another man's step, a lot faster than he'd been ready for. As he turned back to the shed's entrance, he pulled the pistol from the back of his belt line. But it was met with the heavy end of a baseball bat and went flying into the gasoline-soaked pile to his right. The man holding the bat was a familiar face. The same man who'd used that same bat to knock Walker out back in Leila's house.

"Hank," Walker said.

Hank's brother Jason limped around the corner. Then Greg.

"Well, hello there, feller," Jason said. "You're s'posed to be dead."

"Hate to disappoint you," Walker said.

"Nah, I ain't a bit disappointed. I'll be happy to watch Hank beat the shit out of ya again."

"Put that bat down then, Hank. You don't need any help with me, now do you?"

Hank looked over at his brother.

"Don't look at me," Jason told Hank. "Whoop his ass. Ain't no rules in fightin'. Use what ya got."

Hank stepped forward and swung the bat. Hard. Walker jumped back, and the bat whizzed by.

"Ole Hank here," Jason said. "Before he got all fat, he was first-team All-State with that bat. This is gonna hurt."

Walker could see the power in the swing. The problem Hank had was his recoil time. It was much too slow. Hank swung again, with even more force this time. Walker jumped back just enough, then immediately jumped forward, using Hank's slow recoil time against him.

Hank went down easier than Walker had calculated. Must have still been off balance from the swing. This resulted in Walker sliding too far forward, and Hank was able to shuck him off. Walker slid on his stomach all the way outside the shed, then jumped to his feet. Hank was on his way up too. This time without the bat. Walker noticed Alison and Larry at the side of the shed, about to make a move. Walker shook his head, shaking them off. The last thing he needed was them shooting when it wasn't necessary, sending the wasps buzzing down below swarming up from the nest.

"Hank, he's faster than he looks," Jason said. "You don't need my help, do ya?"

"Shut your mouth, J." Hank looked at Walker. "Come on, boy."

"He speaks?" Walker jabbed.

"He's better without that bat anyway," Jason said. "I'd

tell ya to run, but then you wouldn't get to watch your lady friend down there burn to death."

That sentence sobered Walker. He was done playing games. He stalked toward Hank. When Hank raised his hands to fight, Walker kicked him in the groin. When Hank doubled over in pain, Walker brought his knee upward as hard as he could. He could hear Hank's teeth rattle as his knee smacked his forehead. Hank wobbled, then fell onto his back.

"What in the . . ." Jason couldn't finish the sentence. He wasn't used to Hank, the battering ram, being broken.

Walker stepped over Hank and picked up the baseball bat. "Which one of you first?"

Jason turned and looked at Greg. "Get his ass, Greg. Don't just stand there!"

Greg stepped away from Jason. "Uh-uh. I didn't sign up for all this shit. You fight him if you think you can beat him."

"What?" Jason said as he pulled the two-way radio from his belt. "Y'all both gonna die."

There was a good fifteen feet between Walker and Jason. There was no way he could close the distance before he alerted Tim. Jason pressed the call button as he backpedaled.

"Tim, that Walker fella ain't dead. He just beat the piss out of Hank. Get up here before he kills me!"

Things were about to get ugly thanks to that radio call. Walker's clandestine moves were finished. Unfortunately for Jason, he was finished too.

42

W alker was on Jason before he ever even let go of the radio. The bat struck Jason's arm that was holding the radio and broke it in half. Jason screamed in pain. He didn't have to hurt long because he went out cold when Walker's second swing landed just behind his ear.

Walker looked up at Alison and Larry. "Post up on both sides of the garage door and be ready. They might come up guns blazing." Then he said to Greg, "Get in your truck and leave right now. If I ever see you again, I'll kill you."

Greg nodded and walked away.

"Wait," Walker said. Greg turned to face him. "You have a lighter?"

Greg fished inside his back pocket, produced a lighter, and tossed it to Walker. Walker nodded him on. Walker dropped the bat, pocketed the lighter, and began dragging Jason over to the gasoline-soaked pile in the shed.

"Watch my back while I get these boys on the fire pit," he said to Larry and Alison.

He pulled Jason up and laid him on top of the fueled

corn-and-hay pile. Then he went back for Hank. The first pull didn't budge the big man much, but another couple hard tugs got him moving. As Walker passed by Larry, he asked for his help getting Hank on the pile. Larry ran over, and they quickly got him there beside Jason. When Walker looked into the pile, he could see the face of the Mexican man he'd shot earlier, down in the pill room. Walker shook it off when he heard something coming from the steps leading down to the pill mill, so he jogged over, picked up his pistol, made sure it was in working order, then jogged back over to the pile. Lighter and gun in hand. He nodded and pumped his hand out to Larry and Alison, a gesture telling them to stay back and let him handle it.

Walker noticed some dark hair bobbing around where the floor gave way to the trap door. The yellow light was dim inside the shed, but it was still easy enough to see something moving toward the surface.

"Jason!" Tim's voice came up from the room underground. "Everything handled out there?"

"Ah, Tim!" Walker said. "Everything's great. Now get on up here or you're going to miss the party."

Leila came up first. Her tear-soaked cheeks glistened in the yellow light. Her hair was a mess, her mouth gagged. Then Tim came up behind her, his left hand in a death grip around Leila's arm, his right holding a pistol. He gave the shed a once-over. If seeing the dead men in the corner and his two brothers on the gasoline pile shook him, he did a good job not letting on.

"Looks like you've been busy, Mr. Walker," Tim said.

"Yeah, I ran into a few snags along the way, but ended up right where I wanted to be."

"Yeah?" Tim said as he pushed Leila out a little farther

to let two more armed men come up behind him. "And where's that, exactly?"

"About to get Leila back. About to watch you die for taking her."

Tim laughed. One of those slow villain laughs. "You see, Mr. Walker, I learned a long time ago that when people hear me talk, all hillbilly and such, well, it tends to make them underestimate me. Now, I don't know if that's what did it for you, Walker, but I can see that either way, you have underestimated me."

"Maybe," Walker said. "But just make sure you don't underestimate this lighter in my hand, and just how willing I am to burn your unconscious, feeble-minded brothers alive."

Tim eyed Walker for a moment. Walker had been looked up and down this way many times as other men have tried to judge just what he was capable of and what he wasn't.

"No, that was a pretty good scheme coming in here dead. You were able to thin the herd without a whole lot of resistance. Smart. And well executed. Am I safe in assuming you've been to this sort of deadly rodeo before?"

"Not my first time, as they say."

"Yeah, I figured," Tim said. "Then I'm sure you aren't surprised that I had men watching the back of Leila's house, just to make sure you didn't have any backup. Right?"

Walker looked over at Alison and watched a man come up behind her and put a gun to her head. Then the same happened to Larry, who stood on the opposite side of the large open door. Both men pushed Alison and Larry just inside the shed. Walker took it all in, then looked back at Tim. Tim was wearing a wide smile.

"I don't know who you are for real, Mr. Walker. But I get

the feeling, from the word I just received about what happened back on my property to all my men you disabled or killed, and from how you've handled yourself with my men up here, that you don't let people get one over on you very often. And if I'm counting right, between us taking you from Leila's house earlier and now your failure to see these backup men, that makes two times I've gotten one over on you. That can't sit well."

Walker stood silent for a moment. He looked back and forth from Larry and Alison to Tim, then let a smirk of his own cross his face.

"Well, if I'm counting," Walker said, "you did get me back at Leila's house. But let's just say, that wasn't *really* me. For reasons you wouldn't understand. So, okay, I'll give you that one. But this?" Walker looked back over at Alison and Larry being held at gunpoint. "This I can't let you count."

Tim laughed again. "No? Looks like our point systems are different."

"They're not different, Tim. You just don't see the entire chessboard the way I do."

Walker finally let his outstretched arm holding the lighter fall to his side. A crack echoed in the humid early morning air from outside the barn. And in a blood-splattering heap, the man holding his gun on Alison dropped to the floor. Before Alison could even scream from the surprise, another crack echoed along the darkness, and the bullet passed through the head of the second man who'd been holding Larry hostage. He, too, collapsed to the floor.

For the first time, Tim's face showed panic. He shoved Leila to the floor and began firing at Walker. Walker anticipated that this might be his reaction, so he ducked behind the pile Tim's brothers were lying on as Alison and Larry ran back out and around the door of the shed.

Walker put the lighter back in his pocket and readied his pistol. "Stop shooting or I'll toss this lighter and turn your brothers into a bonfire!"

A couple more shots were fired by his men; then Tim shouted, "Stop!"

Walker stood, holding the gun on Tim who had pulled Leila back up and held her close, using her as a shield. The two men stared at each other for a moment.

"Larry, get over here, please. Tim won't shoot you, because if he does, I'll barbecue his family."

Larry stepped inside the shed, hesitant at first, then hurried over.

"Now you've got Larry's sister, and I've got your brothers."

"Yeah, and what the hell do you care about any of this, huh? This ain't your fight. Just mind your own damn business."

"Well, I thought about doing just that," Walker said. "Problem was, you made it my business when you included me in your little abduction. Why did you take me anyway, Tim? That's one of the things here I'm having a little trouble understanding."

"What do you mean why did I take you? You said you worked for the cartel that ran this pill mill that is stealing my business. How could I not take you?"

"Now, Tim . . ." Walker moved around the pile of Tim's brothers' bodies and accelerant-filled vegetation. He kept his gun trained on Tim's chest. "You don't think I see past what you're doing here?"

"I don't know what the hell you're talking about, but I do know that I'm going to shoot this bitch if you take another step toward me."

"Yeah, you see, Tim, since I've recovered all my faculties,

thanks to your brother here hitting me *really* damn hard in the head with a baseball bat, I've been able to see things a lot clearer. Take information in, in a way I wasn't able to before you brought me back to your property. Albeit with a not-so-comfortable headache."

"So, you saying you don't work for the cartel that's been stealing my business?"

Walker laughed. "You going to make me say it?"

"Say what, you arrogant prick?"

"You know the cartel doesn't have a damn thing to do with this drug operation here on Leila's farm."

"Bullshit," Tim said.

"You know how I know that you know that?"

Tim didn't have anything to say.

Walker continued. "I know this, Tim, because I know that *you* are the one running this little operation here on Leila's farm."

"You don't know what the hell you're talking about. If that's the case, smart-ass, then why the shit am I here to burn it down?"

"I'm glad you asked. You're here to burn this down because this was just your temporary setup, until you could move things over to the nice, shiny, much more secure place you've been building onto your barn on your property over the last few months. You're just here tonight for the product, and a fall guy"—Walker pointed to himself and then to Leila—"and to give the police evidence that the pill mill that has been killing people like Larry's daughter and Leila and Larry's father has officially been put out of business."

Tim stood in place, holding his gun on Walker.

Walker just stared right back at him.

"Well, damn, Matlock," Tim finally spoke. "You pretty

much just solved the shit out of that mystery there, didn't you?"

Walker didn't gloat.

Tim's curiosity got the best of him. "So tell me, before you die here tonight, how did you figure all that shit out?"

"I'll indulge you," Walker said. "Just because it seems you have a need to be humbled."

Tim waved his gun in a manner that told Walker to please proceed.

"I first got suspicious after I killed your two guards—not the best at looking out, by the way—and moved into the 'new' part of the barn. One thing was not like the other, and the hallways and building itself were clearly much newer than the barn all of your vehicles were parked in. Next clue was all the empty pill bottles in the first room I came to that were hidden under the false bottom of the boxes. If they hadn't matched exactly the ones in the room right below you here, which I saw earlier today, I might not have begun to put things together so quickly. There's one more thing that really sent it home for me, but I'm getting bored with this."

Walker brought up the lighter and flicked the flint to spark the flame.

"Just a minute now," Tim said as he looked from the flame to his brothers, then back to Walker. "You're a smart man, Mr. Walker. That much is clear. Very perceptive. But you missed one very important thing . . ."

Tim nodded his head to Larry. Larry immediately brought up his pistol and pointed it at Walker's head.

Leila shouted, "No! Larry! What are you doing?"

Larry looked straight ahead at Walker.

Tim let go of Leila and walked away from her, making

his way around the pile his brothers were on, about ten feet from Walker.

"Put your gun down, Larry," Alison said. She was pointing her gun at him.

"It's okay, Alison," Walker said. "Don't do anything. If you shoot Larry, Tim's men will shoot both of us."

"Now put the lighter down, Mr. Walker. To hell with your chessboard . . . and to hell with you. You ain't so smart after all."

Instead of putting the lighter down, Walker tossed the lighter next to Hank, and a blazing fire rose up from the pile. Simultaneously, Walker shot Tim right in the hand that held his gun on Leila, then moved his gun to the left and shot both of his other men dead where they stood, two in the chest and two in the midsection.

Tim was shouting in pain as blood ran from the hand he was holding by the wrist. Walker moved around the rising flame and grabbed Tim by the shirt as he looked over at Alison. "Get Leila out of here!"

Walker yanked on Tim's shirt, pulling him toward the open door.

"What are you doing, Larry?" Tim shouted. "Shoot him! Shoot this son of a bitch!"

Larry moved his gun over to Walker as Walker threw Tim onto the dirt outside the shed.

"I said shoot him, Larry! My brothers are on fire!"

Walker stepped right past Larry like he didn't even exist. Tim's face, glowing in the orange flames that were climbing the shed, was full of shock.

Larry tried to pull the trigger over and over again on his pistol, but it never fired. Tim looked at Larry's gun, then back to Walker, who was pulling Tim up to his feet. Larry threw down the gun and ran at Walker. Walker let go of

Tim, took a step back, and hit Larry so hard in the side of the head as he went by that it knocked him completely off his feet.

Tim got to his feet and looked up the gravel road like he was going to make a run for it, but that was when three squad cars, red-and-blues flashing, slid sideways down the rocky drive and blocked Tim's only way out.

The shed was ablaze behind them. Tim's trucks were full of the pills that were made down in the room beneath that shed. Walker had kept Tim and his men from killing Leila. And though he knew the police were still going to have a lot of questions before they let him go, he was just happy he'd at least seen it through to that moment.

Whatever happened after that would hopefully be Evan Marshall's problem.

43

The sun was just starting to rise over Ashland, Kentucky. It had been a long night, but its rays were finally lightening the dark curtains covering Leila's windows in the living room. It was a full house. Several police officers were strewn about the property, and a couple more were milling about inside where Walker was pouring himself and Leila a cup of coffee. She leaned into him as he took a sip from his mug.

"You okay?" Walker said.

"No. Not yet. I can't believe my own brother was—"

"You don't have to talk about that right now."

Sheriff Taylor walked into the kitchen. "Sorry to interrupt, but we really need to go through everything else. The quicker we do, the quicker we can make sure Larry Ward and Tim Riggins stay in jail, right where they are supposed to be."

The last person Walker imagined being on his side at the end of this was Leila's recent ex. But Andy had been instrumental in making sure everything Walker told him about Tim and his new facility was tied up in a nice neat bow for the district attorney who would eventually be sorting through all of the mess to prosecute all who were involved. Walker was happy the first part of the interrogation was over with the sheriff. If Alison hadn't been there in the form of an FBI agent, Walker would have been doing the interrogation in an orange jumpsuit. Or whatever color they had the inmates wearing at the Federal Correctional Institution in Ashland. Telling Sheriff Taylor that Walker was actually Evan Marshall, an undercover agent who was after the men in the car crash, bailed Walker out in a number of ways. Alison told Taylor that Walker was actually not supposed to kill those men in the car, so she had to take him into custody with her as soon as the sheriff was finished with him, and let the Bureau sort it out. Walker knew Andy would look into everything Alison had said, but Walker would be long gone before anything could come of it. In short, Alison—the FBI agent—Brookins walking him out of there in cuffs like she had promised Taylor she would when they were done with their questions was going to be a literal lifesaver.

Walker put his arm around Leila. "Let's get this over with."

The two of them walked into Leila's living room. Everyone made room for them to sit on the couch. Greg was in the chair next to the couch, getting treatment on his gunshot wound by an EMT. Walker gave him a nod as he and Leila took a seat. Walker looked over to the far corner of the room. Alison was holding up the wall, acting as if she were a fly on that wall for the FBI. But Walker knew her insides were churning, worrying about what was next with Karen Maxwell and her clandestine, government-funded operation. Walker was just happy Sheriff Taylor was asking the questions, sitting in for

Detective Pelfrey, who had his hands full at the Riggins property.

"Mr. Walker," Sheriff Taylor said, "you mind picking up where we left off?"

Walker nodded as he sipped his coffee. "You mind refreshing my memory?"

Leila looked up at him and laughed. He was happy to see she could still smile under the circumstances. His memory, or lack thereof, had been the source of a few laughs over the past twenty-four hours.

"Um," Andy said, "when you finally understood who all was involved. Before you called me."

Walker nodded. "After I found the new pill mill—or what I thought was the new pill mill—attached to Tim Riggins's barn, I was making my way back through Tim's house to try to save Larry and Alison when I noticed something that hadn't registered before. The first time I'd walked down Tim's hallway to the front door, I was so hellbent on finding Leila that I didn't register the family photos on the hallway walls. But the next time I went by, after my first confrontation with Greg in the basement, I noticed one photo in particular."

"A family photo," Andy said, "on Tim's wall?"

"A photo beside the family photos. It was taken at a UK basketball game. More recent than the other pictures."

"What was special about this one?"

"It was of Tim, and he had his arm around . . ." Walker looked down at Leila. "Larry Ward. Leila's brother. The two looked like peas in a pod."

Leila hung her head.

Sheriff Taylor moved even closer to the edge of his seat. "So? How would that help you draw such a monumental conclusion? That Larry was working with him on his illegal business?"

"Well, that photo alone probably wouldn't have done it. But yesterday, when I was walking out back, on my way off Leila's property, I heard some men talking about some sinister things, and one of the men was a police officer."

"Okay?" Andy said.

"At the time," Walker elaborated, "I didn't know what to do. I saw the police car, and I heard the officer driving the car talking to the Mexican men, but I never saw his face. But he knew about the drug operation. And when I saw Larry with Tim on that wall, it all came together for me."

"So why didn't you just confront Larry at Tim's house before you went to save Leila? Why take him along for the ride?"

"Because the only thing I didn't know was how deep Tim's entourage was at Leila's shed. I was hoping it would come down to Larry being Tim's last hope. That's why I emptied the gun of rounds before I gave it to Larry to use to help me. I told him it was locked and loaded, hoping he would just trust that it was and not check. When he said he wasn't military, well, I hoped his training was lacking enough to not press-check the gun himself. Worked out, I guess."

"Son of a bitch," the sheriff said. "So, when did you call me then?"

Walker nodded over to Alison. "When I sent Alison and Larry down to the shed, I had some alone time with Greg. All of this was still mulling in my mind, but when he covered me up in the back of that truck bed with that tarp, I stopped him before he backed the truck out onto the road."

"All right," Andy said. "Why?"

"I don't know really. I just sensed something in him.

When I asked him just before that about his hunting rifle and he told me he was a good shot, I told him to make sure he taught his son. There was a sense of pride in his eyes that I've never seen a bad man have. And I've looked into the eyes of many a bad man."

"Okay . . ."

"So I brought him in. I told him that not only would I let him live if he helped me, but I had plenty of money and I'd pay him for his efforts."

"Efforts?" Andy said. "Which were?"

"I told him that I was going to right some wrongs. And then I asked him that if I signaled him to shoot some bad men at just the right time, would he do it?" Walker looked over at Greg in the chair beside him. Greg gave a weary half smile and a nod. Walker nodded back. "He said he would. Said the only reason he was caught up with Tim Riggins and his family was because Tim blackmailed him when Greg's wife got into a little trouble. I took a chance on Greg, and he bailed me out of a bad situation."

"Right," Andy said. "Okay. What then?"

"That's when I called you," Walker said. "Right after I told Greg the plan, from under the tarp, before Greg pulled away. I told you about what I found at Tim's property. And what I told you that you would find in the boxes in his trucks would be pills to fill all those empty bottles he was hiding. And it was all there, right?"

Sheriff Taylor nodded. "It was. That and then some. We also found the raw product there that he was set to use to start producing the pills on his own property instead of making them under Leila's shed."

"There you go," Walker said.

"Yeah, but there I don't go, Mr. Walker," Andy said. "We found your bag in a car on Tim's property. The one parked outside now, which the other FBI agent had rented. Agent Brookins said she put it there after she checked this house for you, but you weren't here. The only reason you aren't in handcuffs is because you're the reason we were able to shut down Tim's drug operation. But I can't let what we found go. The passport in that bag, along with the *thick* wad of cash, says that your name is actually Evan Marshall. Just like Agent Brookins mentioned earlier."

Alison cleared her throat and stepped over to the conversation. "And remember what we talked about, Sheriff. That's where it's going to have to stay." Alison produced a set of handcuffs. She dangled them from her hand. "Evan, as fantastical as this night has been, you're going to have to come with me and answer for stepping over the line by killing those men in the car." Alison played it up.

Sheriff Taylor stood up. "I know what I said, Agent, but you can't take him anywhere. He is a part of this investigation as well as the murders in that car back in the creek."

"Sorry, Sheriff. It's really not my call. And certainly not yours. But Evan Marshall is of federal concern. We'll make sure justice is done from here."

"You can't do that!"

"Sheriff, I've already cleared this with your police chief as well. Feel free to call and check with him if you like."

The sheriff set his hands hard on his hips as he shook his head. "Damn Feds," he scoffed. Then he turned and walked into the kitchen.

Leila stood up. "Alison, do you mind if I have a word with Walker before you take him? Just to thank him properly without everyone around? I mean, he did save my life."

Alison looked at Walker. He was standing in front of Leila, so she couldn't see him wink at Alison.

"All right," Alison said. "But don't be long. We have a long drive ahead of us."

Leila took Walker by that hand and led him toward the hallway. He didn't really want to have an intimate talk with Leila, because he knew he was going to have to leave with Alison, but he felt after all they'd been through, he at least owed her a conversation.

44

L eila led Walker down the hall to her bedroom. She pulled him inside and shut the door behind him. Walker wasn't much of an intimacy sort of man, so he couldn't help but feel uncomfortable.

"Crazy night, huh?" he said.

Leila walked over and sat on the bed. She patted the empty spot beside her. Walker begrudgingly took it. The water bed sloshed when he sat down.

"Crazy is one way to describe it. So many things happened with so many different people, it's still making my head spin."

"I can imagine," Walker said. "Speaking of, one person I never saw in all the chaos was your farmhand, Tyler. I just figured he would have been in the mix since we know he knew what was going on after he came to the door last night."

Instead of answering him, Leila leaned in and kissed him. Walker didn't really want the kiss to happen. He liked Leila, but he knew that sleeping with her had been a mistake. And he didn't want to exacerbate that mistake with any more intimate encounters, even a kiss. Apparently, Leila could feel that his mind was thinking that way.

She pulled back. "Not the same?"

"It's not that, Leila," he said. "I'm leaving. And though I may pass through here from time to time to check on Kim, I'm never going to live here. Too many bad memories."

"You could make some new ones," she said with a delicate smile. Then she hung her head. "I understand. I do. I just appreciate so much what you did for me, and now I won't really get to properly thank you for it."

"You already have. I promise. Taking me in and giving me a chance when I was at my lowest is something I'll never forget."

She stared into his eyes. Then she covered her face with her hands. "Oh my God, I can't even imagine what I look like right now." She stood up. "I'm an absolute mess. And if I never see you again, I'll be damned if this is the last memory you have of me. Give me just a minute, please."

Walker laughed. "You look great, Leila."

She shooed him away and walked around the wall into the bathroom. "I never wear much but just a little makeup. I'll be right out."

Walker smiled. He stared up at the ceiling, then rolled his neck around to relieve some of the tension he'd been holding there. His head was still pounding from the nonstop beatings it had taken over the last couple of days.

"So, what now, Tom?" Leila said from the other room. "You said earlier, before the cops invaded us, that Alison works for the same, what, spy company you do?" She poked her head around the corner. "And I told you, you were a spy yesterday, now, didn't I? Huh? Didn't I?"

Walker laughed. "You did, but I'm not exactly a spy."

She disappeared around the wall again. "Tomato, tomahto."

Leila's phone lit up where she left it on the bed beside him. Walker paid it no mind.

Leila continued, "Anyway, you both are, what, in trouble with them?"

"I guess you could say that. I mean, they have tried to kill me . . . twice now."

"Good Lord. Okay, well, what does that mean then?"

Leila's phone lit up again beside him. Again, he ignored it.

"This isn't stuff I should be talking to you about. To anyone about, for that matter. But let's just say, we have to take matters into our own hands."

Leila laughed at first, then let out a sigh. "Sounds dangerous."

Leila's phone lit up again.

"Yeah, probably will be dangerous," Walker said. "Par for the course."

He glanced over so he could tell her who was messaging her, and it was something he would come to wish he had never done.

She had four missed messages. All from the same contact: Tyler.

Walker's stomach dropped, and his mind began to reel. Why would Tyler be messaging Leila now if he was part of Tim's drug operation? Why was he nowhere to be found last night? And why, when Walker brought him up a minute ago, did Leila just kiss him? To shut him up because she didn't want Walker asking about him?

"Well," Leila said from the bathroom, "I'd tell you to be careful, but I think I know you well enough by now to know you won't be."

Walker was in his head and wasn't really paying attention. Leila poked her head back around the corner. "Hello? You still there?"

Walker shook his trance. "Yeah, sorry. Just thinking about what still needs to be done."

Leila released a sad moan, then walked out and held his head to her chest in a hug. "I'm sorry you have so many dark things in your life, Tom."

The phone lit up again. Again, it was Tyler. Walker stood up and turned Leila's back to the phone. "Don't worry about me. It's all I've ever known, so it isn't any more of a burden now than it ever has been."

"It just must be such a heavy weight," she said.

Walker stared down at her brown eyes. But that isn't what he saw. He was trying to look deeper. To see if there was a lot of darkness in her life too. He saw nothing. A mind reader he was not.

"You finished freshening up?" Walker said. "Because I really need to get going."

"Oh. Right. Sorry, just one more quick thing. I don't think I've had the chance to use the restroom since sometime yesterday. And of course it's pressing on me now. Be right back."

Walker nodded. Leila went into the bathroom and shut the door. She turned the faucet on so that he wouldn't hear her. But Walker wouldn't have heard her anyway because his mind was elsewhere. He moved over to the bed and picked up her phone. He swiped up on the screen, then hit the green Messages app at the top left corner. The unread messages from Tyler were the top contact. He tapped Tyler's name. The last message confirmed what Walker had feared when he first saw Tyler's name pop up as a message. He read it three times just to let it sink in.

"Mom, we did it."

Mom. Not only did Leila have that darkness he'd just tried to find in her eyes, but she was the darkest of them all.

He went up and read the three messages sent before that one.

"I'm safe."

"I managed to get all the pills out, so we're good. All they're gonna find in the pill bottles in Tim's trucks are baby aspirin."

"I can't believe you were able to get that guy to take down Tim's entire operation. It's free and clear for us to grow now like you wanted to. You're a genius."

And then for good measure, he read the last message again.

"Mom, we did it."

Walker's mind was jumping all around. He heard the toilet flush in the bathroom, so he was running out of time to understand the entire truth. He feared he already knew it. Leila hadn't helped him when he was down; she saw an opportunity and used him. His mind jumped to how often she'd asked about whether he could possibly be a spy or not. Then it jumped to when she had him take apart the gun and put it back together. She wasn't trying to help him regain his memory; she was testing him to see just how much she could use him.

"Almost finished," Leila said through the door. "Just washing up."

Then Walker's mind jumped to when he'd come back from the shed last night after discovering the subterranean pill mill. How Tyler had come to the door. How did he know not to say anything?

Walker scrolled past several messages between Leila and her son, Tyler, until he came to the time stamp that would have been around the time Walker got back to the house last night. He stopped when he found what he was looking for.

TYLER: He just came running out of the shed. He should be back to the house in just a minute.

LEILA: Okay, good. He must have taken care of the men down there. I knew he could handle himself. Come to the door in about twenty minutes and say you just wanted to check on me. When I ask why, say a drifter came along and tried to rob your workers but he ran off. No way he'll suspect me after that.

TYLER: You sure I just shouldn't leave it alone and stay away?

LEILA: Just do what I say. The drugs are on my property. It's only natural to suspect that I know they are there. This will throw him off the scent. He's at the door now. Just do it.

TYLER: Okay. Be up in a bit.

Leila had played Walker like a fiddle. Walker would have liked to think that if he had been himself when all of this was happening, he would have caught something that would have made him suspect her. That she couldn't have taken advantage of him like she had. But he had always been desperate to help a woman in need, ever since the day he watched Kim get beat on by Jim all those years ago. Leila probably knew he had that tendency, too, after he told her about his foster situation.

Leila walked out of the bathroom, but Walker didn't try to hide the fact that he had her phone.

"I thought your phone was busted from all the water?" she said.

Walker extended the phone out toward her, holding it to where she could see the messages he'd pulled up on the screen. "Not my phone."

Leila moved fast. "Those are none of your business!" She swiped at the phone to try to take it, but Walker pulled away in plenty of time.

"I think the sheriff would disagree," he said.

Walker held her at bay as she fought to get to the phone. After a few seconds, she stopped and stepped back. "It's not what you think, Tom."

"It isn't? You didn't play me to gain control of your competition's drug business?"

"Competition?"

"You playing dumb again?" Walker said. "You must have really been laughing under your breath as I explained to Sheriff Taylor in there a minute ago how I discovered that it was Tim's pill mill all along on your property."

"It is his pill mill. I swear. I was just trying to get Tyler out of trouble! That's all!"

Walker had already turned any emotion he had for Leila off. He felt nothing as he casually scrolled down to the last few texts.

"And I quote," Walker said, reading from the phone, "I can't believe you were able to get that guy to take down Tim's entire operation. It's free and clear for us to grow now like you wanted to. You're a genius." Walker closed the phone and put it in his back pocket. "It was pretty genius, Leila. The only thing I'm curious about is do you feel bad at all for killing your father and your niece?"

Leila charged forward and raised her hand to slap him. Walker caught her arm at the wrist and, as gently as he could, brought it back down.

"That a yes? No? Or I don't give a shit?"

Leila tried to yank her hand away, but Walker held on. "How'd you get the cartel to start supplying you? Hearing the cartel mentioned down by the shed is what really threw me off. Tyler must handle all of that for you too. Because you really didn't know those Mexican men."

"You have no idea what you're talking about, Tom. Now let me go!"

"I know that all this time it's been you who isn't who you say you are. Thirty-two, you said you are? You even lied about your age. Tyler is at least twenty." Walker let go of her arm. "You lied about the sheriff beating you up, too, didn't you? Even to your brother who you were in cahoots with. Why? So he would owe you something?" Walker shook his head. "You got me. Hook, line, and sinker. Too bad it's all going to crumble now."

Then something else hit Walker that he hadn't thought of.

"Wait, you didn't know your brother was working with Tim instead of you, did you? Larry is the reason Tim and his crew came to your house last night. So it runs in the family. He played both sides on you, just like you played me. It almost worked. But it didn't. You're going to jail, and unfortunately, you're taking your poor son with you."

She came at him again, but he just blocked with his arms. Then she pulled back and took a deep breath like she was calming down, then bolted for the door. She had it open before Walker could grab her, but he didn't have to chase her. Alison was standing in the hallway, pistol drawn, holding Leila dead to rights.

"Andy!" Leila shouted. "They aren't who they say they are! They're trying to kill me!"

Walker stepped into the hallway behind Leila.

The sheriff ran over with his gun drawn. "What in the hell is going on in here?"

Alison's tone was even. "Sheriff, there are all kinds of penalties against holding a gun on a federal agent."

Andy lowered his gun. "Then tell me what the hell is this? Why are you holding a gun on Leila?"

Walker stepped around Leila, took her phone from his pocket, and handed it to the sheriff. "Andy, you're going to want to look through Leila's phone. Particularly the texts between her and her *son*, Tyler."

Shock morphed Sheriff Taylor's face. "Son? Tyler? What the—?"

"She's all yours now, Sheriff," Alison said. "I need to get Mr. Marshall here back to DC to answer for his own transgressions."

Andy barely even looked up. He was reading the texts from Tyler. Right where Walker had left the phone open.

"Leila? Is all this true?"

There was desperation in Leila's eyes. "I've been set up, Andy. You know me. You know I'm not capable of any of this!"

"Good luck, Andy," Walker said as Alison put the handcuffs on his wrists in front of him.

Sheriff Taylor just stood there shaking his head.

"You son of a bitch!" Leila shouted as she ran for Walker's back.

Alison stepped around Walker, cocked back her right arm, and hit Leila hard enough in the forehead to knock her off course.

Walker looked down at Leila, then back up at Alison, who smiled. "She deserved that much at the very least. And God knows you weren't going to do it."

Walker turned around, shuffled over to the chair, and picked up his jacket and his bag that the police had brought in, throwing it over his shoulder. He opened the flap enough to reach inside and grab the roll of cash. Leila rubbed her forehead as she struggled back up to her feet.

Alison moved around behind Walker and nudged him toward the door. He paused just before walking out and looked over at her.

"Leila, thank you for patching up my leg. I hope they aren't too hard on your son. I know what it's like to grow up like he has, with someone not thinking of what's best for him. I just hope he turns out better than I did."

Leila didn't react. The realization of her own fate was setting in.

Walker looked over at Sheriff Taylor and nodded his head. "Sheriff, mind if we have a heart-to-heart outside? Just me and you?"

Andy nodded back. "Let me make sure Leila's not going anywhere. Then I'll be right out."

Walker turned once more, this time to face Greg. Walker tossed him the roll of cash. "Thanks for your help, Greg. Sorry I had to shoot you."

Greg eyed the large roll of cash, then looked up at Walker with a crooked smile. "It felt good to do something for the good guys for once."

Walker appreciated what he said, but he wasn't sure he was entirely correct about the "good guys" part. It's what Walker always wanted to be; he just wasn't sure he was ever going to fully get there.

Walker smiled. "Buy your boy a nice new fishing rod, would you?"

"I sure will."

Walker turned and stepped out the door. It had been a wild ride on Leila Ward's property, but it was the type of ride he never wanted to go on again.

45

Walker stepped outside Leila's house into the rising heat of the morning. The cicadas' chant from last night had given way to the charming song of a few robins milling about in the trees across the street. Probably feeding their little ones. Their only concern in all the world. What a wonderful life that must be.

"You okay?" Alison said. "You want to lose the cuffs?"

Walker held out his arms. She inserted the key and set him free. "I'm good," he said. "It is amazing how, in life, sometimes you only see what you want to see."

"You mean with Leila?"

"Yeah. I obviously wasn't in my right mind, but if I went back through my time with her, I'm sure there were things that even memory-deprived me should have noticed. But I never suspected her for a second."

"Because you didn't want to?"

"Right. It all makes sense now, in a deranged, manipulative sort of way. But I still should have caught it. Maybe I wouldn't have had to kill so many people."

"You can't live backward, Tom," Alison said. "Rewind

285

only serves to play the same pain you already lived through all over again."

"Thanks for your help. It was a stroke of luck, Maxwell having had you tag along with Mike."

"Not as much luck as you might think."

Walker looked at her, perplexed.

"I was in Maxwell's building yesterday morning when word came through that you had escaped your death plan in that car. I just so happened to have been getting a new assignment from Karen Maxwell when the call came in. As soon as she hung up the phone, I told her that I wanted to be the one to go and get you."

"Maxwell didn't ask you why?" Walker said.

"She did. I told her that word had gotten around about what you'd done last week, interrupting a fellow assassin, getting him killed and all, and I told her that tracking down traitors was my favorite job in the Army. She was angry, and I'd caught her in a weak moment. But that's why she put me with Mike, even though he notoriously works alone. I didn't know if I could affect the outcome of the situation or not."

"I think we both know the answer to that now," Walker said. "I owe you my life."

"Well, I owe mine to Kim. She saved me from Mike last night."

"I don't visit very often, but when I do, I try to always teach her something. I think it makes her feel better about me getting shipped off into this underworld life I was sentenced to for killing Jim. She doesn't really know what I do, or who I do it for, but because I am good at something and not just rotting in a jail cell, I believe it eases her guilt."

"How'd you get over the fact that she looked the other way when your foster dad hit you?"

"It wasn't easy, and it took a long time," Walker said as

he wiped a bead of sweat from his forehead. "But time offers a lot of lessons. A big one it has taught me is that we are all battling something. And most of the time, we don't have any idea how to deal with it. We make mistakes while we're trying to figure it out, and all we can do is hope we don't hurt other people in the process. But sometimes that happens too. Then all we can do is hope the people we hurt give us the grace to be human. Kim is a good woman who was stuck in a bad situation. She was lost and drowning. I decided to give her the grace of being human."

"You're a very unusual man, Tom. And I mean that in a good way."

"I've been called worse."

They both smiled at each other as Sheriff Taylor came walking down the steps of the front porch. Walker pulled his bag around in front of him, dug inside, then pulled out Evan Marshall's passport. Then he looked at Alison.

"Can I see your FBI credential?"

Alison looked confused, but she handed it over without questioning him.

"No handcuffs, I see," Andy said as he pointed down at Walker's wrists.

Walker turned to face him. "Will you allow me to be straight with you, Sheriff?"

"Well, Tom, or Evan, that would be awful nice of you for a change. And call me Andy."

Walker had a feeling that Andy hadn't really bought the entire story. Seems as though he may have been right.

"She even FBI?" Andy looked at Alison.

"She is not," Walker admitted.

"Tom?" Alison looked surprised.

Walker didn't respond.

"This better be good," Andy said.

"Andy, what I'm about to tell you has to stay between me and you. Even if you have no interest in what I'm about to suggest. And the reason I have the audacity to even ask you to keep it between us is because you know that the call for Mike and Alison to come down here as FBI agents came from the office of Senator Davidson."

"Yes. Detective Pelfrey did inform me of that when I checked in with him about the two of them."

"Right," Walker said. "So in short, all of this is above both of our pay grades. Alison and I are a part of a clandestine program that is overseen by a *very* small oversight committee—"

"Let me guess, Senator Davidson is the one who oversees this little secret program."

"That is correct."

Andy folded his arms across his chest. "I'd ask just what it is that you do for this secret program, but I don't imagine that's something I'm allowed to hear?"

"Correct."

"Yeah. Well, judging by what you were able to accomplish here and over at the Riggins property, I think I can pretty well fill in the blanks."

Walker nodded. "I think you can too."

"Let's get to it then," Andy said. "Why are we having this conversation about things I'm not allowed to know about?"

"I need your help," Walker said. "And I don't take asking for help lightly."

"You don't think I've done enough?" Andy said. "The only reason I was letting you leave was because of how Alison here was introduced to us. And you best believe, I had it double-checked that it really came from the senator's office."

"Good," Walker said.

"And the three men who were killed in your little car accident? They just so happened to have rap sheets sent to us late last night. Rap sheets that didn't exist when Detective Pelfrey and I looked into them yesterday afternoon. If that doesn't scream that a cover-up of that accident was being installed by an entity of the federal government that I'm not supposed to know about, I don't know what does. Especially after I saw what you did last night."

"And, Andy, how our program burned those three employees like that, with those magic rap sheets? That's what they are going to do to us. But much worse."

Andy's arms unfolded, and his hands went to his hips. "And that has what to do with me exactly?"

"That?" Walker said. "Nothing. But it is why we need your help."

"Even if I wanted to, how the hell could I help you?"

Walker handed Andy his Evan Marshall passport. Then Alison's FBI credentials. Andy opened them both up, looked them over, then closed them.

"And?" he said.

"Andy, both of those people died last night in that fire."

Andy began laughing. Deep-gut belly laughs. So hard that he had a small coughing fit before sobering up. "And you think I can help with that? You're crazy."

Walker nodded. "I might be crazy, but you absolutely can help with that. And when you do, it will help you too."

"Me?" Andy said. "Okay. This ought to be rich. Go on. I can't wait to hear this."

"Down in that burned-up shed just past the rows of corn, you've got what, Sheriff, seven, maybe eight dead bodies? All of them burned up beyond recognition."

Andy did some figuring in his head. "Sounds about right. So?"

"So, I need two of them to be Evan Marshall and Alison Brookins." Walker reached over and tapped on the IDs Andy was holding.

Walker looked over at Alison. She no longer looked surprised. Instead, she looked at Andy with great anticipation. She knew this might just be the only thing in the world that could spring her from Karen Maxwell's termination list.

"How the hell do you suppose I can do that? Those bodies down there all have families who will know they are missing."

"Not Mike Hudson. The man who was sent by my program to kill me. He doesn't have a family. And today he won't exist anywhere on the planet. Our boss will erase him."

Andy laughed. "Okay. Say I call this Mike Hudson, Evan Marshall. What about her?" Andy motioned to Alison.

Alison looked at Walker. Bated breath.

"There was a man I had to kill yesterday that got all of this started. He was a cartel member. The cartel was supplying Leila. No one will know him or come looking for him. He was in that fire. That can be Alison."

Andy let out a breath. Walker knew it was a lot. Andy kicked at a couple of rocks that were lying in the driveway.

"Man," Andy said. "That's a lot of asking you're doing here."

"I know it is, Andy. I was hoping that handing over the local drug operation and getting God knows how many pills off your streets might buy me a little good will."

"What you're asking me to do is illegal. Would you be asking this if Detective Pelfrey was here instead of still over at the Riggins place?"

"Does it matter?"

Andy looked around. It was quiet out front. Most of the busy work was going on down at the shed.

Walker expanded the plan. "What if I tell you that putting Evan Marshall in that fire also sweetens the pot for you too?"

Andy looked up. "For me? How the hell could that help me?"

"You've got a double homicide you're investigating down in that creek, right? And Evan Marshall is the prime suspect?"

"The only suspect," Andy said.

"What was the sheriff's department planning on telling the public about what happened to the suspect? How will your citizens feel safe if Evan Marshall is never apprehended and a killer is on the loose? You put Evan Marshall in that fire, and not only does it tie that crime off for you, but you get to be the one to take credit for it. You shot Evan Marshall in that shed just before the fire started, didn't you? You took down a murderer. You kept your citizens safe."

Walker was trying to play to Andy's ego. He knew it was there. Walker had seen it on full display the first time he'd met him when he rolled up on him right there in that driveway.

Walker spoke again before Andy could make up his mind. "Have you ever wanted to be more than sheriff, Andy? The kind of stuff we're talking about looks real good to a mayor when he's looking to appoint a new police chief."

"Our chief *is* stepping down this year . . ."

There was a lot riding on this for Walker. And for Alison. Walker just wanted to disappear after all of this. And after all he'd done in his career. He wanted out, but he didn't want to have to take on Maxwell, or worse, Senator Davidson. This was the only way he would get to avoid all of that and just move on with whatever came next in his life. Otherwise, they would have Walker and Alison killed. That's just the way this business worked. If Andy agreed, he and Alison could disappear separately and each start a new life, away from all of that mess. At least for the time being.

"Okay, Tom Walker. I'll do it. But you've got to get the hell out of here. Detective Pelfrey is on his way here. If he sees you, either one of you, this ain't happening."

Walker was about to extend his hand when Alison rushed past him and threw her arms around Andy. Andy stumbled back, patted Alison on the back, then separated from her.

"Thank you, Andy. You just saved my life. I'm not like Tom here. I can't fight these people. They would have killed me."

"Well, you're welcome. Now do me a favor and never let me hear from either one of you ever again."

"Done." Walker extended his hand. Andy gave it a hard shake. "I'm sorry about Leila. I know you two have a history."

"Yeah, but it is not a good one. I don't know what she told you, but she was impossible. But now it makes sense why. She was living an entirely separate life. With a son I never even knew she had and, of all things, a drug operation."

Walker backed away toward the car Alison had driven in. "Good luck, Sheriff."

"Both of you too," he said.

Walker got in the passenger seat, and Alison drove them away from Leila's farm. All he could do was hope that Andy could pull it all together smoothly. But either way, he and Alison were not going to be around to find out.

46

Walker sat back in his chair and wiped his mouth with a paper towel. He and Alison had stopped by his favorite pizza place as a kid, Giovanni's, and grabbed a pie on the way to Kim's house. She was beyond excited to see him. They sat at the kitchen table together, eating and laughing, as Kim told Alison stories of when Walker was a "quiet kid who just loved his books." Of course, every story she told, Walker couldn't help but remember the reality around those fairy tales—all the beatings—but he kept that to himself. It was nice to see Kim happy. And watching her laugh with Alison brought Walker a sense of peace he hadn't felt in a while. If ever.

The pizza didn't hurt matters any either.

The entire time they were enjoying the pizza and each other's company, however, there was a dark cloud hanging over Walker. The deal he'd struck with Sheriff Taylor to help Evan Marshall and Alison Brookins die in the fire on Leila's property was great. Life changing. And for now, it would take him off Karen Maxwell's radar. But Karen Maxwell wasn't ever going to be removed from Walker's radar. Not completely. Not until she was dead. Walker didn't know when, but one day he would be standing over her dead body. His mentor, John Sparks, would tell Walker that she wasn't worth it. But John wasn't here to have a say in Walker's life anymore, and Maxwell killing him was the reason why. Walker didn't know when, but one day he was going to make her pay for it.

Walker cleared his throat as he tossed down his napkin. "Well, this has been nice, but—"

"Don't you say it, Tommy," Kim said. "Don't you say it's time to go."

"Sorry, Kim. It's time to go."

"Humbug," she said. "At least I got to see you. And got to see you enjoy that pizza you love so much."

"Good, right?" Walker said to Alison.

"Delicious."

"So, what now, you two?" Kim said.

Alison sighed. "I wish I could give you some fairy-tale answer, but I have to figure out a way to get my money without being noticed and my stuff without being seen."

"I know someone who can help with your money," Walker said. "The stuff? Leave it."

"But it's everything I have."

"Is it worth dying over?"

Alison frowned. "Well, not when you put it like that."

"What about you, Tommy? Where will you go?"

"Not sure, really. I'd like to just find someplace quiet for a while."

"So you can just sit and read," Kim said, laughing. "I know you. You should really try to write. I remember reading your notebooks. They were good. Real good. Not that I'm a critic or nothin'. But I liked 'em. You still do that?"

Walker thought about all the notebooks in his bag. It

was one of the few ways over the years he could truly escape the world that others had created for him. Now, being on the cusp of actually escaping that world, he was both excited and anxious. Change, even when it's good, always hurts at first. And he had a lot of demons rattling around in his mind.

"I still do it," Walker said.

"Somewhere quiet, huh?" Alison said. "You said you could find someone to help me get my money without leaving a trail?"

"I know a guy."

"All right. You put me in touch with him, and I think I have someplace quiet for you."

"Really?"

"You like the water?" Alison said.

"Sure," Walker said as he leaned forward.

"I have a cousin in Tennessee. She and her husband have a beautiful house on Chickamauga Lake, just outside Chattanooga. They're spending the next couple months in Europe and beyond. I just spoke with her two days ago. She called asking me if I had any interest in house-sitting for them. I'd go stir crazy out there, but sounds pretty perfect for you."

Walker thought about it for a minute.

"It's right on the water. Beautiful sunrises. Even has a boat. Good place to read . . . and write."

That sounded about as good as it could get for Walker. "There a catch?"

"No catch. They're great people. If I tell them you'll take great care of it, they will welcome you."

"Sign me up," Walker said.

"Done. I'll call them in a bit and get you situated."

Walker stood and looked at Kim. "You got the keys?"

Kim smiled. "Of course. I'll go get them."

Walker watched Kim scamper away, then smiled at Alison. "Lake sounds nice. Thank you. Thank you for everything really."

"I'm the one who should say thank you. If your little scheme you convinced the sheriff to go along with actually works, I can start over. And get a redo on choosing my own path in life. So, I can't even imagine how you must feel about the prospect of being free."

"I don't really even know what that means."

Kim came bounding back in. She had the energy of a teenager. Always did, as Walker remembered.

"Let's follow Kim," Walker said. "I've got some things that might help you get started on that freedom."

"Ooh, mystery. I like it."

They both followed Kim out the back door and down the back porch. Walker had hoped that one day the day he was currently having might come, so he'd decided to plan for it. He had been paid handsomely for doing violent things for many years in the name of justice, and he had kept almost all of that money. One of the biggest influences that John Sparks had on Walker was how to prepare for the inevitable ending of his time with Maxwell Solutions.

John's first advice was never to put any of that tax-free money the government was paying him in the bank. So, every time Maxwell Solutions wired money to his bank account after a job well done, Walker removed 90 percent of it as cash. Kim always knew when Walker had finished a job because he always came back to her place to make a deposit.

"I'm surprised you're going to let her see this, Tommy," Kim said as she put the key into the rickety old door of the medium-sized and equally as rickety old barn that wasn't far from the back of the house.

"Oh, I'm the first?" Alison said.

Walker laughed. "You're the only."

Kim pulled back the dark and deeply weather-worn wooden door. Only to reveal a very brand-new door behind it.

"Well, didn't see that coming," Alison said.

"Just you wait," Kim laughed.

Walker stepped forward and punched in an eight-digit code on the keypad fixed to the metal door. The red light went green, and he pulled the handle down while he pushed it open. He reached in and flipped the three light switches on the wall. He heard Alison gasp behind him. Walker had only ever spent his money on two things: modernizing while disguising the inside of that old barn and the car that was sitting beneath its cover in the middle of the barn.

"This is amazing."

"Only thing the poor boy ever spent any of his money on," Kim said. "Looks good, don't it? All fire proof, thief proof, and every other kind of proof they make."

Alison was looking at a modern and pristine garage. The floor was a gray polished concrete. The rest of the walls were white. The window in the back was still there from the old barn, about twenty-five feet high in the vaulted ceiling. The only other thing inside it, other than the covered car, was another door to a different room at the back right of the space.

"This is insane," Alison said. "Who would have thought this old barn looked like this inside. I want to see the car!"

"In a minute," Walker said. "First, I have to get a few things, and I have something for you."

Alison looked over at Kim with a smile. Kim grinned back with an excited shrug of the shoulders.

Walker had never brought anyone else into his circle of trust, but if anyone had earned it, it was Alison. And he wanted to make sure she was taken care of. One, because he liked her. But two, and probably the real truth, he didn't want to have to worry about her once he was gone.

47

W alker stepped around the car and made his way back to the door leading to the only other room in the entirely renovated old barn. There was another keypad on that door. This time, however, it was thumbprint only. And the door itself was twice the thickness of a normal door and auto-bolted more like a high-powered safe. Walker put his thumb over the screen, unlocked it, and pushed the door open. Inside looked like an oversize closet, but only a very small portion of it was for clothes. The rest was a weapons cache, full of all of Walker's favorite tools of the trade. The last section was his money. When he walked in, the lights came on. He walked over to a cabinet where he kept his money. When he opened the cabinet, he revealed a lot of wrapped stacks of one-hundred-dollar bills, but most of his money, over the years, he'd been converting to gold bars.

"I've always been a James Bond fan," Alison said. "This is James Bond kind of cool." Then she looked over at Walker. "You have the looks, Mr. Walker. Too bad you don't have that Bond charisma." She winked and punched his shoulder.

Walker cracked a smile. "Yeah, no. I'm too much of a man for vodka martinis."

They all laughed. Walker moved over to a different cabinet. He opened it and pulled out a black duffel bag, along with a small messenger bag as well. He took both of them over to the center island in the middle of the room. It was white wood, matching the rest of the room. This was topped with white carrara marble. He filled the small bag with cash and half of his duffel bag with the rest of the bills.

Walker then moved over to the weapons. He pulled a Sig Sauer P365 XL off the wall for himself. John Sparks was Walker's biggest influence, and when he made the easy to conceal P365 his own standard issue, so did Walker. It was his go-to. He then opened the drawer below the one holding the guns. Inside were rows of field knives. Walker chose his favorite, the Spyderco Yojimbo 2 Tactical, folded it, and put it in his pocket. Finally, he pulled a Daniel Defense DDM4V7 5.56 NATO semi-automatic rifle from the wall, three spare magazines from a separate ammunition cabinet, and brought them over to the island.

"Damn, Tom," Alison said. "You going to war?"

"Not yet. But I'll be gone for a while. Always good to have a few of my favorite things. Go ahead. Pick out a knife and pistol for yourself. You might need it."

"Really?" Alison walked over. "Any suggestions?"

"Grab the silver CR Sebenza knife on the left there. Probably the Glock 19 for the pistol. There's a spare mag in the cabinet."

Alison brought them over to Walker. He placed them in the messenger bag with the money.

"Wait, I'm not taking your money," she said.

"You're going to need it. Might be a minute before you can pull yours out of the bank without people noticing. Trust me, I won't miss it."

"I-I don't know how to thank you."

"You've already done enough."

Walker grabbed some clothes and stuffed them in the duffel bag. He put the bag on his shoulder and the rifle over top of it. Then he pulled open the drawer in the middle of the island. He produced three iPhones. He powered them on and handed one to Alison and one to Kim.

"Get rid of your other phones. As in destroy them."

"You knew this day was coming, didn't you?" Alison said.

"John used to ask me once a month if I was ready for this day, 'because it's coming,' he would say. Every month for almost twenty years he said it."

Alison gave Walker a pat on the shoulder.

"Kim," Walker said as he went over to the money, "is there somewhere you always wanted to go?"

Kim smiled. "Girls like me don't dream about going too many places, Tommy. We watch that stuff on TV."

"Okay," Walker said. "Anywhere on TV you saw that you thought you might want to go?"

"I do like my stories on the ole boob tube. Hmm, let's see . . . I sure liked *Hawaii Five-O*. That Jack Lord was a real fox. And the way them mountains sank into the sea, ooh wee, I thought that would be somethin' to see."

Walker handed her two stacks of hundreds. "Go see them. And stay a while. Safer that way."

"I-I can't—"

"You'd be doing me a favor. I won't have to worry about you."

"Well, hell, Tommy. Since you put it that way!" She

smiled, then wrapped him in a hug. He didn't return the hug, but he appreciated her excitement.

"You're like Santa Claus, Tom," Alison said.

"I haven't had the chance to do too many nice things for anyone in my life. I figure it's about time I fix that."

"That your plan?" Alison said. "Find trouble and try to fix it?"

"I don't exactly have too many other skills. And even though Leila turned out to be something other than help worthy, it felt good to finally use the only skills I do have for good. Well, at least what I thought was good."

While they were talking, Walker had been inputting his new number in Kim's and Alison's new phones. "Both of you can reach out if you ever need anything. But I'm going to do my best to get lost for a while. You think the lake house is the real deal?"

"I'll call right now."

Alison walked away to the other part of the barn.

"She's a good one, Tommy," Kim said. "Maybe you should stick with her. I can see the chemistry between ya."

Walker motioned toward the door. Kim walked that way, and he followed.

"I'm just sayin'. Hard to find a good woman. 'Specially one with legs that long."

Kim looked back as Walker shut the door, a shit-eatin' grin on her face. Walker returned it in kind.

"Last thing I need is to be involved with anyone right now. I have to start this new chapter on my own."

Walker moved over to the covered vehicle. He walked around, loosening the cover at each corner, then back at the trunk where he pulled it the rest of the way off. He could see Alison standing on the other side of the car. When she saw the completely refurbished 1967 Shelby Mustang

GT500 Fastback, shining in all its silver glory, her jaw just about hit the floor.

"This is the only girl I need, Kim," Walker said with a smile.

Kim looked the car over from front to back, and top to bottom. "Well, I can't fault ya none there."

Walker took out the keys and unlocked the trunk. He put everything inside except a little money and the Sig Sauer. Both Kentucky and Tennessee are open carry, so he felt good about keeping his pistol up front with him.

Alison ended the call and walked over to him. "Good to go with the lake house. I'll text you directions. They've already left, but they'll have someone leave a key for you. I gave them your new number. Told them you'd call them on your way down." Alison stepped back and took in the car once again. "All I can say is wow. Wouldn't have pegged you for a classics kind of guy."

"Thanks for making the house arrangements," Walker said. Then he looked at the car himself. "And I wouldn't say that I'm a classics guy necessarily, but when I was twelve, I saw the movie *Gone in 60 Seconds* and promised myself I'd own one of these one day. They just finished it for me a couple of months ago."

"Good timing," Alison said.

Walker nodded, then went outside. He undid the padlock on the oversize barn doors, and pulled the old, beat-up entrance apart. Kim hit the button on the shiny new garage door that had been hiding behind the old doors. Alison walked out of the barn to greet him.

"Thanks again for the fresh start," she said. The green around her hazel eyes was really shining in the afternoon sun.

"Make the most of it. And like I said, if you need something, call me."

Alison wrapped her arms around his neck. "You do the same."

When she pulled back, she went back in for a kiss. Walker didn't mind. Kim whooped and hollered from the garage, comically ruining the moment. Walker didn't mind that either. It saved him from an awkward good-bye. Alison laughed as she pulled away.

"Be careful, Tom Walker," Alison said.

"You too."

She moved so he could get to his car. He walked over and opened the door.

"Have fun in Hawaii, Kim. Take a friend. People say it's more fun that way. I really have no idea."

Kim blew him a kiss as he got in and shut the door. He fired it up, and that Mustang sounded like the roar of the gods. He popped open the glove box, and inside were a passport and a driver's license. His face on both but a different name. He placed the Sig Sauer and some cash in the glove box and closed it up.

In the passenger seat was a shoe box of cassette tapes. He'd had the original 8-track player replaced with a cassette player. Most would have upgraded all the way to discs, but he thought the tapes he grew up listening to just sounded better. Probably just nostalgia, but he didn't give a damn. It's what he liked.

The only good thing that one of his foster homes had rubbed off on him, in his estimation, was his great taste in music. Maybe Alison was right about him being a classics guy, because the music he loved were all classics too.

Walker pulled off the lid of the shoe box, finger-surfed through the tapes until he found the Led Zeppelin II cassette. He took it out and pushed it into the player. The song "Whole Lotta Love" blared through the speakers, over-powered only by the purr of the powerful engine as he pulled the Mustang forward. He waved good-bye and watched Alison and Kim get smaller in the rearview mirror as he eased his supercar out through the grass. He rolled down his window, and as soon as his tires hit pavement, he turned right and gave it all she had.

Walker didn't have any idea what was next for him. But that was a hell of a lot better than the life he was leaving behind. All he cared about now was finally living life on his own terms, and maybe he could help a few people along the way.

But first he was going to enjoy the ride down to the lake in Tennessee. Then he was going to see which of two things happened the most in the coming months. Could he read more books or finish more bottles of bourbon?

Walker couldn't wait to get started on finding out that answer. And he was looking forward to taking his time doing so.

Holy Water
by
Bradley Wright

Book two in the Tom Walker series.
Coming May 2023

ACKNOWLEDGMENTS

First and foremost, I want to thank you, the reader. I love what I do, and no matter how many people help me along the way, none of it would be possible if you weren't turning the pages.

Thank you to my editor, Deb Hall. You make me look good with the way you turn my inconsistent writing into a legible piece of reading material. I'm forever grateful.

To my family and friends. Thank you for always being there with mountains of support. You all make it easy to dream, and those dreams are what make it into these books. Without you, no fun would be had, much less novels be written.

To my advanced reader team. You continue to help make everything I do better. You all have become friends, and I thank you for catching those last few sneaky typos, and always letting me know when something isn't good enough. Tom Walker appreciates you, and so do I.

About the Author

Bradley Wright is the international bestselling author of espionage and mystery thrillers. KILLER INSTINCT is his nineteenth novel. Bradley lives with his family in Lexington, Kentucky. He has always been a fan of great stories, whether it be a song, a movie, a novel, or a binge-worthy television series. Bradley loves interacting with readers on Facebook, Twitter, and via email.

Join the online family:
www.bradleywrightauthor.com
info@bradleywrightauthor.com

Made in the USA
Coppell, TX
06 January 2024

27340814R00194